A RELUCTANT PUPIL

A devil inside Ariel prompted her to go ahead and teach the Amitan prig a lesson.

Her lips curved in a slow, sensuous smile and she nudged forward, pushing her breast deeper into Dekkan's hand. She stroked his cheek, running her fingers along the tempting sun-browned creases there before spearing them through his cornsilk hair. As thick and fine as a kitten's fur, it sent shivers of sensation up her arm, sensations that collected deep inside her.

A groan slipped from his lips like distant thunder echoing in the hills. She leaned yet harder against his hand, not wanting to break the unbearably perfect contact.

His gaze locked with hers as she drew in a sharp breath. Brown eyes turned black as the darkest night and a fierce yearning filled his face.

Ever so slowly she rose on tiptoe, bringing her lips closer and closer to his. She shifted her arms so that they clasped him fully around the neck, tugging him downward to meet her halfway.

Tantalized, she moistened her lips again and let a puff of air escape from her mouth to caress his. "Dekkan," she whispered again. "Dekkan, I want—"

"No!" With agonized haste, he released her before pushing her away and stumbling backwards into the salon. "No! I won't let you bewitch me!"

Ariel's Dance

Chloe Hall

LOVE SPELL BOOKS   NEW YORK CITY

In Memorium
Harriet L. Caudill
You'd have loved this one.

LOVE SPELL®

November 1998

Published by

Dorchester Publishing Co., Inc.
276 Fifth Avenue
New York, NY 10001

If you purchased this book without a cover you should be aware that this book is stolen property. It was reported as "unsold and destroyed" to the publisher and neither the author nor the publisher has received any payment for this "stripped book."

Copyright © 1998 by Maureen Caudill

All rights reserved. No part of this book may be reproduced or transmitted in any form or by any electronic or mechanical means, including photocopying, recording or by any information storage and retrieval system, without the written permission of the Publisher, except where permitted by law.

ISBN 0-505-52285-3

The name "Love Spell" and its logo are trademarks of Dorchester Publishing Co., Inc.

Printed in the United States of America.

Ariel's Dance

Chapter One

Dekkan um Stonnor's hand froze as the dressing room door behind the stage of the Tweeter Theater opened. He'd never imagined his father would have chosen a dancing butterfly for a lover. For that matter, he'd never thought his father would take a lover at all. How could his father have so betrayed the expectations of his family? But when presented with the tempting little morsel with copper skin and aquamarine eyes that glared at Dekkan from the now dilated doorway, he discovered that even the most staid of men could go haywire.

Especially when that beautiful little lady was most definitely naked.

His jaw dropped as he stood on the threshold, but he could do little about it. Surely even here on the free-spirited recreational planet of Mariposa it was . . . unusual . . . to greet strangers while so inadequately attired? He swallowed the lump in his throat and scrambled for his composure.

"Well?" Her impatient question recalled his wits enough that he could speak.

"Ariel? Are you the dancer Ariel?"

He'd never seen a butterfly frown before. "And if I am?"

He fought to keep his eyes courteously trained on her face. She stood before him, tiny, clearly comfortable with her bareness. In truth, he conceded, she wasn't totally nude. Yet while an elaborate tracing of body paint decorated much of her silky skin, some strategic areas remained shockingly exposed to view. The decoration gave her the appearance of a luscious little butterfly who had landed for a moment in the doorway—and who might flit away at any time.

An irritated butterfly. He dragged his mind and gaze back to her face as he took a deep breath. He had to convince her to help him, and staring at her undoubted charms didn't seem an appropriate persuasion technique. He started again.

"I am Dekkan um Stonnor. May I talk to you for a few moments? It's about a matter of importance."

Her frown deepened in obvious recognition of his name. Dekkan casually stuck his foot in the door, just in case. Butterflies were notoriously unpredictable, after all.

She opened the door wider and gestured him in. Once inside the dressing room, he shut the door and leaned against it. He wanted no interruptions. He distracted himself from the temptation of her by assessing the room. It was small, not more than three paces in any direction. A peculiar contraption filled one corner—Dekkan had no idea what it might do. A screen concealed another corner. But

Ariel's Dance

the dominant feature was the mirrored wall directly in front of him—and behind her.

To his unrestricted view of her frontal charms was now added a reflection of a delightfully rounded bottom and the delicately curved indentation of her spine, not to mention two dimples that decorated those very enticing globes.

And speaking of enticing globes . . .

"Why are you here?" Ariel's question interrupted his contemplation of just how enjoyable it might be to test the squeezability of certain ripe portions of her body. Again he forced his gaze and attention above her shoulders. For a man on hormone suppressants, he found it remarkably difficult to do so.

"Uh, I think we need to talk. About my father."

"Is he well?" Her voice held a thread of . . . affection? Desire?

Dekkan's temper flared at the thought, and he had to pause briefly. "Yes."

"Good."

The uncomfortable silence grew as Dekkan's attention again strayed to other portions of her anatomy. One bright sapphire line traced her left breast and edged down over her stomach to the ruby-dusted curls between her legs. His eyes compulsively followed that tracing. He gulped again, striving to drag his mind back to his reason for being here. Help. He needed her help.

"Did you have some reason for coming here other than to tell me that your father is well?"

His gaze snapped back to her face, where an angry frown creased her brow.

"Yes, of course. It's just—look, would you mind covering yourself? This is very difficult for me. . . ."

She shrugged and turned away as if to indicate that his wishes concerned her not at all. She sat down on a stool before a low dressing table that faced the mirror. Although she was still naked, less of her was in view, and Dekkan sighed in relief.

"What is it you want with me? I have to go onstage in a few minutes." Ariel applied body paints to her skin, a task he'd obviously interrupted. He watched as she raised her arms in a deft motion to arrange her hair in an artful fall of curls. The motion brought her breasts into prominence in her reflection—lush, sassy breasts that pouted at him in insolent display. He swallowed yet again.

"You . . . knew my father when he visited Mariposa recently."

"Yes, I knew him. He was here for almost half a year." She reached for a pot of emerald green paint and began to draw a serpentine figure around the nipple of her left breast with a delicate brush. "I know many people. So what?"

"I understand you and he became friends. That you were very close." His voice was hoarse.

"Yes." She glanced at him in the mirror, then looked away. Was that a guilty flush on her cheek?

She leaned forward to apply an amethyst-and-gold design just below her right eye. That move drew his eyes back to her round buttocks—and those damned dimples.

In frustration, he turned away and walked over to the odd contraption. He stared at it, puzzling over its use. Anything to keep his mind—and his eyes—off the gorgeous butterfly preening before the mirror.

"I have come to talk about—"

A harsh knock at the door interrupted him. A voice shouted, "Three minutes!"

Ariel finished her makeup and stood. She walked

to the odd device in the corner. "Look, I don't have time to talk right now."

"I'm sorry. But I really need to discuss something with you. It's important."

She stared at him as if assessing his determination, then sighed. "All right. But not now. This is my last performance this week. You can buy me a drink or something after I'm done and tell me what you want."

She snapped the contraption's two plasticine arms downward. A fine jewel-toned web of material spread between the arms and the main body of the device. She turned and backed against the machine, positioning her shoulders and back just so. A quick flip of a lever almost covered her bitten-off "Damn!" When she finally moved away, Dekkan understood why her makeup concentrated so firmly on the front of her body.

She now wore a pair of delicate, full-length butterfly wings.

He couldn't help himself. His hand hovered a breath above her skin, tracing that enticing blue line down her body. "You are utterly beautiful, do you know that?" he rasped. "A gorgeous butterfly that flits and flutters and lures men to their doom. Did you do it on purpose?"

"Do what?" Her eyes stared into his, her voice a mere whisper.

"Rob my family?"

Her eyes widened in shock, then narrowed in violent rejection as she brushed his hand away. "Is that what you think?" Her finger poked him repeatedly in the chest in hard, painful jabs that forced him to step away. "Is that what Stonnor said?"

Of course not. My father would never betray a

woman he'd been intimate with. The words hovered behind his lips, but he sealed them in. No way would he allow her the slightest concession. He folded his arms across his chest and gazed at her impassively.

She eyed him up and down with all the affection of a farmer for a destructive crop-chewer. "Stonnor said his eldest son was a prig. I should have listened to him." She pushed him aside and opened the door. "I can't waste my time with a—" She swallowed unsaid whatever epithet she'd intended, but her fulminating glare said it all. "But you stay here. When I get back I'm going to get an apology from you if it's the last thing I—no, if it's the last thing *you* do!"

She stomped out of the dressing room, presumably to the stage, where she would display that delicate little body for men to leer at and covet. Perhaps even to possess.

Just as his father had.

Damn! Dekkan stood alone in the dressing room, trying to restore his composure. This woman had damaged his family—perhaps irreparably. It was his task to undo the harm she had caused. And if she received punishment for her sins in the process, it wouldn't pain him in the least. The pain she had unleashed on his family could not possibly match any tiny revenge he might apply to her.

No, she deserved whatever he could dish out, puny though that might be in comparison to her crimes.

She was a woman who had no compunction about seducing an honorable man—one with a family and a tradition of loyalty—and stealing the most precious treasure he carried.

Dekkan had always prided himself on his self-

Ariel's Dance

control. No matter that he faced temptation daily in his travels to other, less honorable, worlds than his native Amity. He'd always stood firm and true to his upbringing. He held himself chaste for the fiancée who waited so patiently back home.

Ariel was a thief and possibly his father's lover. Stonnor's evasiveness and obvious discomfort when he'd told Dekkan about the problem and asked—no, demanded—help had sent every one of Dekkan's instincts into alert. He'd originally thought his father had merely hated admitting his own foolishness in losing the ring, but now . . . after meeting Ariel in the flesh, Dekkan knew something more shameful was involved.

Why, then, did he himself want her so?

"Beast! Bastard! Son of a Silurean swamp skunk!" Ariel stomped out of the dressing room and away from the monster. His opinion of her was abundantly clear. She swore it didn't matter to her—but that was a lie. Dekkan's view of her would always matter, if only because it came from Stonnor's son. Stonnor had been special to her, and she hated the thought that he'd disparaged her to his son.

Dekkan's appearance here was no surprise. Stonnor had told her he'd ask his son, a high-powered interstellar trade negotiator, to come to Mariposa and straighten the mess out. She'd even approved of the plan—it couldn't hurt to have someone with proven skills at compromise to deal with the stubborn people involved.

Stonnor had also warned her that despite Dekkan's extensive travels on business, he was true to his strict Amitan upbringing, so she felt no surprise that Dekkan didn't approve of her. How could a repressed, overeducated prig approve of a woman who danced naked three nights a week in front of hundreds of men?

But Dekkan's condemnation seemed more personal to her. He didn't just disapprove of her job; he disapproved of *her*.

Why? What had Stonnor told him that generated that icy blast of disgust in her direction?

"What's got you steaming? You're supposed to be the serene, gentle Yselda, not a warrior queen." Milko's chiding made her grimace.

"I just had an unwelcome visitor, that's all." The omnisound system began the wrap-up of the previous act, and Ariel took a few deep breaths to relax herself.

"Want me to go stomp 'im for you?" The youthful stage manager inspected her carefully, rubbing away a slight smudge here and patting a curl into place there.

A brief grin replaced the frown that had settled there. "Thanks, Milko." She leaned up to give the lanky youth a kiss on the cheek. Although he was at least a couple of years older than she and a good quarter-meter taller, he always seemed so young to her.

The image of this skinny boy "stomping" the well-muscled man in her dressing room was so unlikely as to be ludicrous, but she couldn't hurt Milko's pride by saying so. "You don't have to do that. He's just annoying, not threatening."

She hoped she spoke the truth.

"Go on out there, sweetie pie. That's your music." He swatted her on the rump, straightened a slight wrinkle in her left wing, and nudged her toward the stage, where a single white spot of light waited for her presence.

Ariel's Dance

A thought occurred to her, and she delayed for a second. She had just remembered what Stonnor had told her about Amity, about how everyone there was very upright, very chaste. About how sex was something Amitans did with their marriage partner—and no one else. Ever. Even about the hormone-suppressant skin patches that everyone used from puberty until marriage to make sure their willpower could stand any strain of their virtue.

An impish grin lit her face as she suddenly realized the impression she must have made on Dekkan, as prim an Amitan as any on the planet, according to his father. She'd known he wasn't as comfortable with her nudity as she was. From his incoherence, those hormone suppressants must not be totally effective. The grin turned wicked as she considered that thought. She could use that to her advantage. Yes, she certainly could.

"Go on," Milko urged, interrupting her thoughts.

She smiled at him, then floated out onto the low-grav stage. With practiced twitches of her shoulder and back muscles she made the butterfly wings swish open and closed in a steady rhythm, lifting her off the stage and into the air. She ignored the little jabs of pain that resulted, just as she had long ago learned to ignore men's stares. As she entered the light, a roar of applause greeted her, and she began to dance.

The audience was nearly all male, of course, but she gave her all to them as she danced. She flitted and soared, bringing pleasure into the lives of the men who watched her. They looked at her body, they sighed over her grace, they even lusted after her beauty. But there, onstage, she was the Butterfly Woman Yselda, above all the earthly passions and constraints of mankind.

She sprang into her final soaring leap with her back arched to display proud breasts, her legs spread in a graceful split, toes pointed and muscles clearly delineated. And as she floated gently down to the stage to sink into her closing bow, it occurred to her that Dekkan's blanket condemnation of her when she'd hoped for a little of his father's kindness deserved a little punishment.

And she was just the woman to dish it out.

While Ariel was onstage Dekkan had time to convince himself that his unusual reaction to Ariel's physical attributes was due to the stress of his mission. His heightened pulse and flushed skin were just evidence of the normal concern he often felt when entering important negotiations.

It had nothing to do with the girl, he told himself. It was just that it was so important that he convince her to help him get back the ring. By the time she'd been gone a quarter-hour, he'd managed to regain the calm facade that had stood him in such good stead in the past.

Only to have the facade blown away when Ariel reentered the dressing room.

She looked tired now, as if every milligram of life-essence had been drained from her. Her shoulders slumped, her wings drooped, even her hair seemed to have lost the bounce that had characterized it such a brief time ago. For the first time, his eyes did not linger inevitably on her body, and he had the luxury of inspecting her face.

This time he saw how tension had carved the faintest of lines around her eyes. He noticed the taut way she held her lips, as if refusing to let their

Ariel's Dance

natural curve signal the slightest weakness. Her eyes—those incredible aquamarine eyes—seemed shadowed, the lids almost too heavy to stay open.

His butterfly was clearly exhausted.

His butterfly? Dekkan shoved the unwelcome notion to the back of his mind while he concentrated on the drooping girl before him. It was apparent she'd forgotten that he would be waiting for her. When she realized he was still there, Dekkan fancied he could see her repairing her tattered composure, much as a butterfly might try to mend a broken wing.

This was no hard-bitten woman of the streets; this was a tired child, someone to cherish and protect. Inevitably, Dekkan found his feelings softening toward her.

"Are you too tired to speak with me this evening, Ariel?"

Her chin firmed, and her whole body gathered itself into a stubborn stance. "No. Just let me change out of my costume, please."

"Certainly. Would you prefer that I leave?" Dekkan thought briefly of the other dancers, their bodies lacking even the cover of paint, and knew that he would rather not loiter in the hallway, where he would be subject to unwelcome speculation.

She just shrugged and walked over to the contraption in the corner. He took that as an invitation to stay. Once again she backed against it and manipulated the levers. This time Dekkan noticed her wince of pain as the machine's arms folded back into the wall, the butterfly wings again stowed neatly away. She leaned against the device for a long moment before moving to perch at her dressing table.

Dekkan's breath hissed between his teeth. Before

he could stop himself, his hand reached out to probe with gentle care two small wounds in her otherwise unblemished back. Each seeped a short trail of crimson blood. She flinched under his tender touch and looked up at him over her shoulder.

"Did your wings cause this?" His question was harsh, almost violent. *Of course they did, you fool!*

"Yes. They connect to the shoulder and back muscles. It's how I control them in my dance."

Dekkan reached around her to collect a small cleansing pad. He applied it to the wounds, handling her as delicately as he might his baby sister, Jenna. Ariel shivered under his hands but made no protest.

"You should not wear wings if they do this to you." A closer inspection of her back showed faint signs of a number of scars where similar devices must once have been attached.

She started to shrug, then stopped as if she thought better of it. "It's what I do," she told him, her voice abrupt. "I'll change and then we can go somewhere so you can tell me why you're here."

She rose and moved over to the screened corner. She had a grace all her own, Dekkan thought. It lent her smallest gesture a beauty he'd never noticed in any other woman. There must have been a cleanser behind the screen, because the sound of rushing water filled the small room.

Within a few moments, she reappeared and used a towel to dry herself. Now she truly was naked before him, and Dekkan's body reacted with an unfamiliar urgency to her beauty.

What was it about this tiny creature that affected him so? As he did in all moments of stress, he tried to analyze his reaction logically, a technique that had served him well in the past. Why did this

Ariel's Dance

woman turn him inside out with no apparent effort?

He couldn't keep himself from watching her as she dried herself and moved to dress. Her hair was long and silky, a peculiar deep russet color he'd never seen before in all the worlds he'd visited. It was her natural color, as the silky curls between her legs attested. But more than that, her skin had a fascinating copper sheen that was immensely attractive, particularly when contrasted with her brilliant, aquamarine eyes. Her figure was perfection, with high, full breasts tipped with dusky rose.

She turned away and brushed her hair in the mirror, giving him plenty of time to ponder the temptation of her charms barely covered by a single brief undergarment. He began to fidget.

She was ignoring him, as if he didn't exist. He couldn't decide whether he should demand her attention, or just enjoy the show she provided. He'd never been a man to indulge himself in the sins of the flesh; even in his uninhibited youth he'd never found them all that tempting. But this woman had changed everything.

Perhaps it was just the enclosed intimacy of her dressing room; perhaps it was something about Ariel herself. But whatever the cause, he found himself growing hard—a rare event indeed since he'd attached his first hormone-suppressant patch at the age of fourteen.

At last she stopped fiddling before the mirror. She moved over to a small unobtrusive door and opened it to reveal a tiny closet. She extracted a garment that matched the color of her underclothing and shimmied it over her head. She stepped into sandals and laced them up her calves, then stood, ready and waiting.

Ready for what? he wondered with a gulp. No woman on Amity would even consider going out in public in a garment as revealing as the one she now wore; most would not wear such a thing privately for their spouses. It was shamefully short and clung tightly, with thin material that revealed every curve of her body. Long sleeves covered her arms to end in delicate points on the backs of her hands. The neckline was very low, offering a generous display of her breasts. A similarly low neckline in back revealed her spine down to her waist.

Appalled, he asked, "You aren't going to wear that outside, are you? In public?"

"Why not?" She shrugged and her left nipple peeped up out of the dress before going back into hiding.

Dekkan groaned. He knew how little she wore under the garment, and he realized that he was going to have a horrible time keeping his mind on his business and not on those impertinent nipples. Not to mention that sassy behind within such easy reach under the hem of her shift, or that tiny triangle of silk, or . . . He wondered if she realized what her attire did to him, then met her amused eyes.

She'd done it on purpose! This infuriating slip of a woman had deliberately set out to tease and tantalize him!

What was worse, she'd succeeded.

He took a firm grip on his raging libido and ushered her out the door. His third-meter height advantage allowed him to get an incredible view down the front—and back—of her ridiculous garment, and his jaw tightened. He was going to have to show this little tease just with whom she was dealing in Dekkan um Stonnor.

Chapter Two

"He's where?" Sebella ur Jeriana's voice rose to an unaccustomed strident pitch. Stonnor winced. She was the only daughter of his neighbors to the west. She was also his eldest son Dekkan's affianced bride—a prospect that appalled Stonnor nearly as much as it pleased Sebella's parents.

"Mariposa." Stonnor tried placating her. This situation was all his fault, and he wanted to smoothed it over. He owed Dekkan that much—and more. "He had some, uh, business to transact there."

"Business?? What kind of business could he be conducting at that . . . that pagan place?"

"Now, Sebella, you know that Dekkan is an honorable man. There is no reason for you to take that tone of voice. He knows what he's about."

"*I* know what he's about, too! He's out there carousing! And—and going to lewd entertainments! And–and–and consorting!"

Her stammering rage amused Stonnor, though he tried not to display it. He manfully restrained himself, but in the end he just had to ask. "Uh, 'consorting'?"

The glare he received might have come from a farmer surveying a field infested with choke-borers.

"Yes, *consorting*. With loose women." Sebella's voice carried her firm conviction that Mariposa was little more than a den of ribaldry, vice, and carousing. Which it was, of course, as Stonnor admitted to himself. But he would never admit that to his son's fiancée.

"Now, Sebella, Mariposa is a perfectly honorable place. Just because it specializes in providing recreational and vacation resorts for the Federated Planets—"

"Specializes in Vice and Corruption, you mean!" She made the capitals obvious.

Stonnor realized he was getting nowhere. He decided to take the offensive. "And what would a well-brought-up Amitan lady like you know of such things? You can believe me when I tell you that Dekkan is utterly honorable—he would never betray you with another woman, even if he could, which he can't because he uses the patch. Just as you do."

A faint flush tinted Sebella's cheeks, then faded as quickly as it came. "That's beside the point. I don't want my husband coming to me any less than pure. It—it'd be humiliating to have to take used goods."

"Sebella! How dare you accuse my son of such behavior!"

This time Stonnor was sure she flushed as she gathered the tatters of her composure about her. Her efforts to modulate her voice to a more reason-

Ariel's Dance

able level showed in the fist she clenched at her side. "I'm sorry if I appear to be impugning Dekkan's honor. It's just that he promised me we would be wed when he finished that grain negotiation. Instead, I find that he's chased off to some notorious den of iniquity almost the moment he arrived home. He didn't even bother to tell me he was leaving! It's the outside of enough! I simply won't stand for such treatment!"

"My dear," Stonnor said in an attempt to defuse her rising anger, "I think this is a subject best taken up with Dekkan himself. I'm sure when he gets back—"

"You know, Stonnor, you're right! You're absolutely right." Sebella paced away from him, then back. "And that's just what I'll do. I'll discuss this with Dekkan in person!"

Stonnor sighed in relief. "I'm glad you've come to that decision, Sebella. It's by far the wisest course. When Dekkan returns you can have a candid talk with him—"

"Who said anything about waiting till he comes back?" she asked, cutting short Stonnor's relief.

"But Dekkan's on Mariposa! You can't mean to discuss this over the interstellar comlink! You'd have no privacy at all!"

Sebella's smug expression sent every one of Stonnor's hackles rising. "Oh, I wouldn't do that! I'll just go to Mariposa myself and discuss it with him there!" She flashed a triumphant grin and glided out of the room, carrying her victory with her.

Stonnor ran a despairing hand over his close-cropped hair. Dekkan was going to kill him for this, that was for sure. Worse, Stonnor couldn't even blame him. He contemplated the possibility of Sebella's meeting up with Dekkan on Mariposa and discovering Ariel—defenseless, sweet little Ariel, who'd had such a raw deal in life—and for whom he had such plans.

Stonnor didn't even consider the possibility that five-foot-nothing Ariel could hold her own against an infuriated five-foot-ten Sebella. No, Sebella would chew up Ariel as an appetizer, and then start in on Dekkan for the main course.

And if Sebella ever saw Ariel doing that dance of hers, wearing little more than a smile—

The very thought made Stonnor shudder violently. Like all farmers, Stonnor knew the value of careful preparation and nurturing of his fields. It was not part of his plan for Sebella to mess up what he'd so carefully prepared. But how could he prevent disaster? He knew Sebella well enough to know that she was utterly determined on this folly. Then it struck him.

He'd have to go to Mariposa, too.

Ariel watched Dekkan as he struggled with the menu at her favorite tea bar. He sat across from her in a private, curved booth tucked away in a quiet corner of the restaurant. Not many people patronized the place at this time of night. Apart from themselves, only a self-absorbed couple and an elderly gentleman populated the café. All things considered, this was about as private as any public place could be.

"What does 'Flowing and Drooling' mean?"

She wasn't surprised to hear an irritated note in his voice. Nearly everything seemed to annoy him. "It's a kind of tea."

"Yes, but what kind?"

She smiled. "One that flows and drools?"

"Sounds nasty. Don't they have just ordinary teas

here? How about some Amitan Master Brew?"

"I'm not sure. I'll look." She buried her head in the menu, ostensibly searching for his choice. It was wicked of her to tease him—she knew very well that the tea he'd requested was one of this shop's most popular brands and her personal favorite—but she couldn't help herself, just as she hadn't been able to resist taunting him with her dress.

She'd ignored his protests and insisted on wearing this too-scanty garment just to bedevil him, but it hadn't worked out quite the way she'd planned. He'd been the soul of gentlemanly courtesy—even though his mouth was compressed into a tight line—as he escorted her out of the theater and onto the street. Even when she'd deliberately bent over, getting into the hire-car to flash her derriere at him, he hadn't reacted. Maybe Stonnor was right and he was a man of iron principles.

But then she remembered the unwilling spark of desire in his eyes as he'd watched her dress.

She couldn't delay any further. She dialed their orders into the touchpad on the table. Within a few moments two mugs of steaming tea appeared in the service tray. She passed one to Dekkan and took the other.

"What did you want to talk to me about?" she finally asked.

He hesitated, obviously choosing his words with care. "My father visited Mariposa some time ago."

"That's right. I found him . . . charming."

His mouth tightened still further. She wondered if his jaw ached from the tension he obviously held inside. "I'm aware of your relationship with my father, Mistress Ariel. That is your—"

"Ariel."

"What?" Her interruption clearly distracted him from his prepared speech.

"Ariel. Just call me Ariel. 'Mistress' is not an accepted title here on Mariposa." She sipped her tea. "Or rather, it is accepted, but not in the way you meant."

He nodded once, regally. "Ariel, then. As I was saying, your relationship with my father is between the two of you."

"Big of you," she muttered into her mug.

But he heard her. "If you knew what harm you have caused—" he began angrily, then bit off his words. "Forgive me," he said more formally. "My words were—ungracious."

It was her turn to rein in her temper and nod acceptance of his apology.

"As I was trying to say, you and my father did not just have a, uh, personal relationship. More passed between you than that."

"Are you implying that I entered into a personal pleasure contract with your father?" Her words were low, her tone dangerous. No one got away with accusing her of that. "I don't do personal pleasure contracts. Ever."

He was watching her, and it took all her efforts to keep her expression blank. "It was my understanding," he said, still choosing his words with care, "that such was the nature of your relationship with my father. Was I wrong?"

She slammed her mug down onto the table. "Yes! I liked Stonnor. And he liked me—or said he did. We enjoyed each other's company. It was as simple as that."

"I see." He was silent, appearing to mull that one over in his brain. If he had a brain, she thought.

"Did he tell you that he'd recently lost his wife

Ariel's Dance

when he came here? That he had children?"

She eyed him up and down in her most dismissive fashion. "Not much of the child about you, I'd say."

"No, there's not. But I have younger siblings. A brother and a sister. And they are each young enough to be hurt by a father's breach of trust. Or don't such relationships bother you?"

"Why should they? Stonnor was here for a few months; then he went home. Whatever we had vanished when he shipped back to Amity. He has no claim on me—and I have none on him."

"Ah. There is your error. He does have a claim on you. And I think you know it."

Ariel suddenly found it extraordinarily hard to maintain her cool facade. She took refuge in her mug of tea, taking a deep gulp that scalded her throat.

"I don't know what you mean," she muttered.

"I think you do. Do you recall a certain game of chance? On one particular evening?"

"How am I supposed to remember one evening out of so many?" But she did—and they both knew it.

"A game to which my father escorted you—at your request, I believe."

Now her lips thinned.

"A most . . . rewarding evening, was it not? An evening in which you and my father participated in a unique gamble."

Rewarding wasn't the word she would have chosen. *Frightening. Horrifying.* Even *exciting*. But never *rewarding*.

"A gamble in which my father wagered something of deep meaning to him and to my family."

His words beat at her with relentless accuracy.

"No one held a stunner to his head! He didn't have to do it!" She squeezed her lips together to keep back the words he wouldn't believe anyway—words that described how she had urged Stonnor not to gamble. How she had begged him to escape while they still could. Words that told how he had ignored her pleas.

"No, perhaps no one forced him to enter into this activity." He eyed her with as much pleasure as if she were a caterpillar in his salad. "But you are a woman of unusual persuasiveness. It would not be difficult for you to sway the judgment of an older, somewhat naive man."

She felt herself flush and hated him for being able to make her. In defiance, she leaned forward and sideways just so, allowing her breasts to strain at their sheer covering. She watched with satisfaction as his eyes latched onto the sight. Determined to reveal this hypocritical prude, she scooted around on the curving seat until she was next to him, pressing her breasts into his side, and ignoring the skirt that had hiked up above her hips.

"And here I thought you Amitan men were so upright. So disciplined." One hand grabbed his and brought it around her back to rest on her buttocks; her other hand made delicate tracings over his chest and stomach. "So *moral*."

His breath hissed between his teeth, and he extracted himself from her embrace as efficiently as he could. She sat before him, making no move to straighten her dress.

"Cover yourself!"

She looked at him, wondering just how far she could push. Slowly, she shook her head.

"You are a little pleasure-girl, are you not? Was bedding my father and destroying his honor not enough for you that you have to try to destroy mine as well?" His hands jerked her dress down over her hips and more securely up over her breasts.

"Aren't you tempted to try me and find out? Perhaps your father found the pleasure worth whatever price he had to pay." She barely resisted the urge to clap her hands over her mouth as if to shove the words back in. *How could I have said that?*

"Impossible. Because of you, our family may be all but destroyed. I would never pay that price to scratch a momentary itch."

She refused to let her hurt show. "Do you know what I think? I think you want me a lot more than your father ever did. And I think you can't wait to have me naked beneath you—but you won't ever admit it, not even to yourself. Because then you'd have to admit that you're not some galaxy-busting hotshot who's above the weaknesses of mortal men."

She leaned forward and poked him repeatedly in the chest as she made her point. "You'd have to admit that you're not superhuman—you are a man! And that's all you are. Just like your father is a man. And men sometimes make mistakes. And sometimes they fail to live up to their sons' standards of conduct. But you know what? Men who admit that are the real men!"

She stared at him, knowing the tears gathering in her eyes offered further evidence against her. She sighed, then slithered out of the booth.

"Where are you going?" He hadn't responded to her accusations.

She looked down at him. "Anywhere away from a self-righteous prig like you."

As she disappeared into the crowded nightlife jamming the streets, it occurred to her that at least their whole conversation had left her with one small satisfaction.

She'd stuck him with the check.

Dekkan sat stunned as he watched Ariel leave the tea bar. He'd never handled a negotiation so badly in his life. What had gotten into him? He knew better than to insult someone he was trying to negotiate with. No one reacted well to such abuse.

So why had he insulted Ariel?

Absently he tossed a few credits onto the table as he rose to follow her. He was tall, much taller than she, and at first had little difficulty keeping track of her on the street. But when she ducked between two large Andromedans, he lost sight of her. Despite his anxious attempts to locate her, she had disappeared as quickly as vapor.

It aggravated him. She was out there wandering the streets dressed in a garment that would mark her as easy prey for any of the hundreds of men looking for female companionship. She was so tiny, so delicate. He couldn't imagine how she could possibly cope if attacked by, say, that hulking brute across the street. His brow furrowed with worry. He quickened his steps.

Where would she go? He had no idea, really. The only place he knew to find her was back at the theater. He couldn't imagine why she would return there, but perhaps someone there could give him directions to her home. His pace increased until he was nearly jogging as he shoved and elbowed his way through the crowd of pleasure-seekers. He didn't notice the hucksters calling for his patronage. He brushed aside the peddlers offering him artificial dreams. His eyes and his whole being were intent on only one thing: finding Ariel!

Ariel's Dance

When he reached the back door of the theater, he ducked inside just as a couple of performers sauntered out. No one was at the doorway to challenge him, so he strode down the hall to Ariel's tiny dressing room. He could check for a note or memento there that would have her address on it. Hadn't he noticed a small case in one corner? He shoved open the door, anxious to find it.

And there she was.

For one long moment, he hardly realized that his breath sighed out of him. In his profound relief, he collapsed against the door as it clicked shut behind him.

At his entrance, she spun around. "What are you doing here?" Her voice verged on nasty.

Knowing she had reason for her attitude and that he had to mend some fences fast, he spread his hands in a submissive gesture. "I wanted to apologize. My comments earlier were rude and thoughtless."

She eyed him for a long moment before turning away to fiddle with a satchel. With some relief he noted that she'd changed out of that ridiculously flimsy garment and into something more decent. There was a long pause, and he wasn't sure she would answer him at all.

"They might have been—you might have been rude and crude, but at least you said what you thought." Her admission came out in a husky tone that didn't disguise her hurt.

"No..." His protest lacked the conviction he wanted to project. He tried again. "I mean, I have no right to judge you. You were correct in calling me to task."

She turned back to face him fully. "Big of you to admit it. But you still think I'm lower than a swamp-crawler, don't you?" Her smile slipped. "Go on. Admit that, if you dare."

Years of negotiations had taught him when to cede a losing battle. Despite that, it galled him to acknowledge his own stupidity. "I admit that I was too quick to jump to conclusions. I apologize."

"Try not to choke on it," she muttered. "Have you ever apologized before? And meant it?"

He didn't answer, just nodded his head stiffly. "I still need your help. Are you willing to listen to me?"

"What? No little 'gift' to buy your way back into my good graces?"

Her mockery sent a wave of heat rolling upward from his collar. How did she know just how to push every one of his buttons? "If you feel such is necessary for you to consider . . ." His neck felt as stiff as his words.

"No!" She stalked right up to him and tipped her head back to stare him in the eye. A finger-poke to his chest punctuated each word she spoke. "You are a bigoted, arrogant, ignorant prig!"

"I didn't mean . . ." Dekkan grabbed her fingers, stopping the irritating prodding. The gesture was a mistake. The warmth from her hand trapped in his flowed through his arm and lodged somewhere in the pit of his stomach. He dropped her hand and stepped away. "You know I didn't mean that."

He thought she would continue the argument, but then she relaxed and shook her head. "I know. All right. Why don't we try again to have a civilized conversation? Maybe this time we won't come to blows." Her tone indicated that she held little hope for such an optimistic outcome.

He nodded in acceptance of her proposal. "Perhaps we would do better with a little privacy. Would you honor me with your presence at my hotel? I have engaged a suite there."

Her head tipped to one side as she considered. "No, I think not. Stonnor said you liked your luxuries, but I think a lower profile would serve better here. Why don't you come and stay with me? That should give us plenty of time to discuss this, and it might do you good to see how a hardworking dancer like me lives."

"I would not so intrude on your privacy."

A russet brow angled upward in silent, sardonic comment. "Consider it my contribution to your no doubt formidable education."

Dekkan pretended to think her proposition over, but all the while his raging libido shouted an enthusiastic *Yes!* Forcibly, he tamped down his desires. He was an adult; surely he could control himself around her—even if he'd never encountered a temptation quite like this before. With great discipline, he forced himself to look this gift butterfly straight in her flashing eyes. "Why?" he finally asked.

"Because I'll feel better—maybe even be a little more willing to listen to you—if I'm comfortable in my own surroundings. I suspect our, um, discussion might take a while. Stonnor also warned me that you could be quite stubborn, you see." Her sweet tone of voice didn't disguise the quiet triumph of her words. She was forcing him to negotiate on her territory, not his.

Never let an opponent know of your discomfort. Dekkan had found those to be words to live by in negotiating anything. With a placating smile, he assented to her plan. "Do you mind if we detour by my hotel to collect my things?"

"Of course not."

She could afford to be gracious, he supposed. She'd won this small battle and forced him to operate on her own turf—but he was confident he'd win a few rounds . . . later.

Ariel offered no further protest as he bundled her out of the theater and into a hire-car. It took little time for him to detour by his hotel and collect his baggage; within minutes the car zipped along backstreets to a quiet residential neighborhood a few kilometers from the downtown area.

Ariel's home faced the street with a genteel shabbiness reminiscent of a long-impoverished relative still trying to make an impression. Although he could plainly see the faded paint and chipped stucco, the building exuded an aura of luxury. Maybe it was in the lush blooms that filled the somewhat overgrown garden at the front of the house. In any event, Dekkan paid the driver of the hire-car and courteously escorted Ariel to her front gate.

The inside was as welcoming as the outside. He liked the clean, uncluttered atmosphere she'd created in the bungalow. The interior of the house consisted of a huge open salon with a couple of private alcoves off to one side for sleeping. A small but efficient-looking cooking area nestled in one corner. Only a single door—presumably to the bathing area—blocked access to any part of the home. Walls and floor mats of a velvety cream color provided a serene background to the unexpected splashes of turquoise and paprika that appeared in the *hibus* flower–printed furnishings. An exotic setting for an equally exotic little woman. A butterfly. He could easily envision her lighting on one of the comfortable-looking couches and driving a man crazy with her delicate beauty.

He settled himself among the blossoms on the couch, not quite sure how to handle the discussion. That in itself was a rarity; Dekkan prided himself on always having a strategy for any negotiation. This time, however, he felt off balance and at a disadvantage.

He didn't like Ariel's stillness as she politely offered him a heated mug of wine before settling herself beside him on the couch. Her silence made him suspect she was up to something.

Worse, he suspected he would like whatever it was she planned.

He decided to open on a conciliatory note. "I don't know if you heard me back at the theater, but I want you to know that I apologize for my comments earlier. I didn't mean to hurt or insult you."

She looked at him over her steaming mug with shrewd eyes. "Yes, you did."

He laughed harshly. "You're right. I did. But only because what you were saying was so accurate. My feelings of self-righteousness are ingrained in me—in all Amitans, probably. We are taught to believe that our moral code makes us somehow better than others who do not behave as we do. I thought I'd grown out of such provincialism. Until I met you." It was the most comprehensive apology he'd ever made, and he hoped it sounded sincere enough to melt her reserve a bit.

"I see."

Dekkan couldn't tell whether his words had softened her toward him. He tried another tack. "Would you tell me about the night my father gambled away the ring?"

Her eyes met his briefly, then shifted away. "Will you believe what I tell you?"

"Yes." His voice was quiet, assured.

"All right." She paused to marshal her thoughts. "Stonnor wanted to attend a particular gaming house. It was an obsession of his. I tried to get him to give it up, to ignore the game. But he kept insisting. He knew I could get an invitation to the house, and he kept pressuring me to do so." She rose from the couch and wandered over to the window to look out at the street outside.

"So you got invitations to the house. What happened then?"

Her voice seemed to come from very far away. "We went. It was early in the evening—about midnight, I suppose. Stonnor was having a pretty good time, and even won a little." She shrugged. "I tried to convince him that he should quit while he was ahead. But he wouldn't. He could be stubborn sometimes."

"I know." Dekkan grimaced.

"Anyway, a little later we got separated. I didn't see him for a while. When I did find him, he was in another room, deep in a game of *shallon*. I'd warned him about that game—it's too easy to rig it so the house always wins. But he thought he was smart enough to take them instead. He couldn't seem to understand that being smart isn't enough." She paused. "By the time I'd talked my way into the room, the damage was done. He'd already made the bet."

"The ring?" He wasn't sure why he needed her to confirm what he already knew. "He'd already bet the ring?"

"Yes." Her voice was infinitely sad.

"And he lost." Dekkan's tone was flat.

"Yes. He lost." She emptied her mug and placed it on an end table. She sat back down on the sofa, her pose stiff, her hands clutching her knees tightly. "I thought he'd go crazy. He couldn't believe it. It was all I could do to get him out of there before he did something foolish. I felt so bad! Dekkan, I tried to warn him; I tried to get him to see reason. But he was like a man possessed—he just wouldn't listen to me."

Dekkan's experience as a negotiator had honed his ability to look below the surface, to determine when a person was telling the truth or lying. Every fiber of his being wanted him to believe that she was being honest with him. Before he realized it was happening, he felt something tight and hard loosen within him. He shifted closer to her, letting his hands cover hers in wordless comfort.

"Yes. That sounds like something my father would do. He is sometimes . . . difficult."

She gave him a thin smile of agreement. "Yes. Sometimes he is difficult." She looked up at him and tugged one hand free. "Just as you are sometimes difficult." Her hand stroked his temple, shoving back a lock of blond hair from his forehead. "You have much of your father in you, Dekkan, son of Stonnor." At his quizzical look she admitted, "Stonnor tried to teach me a little Amitan—like the *um* of your name that means 'son of,' and the *ur* used by daughters to mean 'daughter of.'"

He reached up to take her hand in his and smiled. "Yes, I do have much of my father in me. And sometimes it makes me do things I regret. Like insult and snap at you. I am truly sorry, Ariel. I apologize again for my earlier behavior."

This time his tone must have convinced her of his sincerity. She smiled at him more fully. "I understand. Love makes us all behave oddly. And you do love your father."

"Yes, I do." He paused. "So you managed to get him out of the gaming house. What happened then?"

"He was . . . distraught. He insisted he had to get his losses back. That it would destroy his family, even ruin the keep." She shifted away from him slightly. "He asked me to help him get it back."

That surprised him. "He asked you to get back the ring? How were you going to do that?"

She smiled wryly. "He had a plan—he always had a plan. It was supposed to be easy."

"Easy to do what? How did he plan to get the ring back?" His insistence surprised him, but not as much as her answer.

"By stealing it, of course."

Chapter Three

Dekkan's world tipped and spun as he tried to absorb Ariel's confession. His upright, morally righteous father had planned to steal someone's property? The idea was so alien as to be incomprehensible. He pushed himself to his feet and paced the small salon.

"Are you all right?" Ariel's question finally penetrated the haze that enveloped him.

He shook his head slowly. "Are you sure the man you met last spring was my father? I can't believe . . ."

She shrugged. "Sure. That's what he said, anyway."

"Unbelievable." Everything he'd learned about his father since arriving on Mariposa seemed skewed. Nothing matched the mental image of the man he'd known his entire life. Not the heated affair with the naked little butterfly, nor the gambling away of the family legacy. Certainly not this incredible plan for grand theft.

"Dekkan, will you tell me something?"

"What is it?" He still contemplated the bizarre discoveries he'd made.

"Why is this ring so important to you? It didn't look all that valuable to me."

"What? Didn't Stonnor explain?"

She shook her head. "No. He just said it was important that he get the ring back. When he failed, he told me you'd be coming to get it yourself." Her brows knitted in a delicate frown. "So why is it that important?"

Surprised, he considered her. Again, she seemed sincere in her question. "It's a long story, Ariel. Are you sure you want to hear it?"

"What else do you suggest we do?" Her pointed gaze at the bedroom visible through the archway made Dekkan flush.

"I take your point." He eased himself down into a comfortable chair that faced the couch where Ariel still sat. "How much do you know of Amity?"

"Very little. Just what Stonnor told me. That it's an agricultural world that specializes in exporting gourmet foodstuffs to the rest of the Federation." She grinned. "And that its people are very conservative."

He winced in acknowledgment of the truth of her statement. "We are. The population is very small for the amount of land we have. Only a few million people live on the whole world. The land is broken into large family keeps, each of which is responsible for providing its own necessities as well as generating a certain amount of produce for export."

"You mean you don't trade for food among yourselves? What if someone has a drought or a plague or something?"

"It rarely happens. Nearly all the holdings are large enough that local problems don't impact the entire keep. Our own family's keep, Misthaven, is about a thousand kilometers long by about a hundred wide. Also, the climate is uniform over much of the planet, with little variation from year to year. Should any holding get in trouble, its neighbors would, of course, assist them any way they could."

"Of course," Ariel said faintly. "It all sounds very . . . big."

"Yes. It's a big responsibility."

"What does all this have to do with the ring? It was very pretty, with one central gem and red stones in a kind of filigree work, but I imagine its worth is hardly a drop in the bucket compared to the value of the land you've described."

Dekkan steepled his fingers and rested his chin on them as he gazed at her steadily. "Each keep maintains a special talisman that represents its people. The talisman is the symbol of prosperity and hope for the clan. Our talisman is that ring."

"Oh."

"But it's more than that. The ring has been in the family for over two hundred years. It has descended from father to son through seven generations. Losing it is not just losing a valuable trinket. It means the loss of the heart and soul of our family—of the entire holding."

Ariel didn't reply. Dekkan couldn't tell whether his explanation had satisfied her. She just watched him with those damned aquamarine eyes that seemed to see into his soul. He hoped he wouldn't have to be more explicit, that he wouldn't have to tell her of the very personal meaning the ring held for him.

Or that he was supposed to give it to his fiancée as soon as he got it back.

To his relief, she didn't probe further. "What is it you want with me?" she finally asked.

"My father told me that you could help me retrieve the ring. That you know where it is."

"Do you want to buy it back?"

"If necessary. I would hope that whoever possesses the ring will listen to my explanation of its importance to us and allow me to redeem it." He watched her closely.

Ariel gave a short, remarkably harsh bark of laughter. She rose from the couch to pace over to the window looking out over the lush gardens outside. "You can't redeem it. And no one will take your money."

"Then perhaps some other deal can be struck." He kept his voice mild. "I am a skilled negotiator. I represent Amity in interstellar trade negotiations and know how to compromise for a solution that satisfies everyone."

She turned to stare at him in disbelief. "You think you can just walk in and ask to have the ring returned to you and that will be that? Impossible."

"So you *do* know where it is?"

"Yes, I know. For what it's worth."

"I thought you said you and my father stole it back. I assumed—"

"That I had it hidden away somewhere?" The cynical twist to her lips brought a wave of heat to Dekkan's cheek. "You weren't paying attention. I said we planned to take it back. Sort of. But we didn't get it away from where it was kept."

"So the one who cheated my father out of the ring

Ariel's Dance

has it still. A pity." He considered the information. "I had thought that I might be able to deal with you to get it back. I see now that this is not the case."

"That's not quite right, actually."

"What's not right?"

"Well, I'm not positive that Jeccad still has the ring."

"Jeccad? Who's he?"

"You came out here to retrieve the ring and you don't know who Jeccad is?" She eyed him up and down. "You're less informed than I thought."

Dekkan flushed. "So humor me. Who is Jeccad?"

"He's a very respected and powerful local businessman. And he's a fanatic about keeping track of his possessions. He might give something away, but he'd never let anyone get away with stealing it."

Dekkan eyed her shrewdly. "So my father was right when he said that you were the only one who knows how to get it back." Ariel shifted uncomfortably under his direct gaze. The silence stretched.

"Why are you looking at me like that?" she finally asked.

"I'm just waiting for you to confirm what my father told me. Do you know where the ring is? And will you help me get it back?"

Ariel collapsed onto the couch in a fluid, graceful sprawl. "Sure, I know where it is. But why should I help you get it? I could just go after it for myself, you know."

"I don't think so," Dekkan mused. "If you intended to take it yourself, you'd have done so long ago. It's been months since Stonnor was here—you've had plenty of time to do so. No, you either can't get it yourself or you don't want to. I don't know which."

Ariel shrugged, but refused to explain.

Dekkan considered her stubborn expression. "Will you help me get the ring back?"

What's in it for me if I do? I'm not a charity, you know. I've got my own problems—I don't have time to go chasing off after a ring that doesn't belong to me."

"I understand that it would interfere with your, uh, career. I'm prepared to compensate you for your lost wages, and pay you handsomely as well."

"Will you compensate me for my freedom if things go badly?"

Dekkan quirked a golden brown brow. "Is it so dangerous? Just to negotiate the return of a ring with much less value to anyone outside my family?"

She sighed in exasperation and looked away from him. "You have no idea."

"So tell me."

She opened her mouth, then shut it with a snap. "You don't know who or what you're dealing with here. Jeccad sets his heart on things and it's very difficult to change his mind. He also is very dangerous to those who thwart him. In his vengeance, he might do anything."

"Even kill? Would you be in danger if you helped me?"

"No," she admitted slowly. "He's not a killer. He won't kill me, or you either. He doesn't destroy his own property, you see."

The dawning realization of her meaning sent shock waves through Dekkan.

"You mean, you . . . you're his . . ." He couldn't get the words out as they bounced around his jumbled brain.

"Oh, no. I'm not his mistress," she assured him gently. "I'm his daughter."

* * *

Ariel's Dance

Only after hours' more discussion did Dekkan agree to let things drop for what remained of the night. Ariel's yawns finally made him admit that he, too, could use some rest. With unceremonious efficiency she handed him some spare blankets and a pillow from a storage drawer and pointed him toward one of the sleeping alcoves. While she was not the most gracious hostess he'd ever encountered, he had to admit that his sleeping quarters were as clean and comfortable as they would have been at the hotel.

A little while later, *comfortable* wasn't the word that sprang to Dekkan's mind when Ariel wandered out of the bathing chamber, having commandeered the first shift there. He was trying very hard to quash his mental picture of her as he'd seen her at the theater, but when she stood outlined by the bright light from the room behind her, all his memories faded into dust. Her sleeping garment covered her loosely from shoulders to knee. The loose-fitting shirt wasn't transparent or at all provocative. In it, she reminded him a bit of Jenna, his sixteen-year-old sister, with her bare feet and shy expression.

And it touched his heart as nothing about her had yet done.

"I—" He had to stop to clear his throat of its sudden huskiness before he could continue. "I'll just be a few minutes. Go ahead and settle down to sleep. I'll try not to wake you."

She looked at him, as open and vulnerable as Jenna but with an allure his sister utterly lacked, then nodded silently and moved out of the doorway. He brushed past her quickly, determined to forget the large, aquamarine eyes that could draw a man into their depths, and the slim, enticing legs that lured his touch.

Once in the privacy of the bath, he propped himself against the counter, his head down as he took deep breaths to recover his composure. Would she never stop surprising him? Never stop teasing him with what he couldn't have?

Forcibly he called up the image of the woman he was betrothed to. Sebella waited patiently for him back on Amity; like most Amitans she was tall and full-bodied, with warm brown eyes and blond hair that she wore in a tightly braided bun. Sebella was strong and capable, and he was devoted to her.

At least he thought he was. After the six years of their engagement, he sometimes found it hard to tell.

He stripped off his jacket and shirt. With weary confusion he stared at his image in the mirror before him. What kind of man was he to lust so hotly after a little butterfly dancer, while a truly good and kind woman waited for him at home? He filled the small washbasin with cold water and splashed it over his face. He was a heel, a cad, a rake. He was untrustworthy, unfaithful, unworthy. He was—

His breath caught in a sharp gasp as he noticed a bright pink spot on his image in the mirror. Horror-struck, he stared at the spot, then slowly looked down at himself. It was there, all right, glowing pink in warning.

With disbelieving eyes and shaking fingers he traced the small square placed on his abdomen. It was the sign of manhood on Amity, proof that one had moved from the realm of childhood to that of an adult. All Amitans were fitted with the patches as a matter of course when they reached puberty. The skin-tabs released a slow, steady stream of

Ariel's Dance

medication that repressed the wild hormonal swings so typical of young men and women.

In males, the suppressants made the wearer impotent; in females, they acted as birth preventives as well as suppressing sexual urges. It was the Amitan way of assuring that few unwelcome children were born, as well as guaranteeing purity in both sexes until marriage. Dekkan himself had replenished the patches semiannually for almost twenty years. Now the one he wore shone a brilliant pink.

He thought back and realized that he'd been due to replace the patch when he'd arrived home after the just-concluded grain negotiations. But his father had cornered him almost on arrival and poured his tale of woe into Dekkan's ears. The seriousness of the situation had driven all other thoughts out of Dekkan's mind; he'd left the next morning to come here to Mariposa.

He hadn't replaced the patch.

Pink was still safe, he assured himself with near-frantic haste. Pink merely meant that the patch was running low and needed to be replaced. Pink didn't mean he was in imminent danger of losing his protection. Red was the color that meant the patch was useless. Once it turned red, Dekkan might as well tear it off and throw it away.

He wondered if there was any chance that he could locate a replacement patch here on Mariposa, and immediately recognized the thought as a futile one. Amitans didn't publicize their population-control techniques; it was considered ill-bred to discuss such things with strangers. The suppressants were specific to Amitans, Dekkan knew, a special formulation that worked only on the peculiarities of Amitan physiology.

He stared at the glowing square patch on his

stomach and groaned. No wonder he'd had such an extreme reaction to Ariel—the patch was already straining to keep his hormonal balance in line. He contemplated the coming events of the next few days—and his likely proximity to the bewitching woman who'd already thrown his complacency off balance—and groaned again. There was no help for it. He'd just have to hope the patch would endure until he could retrieve the ring—and hope his willpower could stand the strain.

Then he remembered how Ariel had looked standing in the doorway a few minutes ago, and he groaned for a third time.

Slowly, like an old man, he moved through his regular bedtime ritual. His thoughts spun wildly, and he hardly knew what he was doing. Images of Ariel skittered through his mind . . .

. . . as he'd first seen her, naked, covered only by a provocative skin of body paint . . .

. . . fitted with the wings of a butterfly in a sexy, colorful display . . .

. . . her luscious body utterly bare, glistening with moisture from her shower . . .

. . . wearing a scandalous dress that hid nothing whatsoever of her many charms . . .

To his dismay he felt himself growing hard again, his manhood springing proud and strong from his loins.

And the patch glowed a darker pink.

"Do you spend an hour in the bath every evening?" Ariel's soft voice startled him as he returned to his alcove. Her voice filtered easily from her own sleeping area only a few meters away.

Dekkan muttered something in response but couldn't compose a coherent answer. He climbed

Ariel's Dance

into bed and lay rigid as he listened to the soft whisper of Ariel's sheets betray her movements in bed, a bed only steps away from his own. *No!* He couldn't contemplate such things! He had to maintain his control if it killed him—he was not going to succumb to the temptation that had ruined his father.

He turned out the light to concentrate on the complexities of the contract he'd recently negotiated for Amity. He tried to fill his mind with details of payment bonuses and shipping schedules.

Ariel did not speak again. A long while later he drifted into an uneasy sleep—only to be tormented by dreams, of a kind and in detail he'd never before experienced.

It was dark; he could see nothing. Soft hands caressed him, smoothing open the loose sleeping robe he wore. Gentle fingers probed each muscle and nerve. He felt tender strokes over his whole body, fingering their way through the soft hair that covered his chest and arrowed down his abdomen to cluster around his burning erection.

He kicked the covers off in restless desire, but a soft voice urged him to lie still, to let himself enjoy the pleasure she gave. He complied, although the ache in his groin urged him to plunge into a welcome, warm wetness that he had only imagined.

A warm weight settled across his thighs, and sweet lips moved over his face. Nibbles on his cheeks and nose tormented him; he strained to move his mouth under the elusive lips, but could not capture them with his. Sweet, hot breath burned his skin as the mouth surged over his cheekbones to gather the tender lobe of his ear.

A heavy groan escaped him as he began to twist under her persistent torture. The earlobe was sucked, licked, nibbled, twisted, each movement sending shock waves throughout his body. With urgent demand, his hands captured the feminine head that tormented him and forced her mouth to his. A sigh of pleasure surged from him as his mouth met hers in delicious mating. Her lips were as sweet as musk-laden honey. His tongue speared a mouth that opened eagerly, permitting him an intimate exploration. He stroked her tongue, her teeth, the wet, hot cavern of her mouth.

Her hands were not idle. Fingers laced through his hair, pressing his mouth more firmly to hers. Other fingers stroked down his neck and side, kneading his muscled frame in wildly erotic motions. His arms moved around her, clutching her delicate body to his; he felt the hot brand of her nipples pressing against his, the surging warmth of her breasts molding themselves to him.

He held her tightly, his hand roving down a delicately curved spine to the dimpled buttocks below. His other hand joined it there, curving into lush hips and urging a soft feminine mound against the rigid thrust of his shaft.

When one of her hands nestled between their bodies and captured the pulsing demand of his masculinity, he thought he would faint from pleasure. He groaned again and buried his tongue in her mouth. Delicious strokes fired his ardor to new heights. He writhed under her ministrations, and his hips began to thrust upward, but he couldn't locate the sheath he sought.

She eluded him persistently, while still stroking him urgently. His excitement grew. Her touch was bold and firm, delicate and tender, all at the same time. He bucked wildly now, seeking a release that he needed, wanted, had to have. . . .

Ariel's Dance

A wet, flaming explosion burst from him, bringing welcome tremors of release from the tension, the torture of wanting and not having. He sighed, collapsing into a limp heap of nerve endings. Only slowly did he relax into deep, sated sleep.

Dekkan awoke late the next morning. He was exhausted from the vivid dreams and from the tension that had surged in him throughout the evening before, so it was no surprise to find that Ariel was up and about before him. He blinked owlishly in the morning sunlight.

She stood by the window of the salon, visible through the open archway of the alcove, her back toward him. Somehow, he hadn't been all that sure that she'd still be there this morning; he'd half expected her to flit away.

But she hadn't, and it was time for him to get up to meet the day. He rolled over to sit on the edge of the bed and was embarrassed to realize that sometime during the night he'd kicked the covers away. Amitans were innately modest, and it bothered him that he'd been exposed to her gaze while he slept.

A hasty check brought relief that his sleep robe was still neatly tied at his waist.

He stood and felt a deep flush rush up his neck and face as he noticed a large, sticky splotch on the bedding. Hastily he tugged the bedcovers over it to hide it from her—and his—gaze. Had she seen it? He would be utterly shamed if she had noticed his loss of control.

"Good morning. You finally woke."

He spun around, searching her face anxiously for signs that she'd noticed his lapse. He could detect no indication that she had, so he relaxed slightly. "Yes. Good morrow to you, Ariel." He felt himself redden. How did one talk to the woman about whom he'd had such incredible—such wildly erotic—dreams? "Uh, did you sleep well?" He felt his cheeks grow hotter at the inanity of his question.

She smiled faintly. "Why, yes, I did. And you?"

"Uh, fine."

The too-polite conversation lapsed into an awkward silence. A glint of humor lit Ariel's face. "I can see you're a man who needs his morning brew to get himself going. Would you like me to make some tea?"

"Yes, thank you." He latched onto her suggestion with relief and watched as she moved with her own unique grace to the cooking area. Now if he could just figure out how to get into the bath without further embarrassing himself . . .

"Why don't you have your morning shower while I wait for the tea to brew?" Her question came while she had her back to him, fussing over the tea brewer. He was grateful he no longer had to look into her face.

Dekkan retreated thankfully to the bathing room and collapsed against the door. If he was such a bundle of nerves from a mere dream, he couldn't imagine how shaken up he would be had he and Ariel actually done . . . that.

For the first time since he'd learned of this fiasco, he felt a grudging respect for his father. Apparently, having an affair was no simple matter. To have survived such torrid lovemaking with this woman and retained his serenity seemed an amazing feat to Dekkan. How had his father done it?

He started to untie his sleep robe and frowned. Was it tied backward this morning? Like nearly all Amitans, Dekkan was ambidextrous, with little or no preference for either hand. Still, he'd developed a habit of wrapping his sleep robe a particular way—left side over right—but that wasn't how it was wrapped this morning.

He frowned as he considered the issue, but finally dismissed it with a shrug. The previous day had been so distracting and unnerving that he might have done any number of peculiar things without realizing it.

He hooked the sleep robe over a convenient door hook and turned on the cleanser spray. Nude, he leaned close to the mirror to check the stubble on his cheeks and found his gaze drawn inevitably to his stomach. The square patch still adhered tightly to his skin in its long-accustomed place. His eyes widened and his hand froze in the act of scraping over his chin.

The patch glowed scarlet.

"You really do like to take a long time in the bath, don't you?" Ariel's amused query greeted him when he finally managed to return to the apartment's main room.

"Uh—" His mind was absolutely blank. He could think of no valid response to her question. All that occurred to him was that the patch on which he'd relied for his entire adult life now lay useless and discarded in the bath's disposal bin. He closed his eyes in despair.

He was on his own.

A hot mug of tea was shoved into his hand, and he opened his eyes to see Ariel standing close beside him. Too close, really. He could see the shining copper glints in her hair, smell the delicate spice that was her skin, sense the glistening moisture of her lips.

She guided the mug to his mouth. "Here. Drink this. You'll feel better."

Obediently he swallowed the hot tea. It scalded his mouth, and the pain proved a further distraction. One sip. Two. Her hands guided the mug back to his mouth repeatedly until he regained enough control to step away from her and lower the mug to a table.

"I think we should get going, don't you?" Dekkan was desperate to get away from the enforced intimacy of this house. Anything to gain a little distance between them.

"Sure." That amused glint shone stronger than ever in her eyes. "But there's just one thing," she began as he sidled to the door leading to the outside.

"What's that?"

"Don't you want to put on your clothes first?"

He looked down at himself, still garbed in his rumpled sleeping robe, and groaned. This was not going to be one of his better days.

Chapter Four

Ariel served a light morning meal to the now fully dressed Dckkan in thc sunny alcove she used for dining. Rather than spending the time dressing herself, she'd taken special pains with the fare, warming the spice-nut rolls to a just-right steaminess and brewing a large pot of Amitan Master Brew tea. She figured her modest sleep-shirt covered more of her than anything else he'd seen her wear—or not wear.

Despite Dekkan's distraction and obviously hard-won control, he'd allowed her to nudge him into a chair. After growing up in her father's house, Ariel knew better than to try to negotiate with a male who had other things on his mind—especially when those other things, whatever they were, had clearly shaken him to the core. Perhaps he had some sort of bathing room fetish, she thought with a carefully shielded grin.

Applying careful strategy, she waited until after

he'd consumed several rolls, drunk a mug of tea, and lost some of his iron-staff rigidity. She refilled both their mugs before opening the discussion. "Are you ready to hear my terms?"

"Terms for what?" The lines beside Dekkan's mouth betrayed a quiver of tension. He had a nice mouth, she thought, sharply chiseled with a sensually full bottom curve. *A mouth made for kissing.*

Hastily, she dragged her thoughts back to the subject at hand. "For helping you get that ring back." She gulped down the last of her tea. "Don't you want to know what it's going to cost you?"

"I'm sure you've got some price in mind?"

Refusing to let his sarcasm distract her, Ariel plunked her empty tea mug onto the table. She faced Dekkan, wrapping her determination around her as she would a cloak. Before he left last spring and told her that his son would return to reclaim the ring, Stonnor had warned her that Dekkan might consider her price too high. She took a deep breath and tried to ignore the musky spice scent that wafted her way from him. "I want you to get me into an academy—one of my choice—and use your influence with the admissions committee to see that my application is accepted."

"You want to go to school?" His voice rose at the end of his question, ending in a squeak he quickly tried to cover with a cough.

"Yes."

"You've left it a bit late, haven't you? Most people go to academies when they're a lot younger than you."

With his words, she imagined gray hairs sprouting and wrinkles furrowing her cheeks. Her temper flared. "I'm not too old!" She stamped out her anger and buried her insecurity with determined skill.

Ariel's Dance

"I'm only twenty-seven standard years old. Academies accept students up to the age of twenty-nine. I checked."

"So they do." He paused. "I can't imagine what good a course in art or music would do someone in your, uh, profession."

His insinuations might have fired her ire again if she hadn't kept her self-control in a firm grip. Stonnor's advice had included a warning against negotiating anything with Dekkan when her volatile nature held sway. She took another deep breath and let it out slowly. "You don't have to pass judgment on my plans. You just have to agree to help me achieve them. I help you and you help me. It's a simple bargain."

"That's it?"

"That's it." No way would she say anything more until he agreed.

A long silence stretched between them while he meditatively sipped his tea.

Her vow of silence crumbled under his stare. "Well?"

"You've made yourself perfectly clear." His deadpan face frustrated her attempts to read his reaction.

"Well?" she asked again. "Do you agree?"

"I'm thinking about it."

Frustrated by his calm deliberation, she subsided, drumming her fingertips against the warm mellowood tabletop. It certainly hadn't taken him long to recover from his earlier disconcertment, Ariel thought as she resisted the urge to shift uncomfortably under his assessing stare. Too bad he couldn't have stayed off balance a little longer—just long enough to get him to agree to her terms.

Instead, she found herself off balance. She

couldn't keep her gaze off the sexy grooves in his cheeks that appeared and disappeared with his slightest facial expression. What would his mouth taste like? Tea? Or just of the man himself?

Before the temptation to find out proved too overwhelming, she clarified her request. She wanted no misunderstandings. "I warn you, it's to be my choice of school and my choice of programs." She leaned forward to drive her point home. "You understand that? My choice—not yours."

His smile was so bland, it raised her hackles immediately. "Of course. You choose the school. You choose the course. I merely have to get you into the program." A quizzical gleam appeared in his eye. "And I suppose you'll hold me to it, even if you choose something like hyperwarp theoretical studies?"

She reared back in her chair. "You think I'm too dumb to understand a subject so advanced?"

"Of course not," he said smoothly—too smoothly. "I was merely speculating on how difficult you'd make my task. After all, a good academy will require that you have a certain academic background, no matter what I say or don't say to the admitting committee."

"Don't worry. I'm qualified for the school I have in mind, and for the program, too. Stonnor said you were familiar with how the committees work because you're on one yourself. All you have to do is see to it that my application isn't rejected for other reasons."

"What other reasons might those be?" The silkiness of his voice didn't disguise the barb in the question.

"Never you mind. It's not your problem—yet."

Ariel's Dance

She rose from the table and collected their dishes from their brief morning meal, making sure his gaze didn't capture hers. To punish him, she let her hips sway just a little too much beneath her thin sleep-shirt and was rewarded when his eyes lingered on the motion. "Are you finished with your tea?" she asked.

"Not yet." He shook his head, moving the mug out of her reach. "And the financing you'll need to pursue your, uh, academic career?"

She whirled to face him. "What about it? I've got money. I've been saving up."

"You don't expect me to provide you with the necessary income while you study?"

"No! I don't need your money." What did he think she was, anyway? She pulled herself up short as she remembered just exactly what he did think of her. With an effort, she forced a more moderate tone into her voice. "I have the money I need. Your credits are perfectly safe from me, don't worry."

He didn't answer, just stared at her for a long moment. She couldn't tell what he was thinking, but it became too uncomfortable to meet that penetrating gaze, so she turned away to finish clearing the table.

Dekkan broke the silence, cupping his mug between his hands. "I don't suppose you'd like to tell me exactly which academy and what course you're aspiring to, would you?"

She leaned back against the cleanser cabinet and felt its subtle vibrations ripple through her as it began cleaning the dishes. Interestingly, his gaze focused again on her, but about a foot too low to meet her eyes. *I wonder if it's the vibration of the cleanser that has him so enthralled?* She suppressed the grin that wanted to surface at the thought. "No, I don't think so. You probably wouldn't believe me anyway."

He opened his mouth as if to protest, then shrugged. "Okay. Your price seems reasonable. I agree to your terms and will sponsor you into your choice of academies. Now, what help can you give me in getting my family ring back?"

Ariel's spirits rebounded with characteristic speed. She let a wide smile break over her face, but managed to keep herself from celebrating too obviously. "Great! Let me get changed and we'll go over and talk to Jeccad."

"As easy as that?" He lifted his mug for another sip.

"Sure. After all, Daddy can hardly refuse to see his only daughter, right? Especially when she's bringing her future husband to meet him."

Tea spewed from Dekkan's mouth and sprayed over the table. "Fu-future *hus*—?"

She tsked as she grabbed an absorbent wipe and cleaned up the mess. "You do have a bit of a problem with eating and talking, don't you?" she asked. "If you'd try not to do both at the same time—"

"I do not have a problem with eating and talking! But if you—"

"Then why am I cleaning up after you?" she interrupted in her most reasonable tone.

He placed the mug on the table with awful precision before enunciating each word with equal care. "If you must dump surprises on me in the future, will you please not do so when I'm trying to drink hot tea?"

She shrugged and turned away, not wanting him to catch the gleam of amusement in her eyes. His reaction had been even better than she'd planned.

Ariel's Dance

Served him right for being such a beast about their bargain.

Dekkan caught her by the arm and pulled her back around to face him. Sudden and unexpected fire surged through her at his touch, and she frowned. What was going on here? Did he feel it, too? She couldn't find the answer in his face, but his hand dropped away from her with unflattering speed.

His stern words almost covered his haste to avoid contact with her. "Explain what you meant about introducing me to your father as your—" He didn't appear able even to say the word *husband* in reference to her.

Her head lifted in proud defiance. "It's simple enough. If you want to get on Jeccad's good side, all you have to do is tell him you're going to marry me. And since we're going to need his cooperation . . ."

"Is he so anxious to find someone to take responsibility for you?"

She didn't want to explain, so she just gave a quick nod. "Like I said, you're going to need his cooperation if you're ever going to get that ring back. And if he thinks you're going to solve one of his biggest prob—" She chopped off her words, but it was too late. Dekkan pounced on her slip.

"Problem? Was that what you were going to say? You think Jeccad might find an unmarried daughter who dances naked for thousands of men every night to be a problem?"

The flush of fury made her cheeks scorch. "That has nothing to do with it! It's not my dancing that bothers him!" With a disgusted glare, she realized she'd again given Dekkan an opening! She forestalled his next question before he could move his mouth. "Look, my relationship with my father is none of your business. All you need from me is help getting that ring back, remember?"

Although he didn't look at all satisfied, he didn't pursue the subject. With a brief nod he stiffly agreed. "Fine. But telling your father that you and I are—are betrothed is not an option."

"Why?" As if she didn't know. "You seemed to like me well enough last night."

Scarlet rolled up his neck and face in a rising tide, and he jumped to his feet. "What do you mean, 'last night'? What are you talking about?"

She tipped her head to the side, wondering what she'd said to set him off. His reaction seemed extreme, to say the least. "You know. Last night. When I told you what happened with Stonnor. You were very pleasant—almost as if you could stand to breathe the same air with me."

A look of the most profound relief crossed his face before he turned away with a muttered, "Oh."

"What did you think I meant?" She couldn't have stopped herself from asking if wild *droogs* had been storming the apartment.

He paced over to the salon area and sat in an overstuffed chair, his rigid form seemingly misplaced upon its cushiony surface. "I'll quote your words back at you," he told her. "It's none of your business what I thought. That doesn't change the fact that you can't tell your father that we plan to marry."

"Why not?" She sprawled upon the sofa and picked up a pillow, kneading it with her fingers. It seemed a safer choice than curling up on his lap, which was her first instinct. "It's a good plan. Jeccad will be grateful. I don't mind. And it'll make it easier to get your ring back." At least I think it will, she added silently.

Dekkan took a deep breath before answering. "You can't tell him that because I'm betrothed to another woman. My intended bride is back on Amity awaiting my return."

"You mean Sebella?"

Astonishment settled over his face like a cloud. "What? Who told you about my betrothed?" Then understanding followed and turned the cloud into a bitter thunderhead. "My father, of course. What other family secrets did he betray?"

"You call telling me his eldest son plans to marry—someday, if I recall, but not anytime soon, given that your engagement has been going on for almost a decade—you say telling me that is betraying a family secret?" She tossed the pillow to the side and stood up. "What is Sebella, some kind of crazy lady you have to keep locked up in the cellars so no one finds out about her?"

"Six years is not almost a decade!"

Her triumphant grin must have given her tactic away, because he too stood and towered over her.

"And I'll thank you not to insult Sebella." Dekkan leaned over her like an avenging angel. "I'm—I'm devoted to her. As she is to me!"

The defiant ring of his voice didn't faze Ariel one whit. "Sure you are," she told him, making no attempt to disguise her irony. "That's why it's taken you six years to get up the nerve to marry her. Maybe you'll wait another six before you actually thread the loop with her."

His hand rubbed over his face. "I don't need this," he muttered. He paced away from her to the window and looked out for a long moment. Finally, he turned to face her. "I don't need to put up with your impertinence. Consider our agreement at an end. I'll recover the ring myself." With long strides, he headed for the door.

"Wait!"

Ariel barely intercepted him before he reached the door, throwing herself in front of it. When he put out his hand to turn the almost shoulder-high latch, he grabbed one soft breast instead. A look of pure agony crossed his face—but he didn't move his hand away from the gentle curve it cupped.

The pleasure that flowed from his unexpected caress took Ariel by surprise. Unwillingly, she felt herself lean against that callused warmth. *He must share some of the outside chores when he's home.* Her thin sleep-shirt did not disguise her body's instant reaction to his touch, and she knew he felt the tip of her breast pebble against his palm before turning to pouting hardness. She looked down at his hand, so strong against her tender flesh, and suddenly wanted to feel that strength against her, within her. "Dekkan . . ." she said softly. "Dekkan."

She might have been surprised by the bud of desire that blossomed between them, but she knew how to foster its growth. The temptation to let herself enjoy this unexpected pleasure mushroomed while she struggled to think things through. Surely his patch would prevent things from going too far. Stonnor had said it made Amitan men impotent.

But it hadn't kept Dekkan from wanting her.

A devil inside her prompted her to go ahead and teach the Amitan prig a lesson. That the "lesson" indulged her own inclinations as well as stoked her pride merely spiced its reward.

Her lips curved in a slow, sensuous smile, and she nudged forward, pushing her breast deeper into his hand. She stroked his cheek, running her fingers along the tempting sun-browned creases there before spearing them through his corn-silk hair. As thick and fine as a kitten's fur, it sent shivers of sensation up her arm, sensations that collected deep inside her.

A groan slipped from his lips like distant thunder echoing in the hills. She leaned yet harder against his hand, not wanting to break the unbearably perfect contact. No, it wasn't perfect. It could only be perfect if his flesh touched hers unimpeded by her shirt. Her breath came in slow gasps that kept time with his heavy inhalations.

His gaze locked with hers and she drew in a sharp breath. Brown eyes turned as black as the darkest night, and a fierce yearning filled his face.

He wants me!

Triumph and something else she was too involved to identify flared inside her. Ever so slowly she rose on tiptoe, bringing her lips closer and closer to his. She shifted her arms so that they clasped him fully around the neck, tugging him downward to meet her halfway. Obediently, he let her pull him into position without protest, watching every millimeter of her approach with complete attention.

She took her time, savoring the anticipation. Would his mouth be hard or soft? Tender or ardent? Skillful or untutored? When only a tiny space intruded between them, she paused. She ran her tongue over her lips, knowing it would leave behind a glistening sheen.

Another groan escaped from him, and his entire body seemed to clench in reaction. Her arms tightened around him, and she smoothed her hands over his back. His muscles rippled under her touch, and upon her breast, his fingers imitated her caress.

Tantalized, she moistened her lips again and let a puff of air escape from her mouth to caress his. "Dekkan," she whispered again. "Dekkan, I want—"

"No!" With agonized haste, he released her breast before pushing her away and stumbling backward into the salon. "No! I won't let you bewitch me!"

Bereft by the sudden loss of contact she'd accepted so quickly as natural, Ariel stood by the door, shaking her head in bemusement. How could he deny the passion that flared between them—passion that even now flared through her veins? Surely he'd felt the same?

She collapsed against the door, finding reassurance in its firm support. A deep breath helped her regain her composure. A second helped even more. Calling on a strength she wasn't sure she could rely on, she slowly straightened away from the door. Her knees might feel like overcooked *ancha* noodles, but he didn't have to know that.

She tried to convince herself that her disappointment arose from the failure of her attempt to teach him a lesson in desire. Given another standard decade or two, she might even succeed in believing the lie.

"I'm sorry." They were the only words she could think of that might convince him to stay.

For long moments he didn't respond. He stood by the window looking out into the rear garden, his fists braced against the frame on either side. In the morning sunlight streaming through the crystal panes, his silhouette exemplified masculine perfection. Broad shoulders tapered into a narrow waist, while strong calves and thighs supported a body Ariel couldn't help but admire for its sheer beauty.

She gulped hard as barely suppressed desire

licked through her again. Maybe her plan to torment him a little wasn't such a good idea.

Then Dekkan turned his head from his silent contemplation of the garden. The look of agony on his face sent another gasp rippling through her. "Don't be," he said, his voice low. "It's not your fault."

She moved toward him, hand outstretched in silent sympathy. "Dekkan, what is it? What's wrong?" Her fingers ached from the need to touch his warm, muscled skin again.

His gaze moved from contemplation of her hand back to her face before he again turned away to stare out into the garden. "It's . . . nothing you can help." A harsh laugh broke from him. "I suppose it comes as natural to you as breathing."

"What are you talking about?"

She saw a deep breath shudder through his frame before he swiveled to face her fully. "Seduction. You probably were born knowing how to seduce a man. It's just an instinct with you."

Her good intentions to comfort his pain vanished without a whimper of protest as she gasped in outrage. "Wait a second, here. I'm not the one who grabbed you! You put your hand on my—."

"Only after you put yourself in my way!" he retorted. "I was reaching for the latch, not you!"

She stalked up to him, fists perched on her hips. "Well, you sure weren't in any hurry to let me go, were you?" By the time she spit out the accusation, she was standing toe-to-toe with him. His spicy scent enveloped her, but she forced herself to ignore it.

"And you didn't even try to pull away!" His ferocious frown belied the stain of embarrassment—or was it anger?—that colored his cheeks.

Their glares silently dared each other to continue

the argument. Finally, the ridiculousness of the situation made Ariel relax into laughter. "I can't believe we're arguing over something so silly," she managed to choke out. "Nothing happened, after all. It was just an accident."

Dekkan's frown indicated he didn't totally agree with her conclusion, but he, too, relaxed. To Ariel's disappointment, he also moved away from her to sink onto the couch. She was getting addicted to the masculine warmth he radiated.

"You did it to me again," he said with a groan. He leaned his head against the pillows of the couch and rubbed his face with both hands.

"Did what? Dekkan, what are you talking about?"

He looked at her with the resignation of a man who knew he'd lost his fortune at the turn of a card. "You've made me look a fool one more time. How many is that so far this morning? Three? Four? I think I've lost count. And it's not even the tenth hour yet. Just imagine what the score will be by this evening."

"No one can make you look a fool. The only person who can do that—" With all her heart, she wanted to pull her words back from the air and stuff them back inside. Too late.

"Is myself?" he finished with ironic courtesy. "Believe me, I know that all too well."

"I didn't mean . . . I only meant . . ."

"Sure you did." He paused while she floundered trying to find a way to take back what she'd so clearly meant. "Never mind." He waved her away. "Why don't you go get dressed while I try to recover from your latest successful attack."

Frustrated beyond belief, she hovered, then spun away to do as he suggested. She grabbed some clothing from the storage closet and stomped into the bathing alcove to dress. No way would she let him accuse her of seducing him again! He'd have to ask her—no, he'd have to *beg* before she'd even consider letting him lay so much as a finger on her again.

A gleeful smile lifted the corners of her lips as she imagined that sweet event. Yes, she'd like to see him plead for her touch. If he did it with enough sincerity, she might, she just might—

The sharp recollection of the wave of desire he'd inspired pulled her back to reality. With absent skill, she pulled off her sleep-shirt, only to have a sudden thought. Nude, she opened the door just enough to poke her head out. Dekkan still sprawled on the couch.

"Dekkan?"

His head turned toward her in wary question. "What?"

"How high can you count?"

"What? Why?" The wariness was in full bloom now.

She smiled with sweet menace. "Because if you're going to keep track of the times you look a fool, you'd better be able to count real high!" Without giving him a chance to answer, she pulled her head back inside and shut the door with a challenging crash.

Stonnor settled himself deeper into the comfortable chair in the ship's observation lounge. Luxury space travel had some advantages, and the plushness of the furnishings scattered around the ship was one of them. While his home at Misthaven had been well furnished by his wife Dolooran when they moved into the newly built keep-house, that had been almost forty years ago. The cushions had grown a little lumpy in the past few seasons, what with Dolooran's long illness. Maybe he should think about doing a little renovation.

He accepted the icy-cold drink he'd ordered from the friendly blue-skinned waiter and took a wary sip. It almost took the top of his head off. Amitan taverns at home didn't serve anything that in any way resembled a hyperstellar strangleblaster. True to the drink's name, the frigid heat of the beverage blasted its way to his stomach, searing his esophagus all the way down. He couldn't have uttered more than a strangled bleat if the galaxy's fate depended on it. Blissful smile in place, he took another, less wary sip.

"Stonnor! What are you doing here?" Sebella's unexpected shrill voice made him realize the galaxy's fate—or at least his life—just might depend on regaining his voice.

With manful effort he tried to respond to his son's outraged fiancée while juggling the tipping drink onto the table next to him. An evil, smoky hiss arose from the drops of liquid that spilled onto the plasticine surface.

"What's wrong with you?" Rather than concern, her tone conveyed deep suspicion.

Gasping and snorting for breath, he tried to force the words out, but nothing emerged except a few gasps.

"Brolla, thump him a little. Maybe he's choking or something." Sebella addressed her words to a large young man looming behind her.

Stonnor's blurring vision caught only a glimpse of the well-muscled man who was one of his son's best friends before a heavy hand thwacked him between the shoulder blades, almost knocking him to the floor.

Ariel's Dance

A second thwack all but toppled him again, but it did provide enough incentive to force his strangling vocal system to work. "Stop!" The third thwack felt lighter—or maybe his back was numb.

"Keepsire Stonnor, are you better?" Brolla's deep voice expressed the concern Sebella's had lacked.

"Yes, Brolla," Stonnor managed to mutter while massaging life back into his shoulder. "I give you thanks. I think."

"What are you doing here?" Sebella's voice might have quieted, but the suspicion in it hadn't disappeared.

"Why, I'm going to Mariposa to see my son." He injected as much innocence into his tone as he could manage.

"May I ask why?" Her words might indicate courteous interest, but her tone demanded an answer. Sebella lowered herself into a nearby double-seated chair in a way that made its plump softness seem as stiff as a durennium-coated plant stake.

Stonnor watched Brolla gingerly lower his massive body into the other half of Sebella's chair. Why had Brolla come? Stonnor ignored Sebella's question in favor of one of his own. "Brolla, it's good to see you again. Are you going to visit Dekkan, too?"

Brolla's cheeks flushed slightly, and he opened his mouth to answer.

Sebella's insistent question cut him off. "I asked why you are here. I'd like an answer."

Stonnor turned a bland gaze on Dekkan's pushy fiancée. "I'm on keep business, my dear."

Her face flushed an angry red, but not even she had the ill manners to pursue the topic. No one with any grace insisted on details of private keep business.

Time to take the issue into the enemy's camp,

Stonnor thought. "I see you are as good as your word, Sebella. I really wasn't sure you'd go to the expense of traveling all the way to Mariposa when Dekkan is scheduled to return within a moon-cycle or so."

Her eyes narrowed. "I always do what I say I will."

He accepted that as the truth he knew it was and nodded. "But I didn't expect you to be accompanied by Brolla. Or is this just another happy coincidence?"

"No. I asked Brolla to come with me."

Stonnor's eyebrow arched upward in gentle inquiry. It wasn't his way to pry, but he would have given half this year's bumper crop of *ingleberra* fruit to know why Brolla had been invited.

Apparently, gentle inquiry worked as well as a direct question. Sebella's gaze shifted restlessly as she added, "It isn't seemly for an, uh, Amitan maiden to travel unaccompanied." Her voice strengthed as she warmed to her explanation. "Especially to a planet such as Mariposa. It's filled with vice and debauchery, you know. I had to have protection."

With the satisfaction of one who had talked her way out of cleaning out a messy stable, Sebella leaned back more comfortably in her chair and patted Brolla on the arm.

"I see." Stonnor eyed the stolid, muscular man beside her. "I can see that Brolla would be a great comfort to a lady concerned for her safety in a strange land."

Brolla folded his arms across his massive chest but added nothing to the explanation.

"So," Stonnor said, "here we are. Three, uh, compatriots all destined to visit the lovely Mariposa."

"To see Dekkan. Not to visit the planet."

"Why, Sebella, of course. I never thought anything else. But surely you'll want to attend some of the more charming entertainments while you're there?"

He thought he caught a spark of interest in Brolla's eye, but Sebella denounced such folly immediately. "I—Brolla and I do not plan to attend any lewd entertainments. I consider this a business visit."

"Business? A visit to your fiancée is business? Surely you meant pleasure, my dear?"

"Business," she said firmly. She caught the eye of the blue-skinned steward, who hurried over. "Bring me a glass of Amitan mineral water."

"Of course, madam," the little man said in formal tones before turning to Brolla. "And you, sir? May I bring you a beverage?"

Brolla's mouth opened and his hand moved to point to the glass sitting by Stonnor's chair, but Sebella again cut him off. "He'll have Amitan mineral water, too. And make sure it's Amitan. We don't drink foreign liquids."

Her condemning glare at Stonnor's glass forced him to pick up the strangleblaster in defiance and take a deep swig. Somehow the prospect of having an excuse not to talk to Sebella held great allure at the moment.

Only a few hours out of Amity and he already knew it was going to be a long, long trip.

Chapter Five

With automatic courtesy, Dekkan held open the door to Jeccad's Milk Bar and Gambling Emporium for Ariel. "Milk bar?" he asked, raising an eyebrow in skepticism.

Her expression was indecipherable. "Why not?" Regally she sailed by him into the plushly decorated chaos of the interior.

Dekkan followed, only to be surprised by the refined luxury he found inside. Customers from a wide variety of worlds sat around small tables furnished with the latest in service machines. Exotic music drifted through the air, and soft lights pulsed in a seemingly random pattern of color.

Dekkan had to concentrate for a moment to realize that the light displays presented an ever-changing panoply of visual art from the far corners of the galaxy. Primitive cave drawings from Old Earth vied with paintings from the neonovan

Ariel's Dance

school of ximobiotic nudes, which rubbed metaphorical shoulders with the brilliant abstracts of Lentazoid pulsar displays. The constantly shifting lights and shadows combined with pulse-stirring background music to make the details of the room surprisingly difficult to discern.

He peered harder at a nearby table. If he hadn't known better, he'd have thought the mauve-skinned Ganizeds seated there were drinking—

"C'mon." Ariel's fingers closed around his elbow, and she started to tug him across the room.

Dekkan's head swiveled to confirm his perception as he obediently followed her weaving progress. "They're drinking milk!"

She nodded, but didn't pause. "Of course. This *is* a milk bar. You saw the sign out front."

"But . . ." Dekkan shook his head. What happened to the den of vice and iniquity he'd envisioned when his father had confessed his sordid loss?

"Now listen," Ariel told him when she at last paused in front of a large, ornately carved door tucked away in a discreet corner. "Just follow my lead and let me do the talking when we're in with Jeccad. You understand?"

She raised her hand to press the announcement stud on the door, but Dekkan reached out to stop her. "Wait a second. What are you going to tell him?"

"Why, just what we discussed, of course."

Ariel's too-innocent look didn't fool him for a moment. "No, you're not. You are not going to tell your father that we plan to marry." Dekkan made his voice as firm as he could in spite of her delicate spicy scent that teased his nose and filled his head with what-ifs. He'd already discovered that this but-

75

terfly's will was as strong as permanum alloy. If he wasn't careful, she'd stomp all over him with size-three hobnail boots.

She shook her head, tsking. "It's really the best way to make him want to help you get the ring back."

"Maybe so—but you're not going to tell him that." He paused and tried to glare her into submission. "In fact, you're going to let me guide the discussion. Aren't you?"

Their gazes locked for a long moment; then she blinked and looked away. "Okay. If you say so," she muttered. "But you're making a big mistake."

She frowned and flipped her dark copper hair back over her shoulders. Unfortunately, the movement drew his attention to the shifting curve of her breast beneath her loose-fitting silk shift. He couldn't have kept his eyes from following that subtle sway for the entire value of this year's grain contract. The delicate, almost-sheer amber fabric and deep armholes of her dress made no attempt to disguise the distressing scarcity of undergarments. Nor did the bounce and jiggle of her breasts whenever she made the slightest motion reassure him.

Although the garment's neckline rose modestly to just under her collarbone, the oversize armholes dipped almost to her waist, allowing him alluring peeks at the side curve of her breast. In fact, if he looked very carefully, he was almost sure he could see the shadowy outline of a darkened nipple pebbling against the fabric. . . .

"Are you quite finished ogling my chest?" Her amusement recalled him to his senses.

Trying very hard to ignore the flush he felt turning his face dark red, Dekkan forced his gaze away from her and muttered an insincere apology. He

Ariel's Dance

heard her voice continue, saying something he didn't bother to follow while he tried to master the embarrassment that filled him. Distance alone wasn't enough, dammit.

"Sorry," he muttered. Reluctantly, he released his grip on her hand and let her press the stud, expecting the tightening in his groin to disappear at the loss of contact with her. It didn't.

A faint humming was replaced by a holo-vid of a bald butler in the traditional green-and-gold formal attire. "May I assist you, gentlepeople?" The man's speech had a peculiar lisping pronunciation Dekkan couldn't quite put his finger on.

"Hey, Gummy, it's me. I want to see Jeccad."

Ariel's cheery greeting brought a wide smile to the man's image. "Missy Ariel! It's been a long time. Enter, enter."

The door clicked aside and the original of the image bustled them inside. As soon as they crossed the threshold, the door shivered into place behind them with a final-sounding thump. The room beyond was obviously the foyer for a large private residence situated behind the public emporium.

Although furnished with excellent and expensive taste, the white marble and gray steel decor left a chill in Dekkan's mind. Not a single rug or tapestry lent the slightest warmth to the room. He couldn't imagine a starker contrast to the opulence of the public area they'd just passed through.

Ariel moved into the doddering butler's arms with an enthusiasm that sat uncomfortably on Dekkan's shoulders. For some reason he disliked seeing her snuggle so eagerly into another man's embrace. A wave of anger swept over him, making him want to rip her away from the older man. He wanted to be the man holding her close, feeling her body press against his.

In fact, he wanted her—badly. The fullness in his groin turned into an actual ache.

"Gummy, it's good to see you again!"

She didn't have to sound quite so enthusiastic, Dekkan thought as he shifted his weight from side to side. Why couldn't she just shake hands with the man? Gummy's hands strayed perilously near the sides of Ariel's full breasts. Dekkan could feel those soft mounds as if it were his hands on Ariel. His imagination soared as he contemplated what the sensation of delicate silk shifting over even more delicate skin would feel like. His fingers curled in anticipation.

A broad smile cracked the butler's wrinkled face, revealing the source of both his nickname and his unusual enunciation. Not a single tooth sullied the interior of his mouth. "Why have you stayed away?"

Ariel pulled a face. "You know what it's like between me and Jeccad, Gummy. He's so determined to make me give in. It's like dealing with a single-minded *boarass*. It's impossible to get him to listen to me, much less pay attention to what I say."

"And you're just as stubborn."

The two stared at each other in silent communication. When Gummy's hands remained too familiar for Dekkan's ease, he decided to remind Ariel of his presence. Intellectually he realized the man's grip on her was more avuncular than ardent, but Dekkan still wanted Ariel out of Gummy's embrace—even if Gummy had at least half a century on Dekkan. His shoulders shifted uncomfortably with the need to stake a claim on Ariel.

As if she realized the tenor of Dekkan's thoughts, Ariel pulled away from Gummy and spun to face

Ariel's Dance

Dekkan. "Gummy, this is Dekkan um Stonnor. He's my—" Dekkan's warning glance must have cautioned Ariel not to push him too far. She grimaced as she reworded her answer with obvious disdain. "—my friend."

Dekkan dredged through his negotiation skills and acknowledged the introduction with a First-Degree Neutral Smile for Dealing with Uncertain Hierarchies. "It pleases me to meet you . . . Gummy?"

A small flush rose over Ariel's cheekbones. "Oh, sorry. Gummy is my father's right-hand man. Right, Gummy?"

The butler/right-hand man just grinned his toothless smile and nodded.

"I see." Dekkan shifted his expression into a Second-Degree Smile for the Opposition's Assistant.

"How is Daddy, Gummy?"

The old man shook his head lugubriously. "Not good. His temper has been sorely frayed since Mistress Floribunda tossed him over."

Ariel shook her head and clucked sympathetically, whether mock or genuine, Dekkan couldn't tell. "I wondered when they'd come to blows," she said. "I can't believe that they ever got together in the first place. She's even more stubborn than he is." Dekkan must have looked confused, because Ariel expanded her comment. "Floribunda is—or was—my father's mistress. But she's an even harder-nosed businessperson than Jeccad, so I've wondered when they'd have a falling-out."

"I see," Dekkan said. He couldn't quite keep the censure out of his voice, and wondered how Ariel must feel having such a licentious father.

Ariel flushed. "You're quite a prig, you know,

Dekkan. You should be glad that your father dealt with me instead of Floribunda. She'd have put you through all nine levels of hell without blinking twice."

Dekkan stepped closer to her, unable to resist the warmth and special scent that was hers alone. "And you think you haven't?" he asked softly.

He reached out gently to brush a strand of that incredible copper hair from her eyes and then couldn't move his hand away. Snared by an urge more powerful than anything he'd ever felt, he lowered his head. He *had* to kiss her. His mouth approached hers, and the flavor and moisture of her breath brushed over his lips, making his head swim and his whole body tingle in anticipation. He paused to savor the sensation—and was shocked when she pulled her head back and stepped away.

Her nose tipped up as she turned from him in grand dismissal. Stunned, Dekkan froze, then awkwardly straightened. This was not the time, nor the place; he knew that. But how had she retained enough presence of mind to draw back from an embrace that promised to sizzle his eyelashes?

"Where's Jeccad?" she asked Gummy. "We need to talk to him."

Gummy. Dekkan wanted to groan aloud. He'd forgotten all about the other man. Ariel scrambled his brains so easily, with just a look, a touch, a hint of her scent. He didn't dare look at Gummy's expression.

"I believe he's in his study, Missy Ariel, but I wouldn't—"

Gummy's warning faded as Ariel grabbed Dekkan by the hand and pulled him along with an eager, "C'mon. Let's go see how you do with my father."

"But Missy Ariel!" Gummy's belated protest fell

Ariel's Dance

on deaf ears and was reduced to anxious muttering as their distance from him increased. The butler's shambling gait left him with no chance of capturing Ariel as she flitted away, Dekkan in tow.

She skittered around a corner and stopped abruptly, causing Dekkan to careen into her. His body rammed into hers, knocking her against the wall. Instinctively, he put his arms out to catch her and break her collision—and ended up with her pressed tightly between him and the wall.

His fantasy of a few moments ago instantly faded into oblivion as the reality of touching her eclipsed it. Without direction from his brain, his hands shifted over her back, rubbing the silk of her dress over her skin. It felt even better than he'd thought, like petting a luxurious fur.

From rapid walk to sensual heat in an instant, Dekkan thought. Every cell in his body felt determined to press against her. Instinctively, he turned her and pulled her closer. Her breasts, unfettered beneath her gown, pressed against his chest in a sensation so evocative that he gasped. The tips of her breasts prodded him and he began to guide her body into a slow, sensual massage of his chest. His thin shirt, despite its formal design, allowed him to feel every movement with penetrating clarity.

He backed her against the wall and pressed his knee firmly between her legs, lifting her slightly until she rode his knee. Her hands, looped around his neck, gently moved to the closure of his shirt and delicately freed first one and then a second stud closure.

"Ariel," he said softly, lowering his head to nuzzle the curve where her neck met her shoulder. "Ariel."

His hands homed in on the sides of her breasts, then, as if drawn by an irresistible force, cupped them entirely. She arched her back to fill his palms more fully and worked more frantically at his shirt. Following an impulse he couldn't resist, he let his hands shift to the sides of her dress. Leaning away slightly from her upper body, he pressed his hips more tightly to hers, letting him see her better. She was smiling faintly while she concentrated on opening his shirt.

With a deliberate movement, he quickly tugged the open armholes of her dress inward toward the middle of her chest. He felt a momentary resistance; then she shifted her hips on his knee slightly to release the strained fabric. The plunging armholes looped inward, leaving her naked breasts exposed to his eager gaze.

It's not like you haven't seen her breasts before. The voice of reason tried to calm him but failed. Excitement surged like wildfire within him, and his breath grew shallow and fast. His shirt hung open now, and Ariel looped her arms around his neck in a loose circle before deliberately arching her back.

His hands cupped her breasts again, this time with no fabric barring the way. Slowly, not sure if she would let him progress to the further intimacy he wanted, he lowered his head. Ariel made not the slightest protest. Instead, her hands moved upward to guide his mouth to its pouting target.

When his lips closed over her nipple, he felt the shudder of reaction ripple through her. A little gasp tore from her throat, and she arched to further bring herself into his mouth.

She tasted like honey and Saurian brandy and nectar and the indefinable flavor of pure Ariel. His tongue swept over the pebbled nipple, savoring every rise and indentation. Fire raged through his veins while he deepened the embrace, taking her

Ariel's Dance

entire nipple into his mouth and beginning to suckle on it. The rhythm of his pull-release-pull matched the pounding of his heart. Ariel's breath came in matching gasps, and her hips began to surge on his raised leg, rubbing her intimately against the fabric of his pants. Her hands pressed his head harder against her breast, encouraging him to continue.

The far-off ting of a bell merged with Ariel's sudden stiffening. Now he'd have to start all over again with the task of relaxing her. The prospect of repeating his embraces made him smile before returning to his avid suckling.

"Someone's coming!" Ariel's words, whispered into his ear, sounded more like an endearment than a protest.

He ignored her. Shifting to her other breast, he let his tongue explore the pouting nipple. It tasted as exquisite as the first.

Her hands moved from his hair to his chest. "Dekkan, stop! Someone's coming!"

"What?" His question was muffled by the soft breast his mouth had no intention of leaving.

She pushed against him. "Stop it. You don't want to be found like this, do you?"

This time her words sank in. "Someone's coming?"

"Yes. I heard the elevator bell." She squirmed around so much he had to drop his knee and let her slide her feet to the floor. Only now did he realize the hard marble wall had made his knee ache.

That's not the only thing aching right now.

Still half-involved with the interrupted embrace, he stood there while Ariel shrugged her shoulders. In an instant, her dress had returned to its correct draping, although the points of her breasts stood out sharp and clearly defined. Dekkan ached to take them into his mouth again.

"Will you fasten your shirt!" she ordered. When he didn't move to obey fast enough, her fingers quickly moved up the row of closures. Dekkan took a deep breath and closed his eyes, enjoying the butterfly-light touches against his chest. His arms still encircled her, and he couldn't resist pulling her closer to him to give her a brief but ardent kiss. "Thank you, Ariel."

With their clothes restored to some sense of order, she relaxed slightly, making no move to leave his arms. "Thanks for what?"

Did she sound a little wary? "For fastening my shirt. For warning me that someone is coming." He tipped his head, hearing the echo of distant steps but unable to tell if they approached or moved away.

"Oh," she said, before making a brief, abortive attempt to step away from him. When he didn't release her, she didn't struggle, but rather reached up to run her finger down the side of his cheek.

He knew he held her far too tightly, pressed his body against hers much harder than necessary, but he had no inclination to do otherwise. She fit against him perfectly, each curve and indentation matching a corresponding arch and protrusion of his. His aching manhood revealed the state of his readiness to resume their embrace, but to his surprise, he felt no shame. Ariel surely understood that she was far too tempting for any man—even him—to resist.

Every texture and curve of her body cried out for tactile investigation, from her tumbled auburn curls softer than sarsilk that wrapped around his fingers in a living binding, to her skin, soft, faintly scented with a delicate spice, that tempted his mouth. He started to lower his head to let his lips begin that exploration.

Galaxy! Had he no willpower at all? He jerked his head back and stared at her. What was he *doing*, for galaxy's sake? The footsteps, though still some distance away, were definitely coming closer. Abruptly, he let her go.

His unexpected release bounced her against the wall, and she banged her head lightly. He tried to catch her again to prevent the collision, but only ended up with her back in his arms.

"Ouch!" she complained without heat. "Watch what you're doing, will you?"

Something inside him flinched from the realization that she felt none of the sensual pull that still enveloped him.

"Sorry," he said harshly, wondering what it would take to break her calm composure. Hadn't she felt anything of the passion that had nearly swamped his senses? He felt a deep reluctance to release her. Nevertheless, he slowly opened his arms and let them drop to his side before stepping away from her. His arms felt empty.

She ignored his apology. "This is your last chance. You can tell Jeccad we're planning to marry, or . . ."

It took him a moment to recall what she was talking about. The recollection stiffened his own resolve, and he took another step away. That was the trick, he decided. All he had to do was maintain a certain distance from her and he could keep a clear head on his shoulders. He took a deep breath to bolster his determination and answered her unstated question.

"Or what?" He considered her with fascinated interest. "Are you threatening me, by any chance?"

"Of course not." A shrug of her shoulders accompanied her instant denial.

Unfortunately, the gesture gave her breasts an impertinent little jiggle and emphasized the still-prominent peaks of her nipples. His gaze latched onto the sight as a starving man would snatch at a feast.

"Are you sure you don't want me to tell Jeccad you're my fiancé?" Her question barely broke through his mental fog.

"Yes. I mean no. I mean . . ." Dekkan turned away and rubbed his hand over his face in utter frustration as he felt his negotiation expertise crumble. All he could concentrate on was how it would feel to slip his fingers inside those gaping armholes and cup his hand around her breast—again. She was all gossamer heat and silken fire. His hand curled with the absolute need to hold that heat and fire one more time.

When he remembered how it had felt to touch her, his frustration rose to unbounded heights. How the hell was he ever going to get the ring back when he couldn't concentrate on anything except Ariel's body?

"I don't know what I mean," he admitted at last. He turned to face her again and pointed an accusing finger. "You are dangerous! I can't even think two coherent thoughts when you're around."

Anger sparked in her eyes. "Me? You're the one who has the problem! I'm a perfectly reasonable human being. It's not my fault you're irrational!"

"Irrational? Irrational? I'll have you know—."

Whatever Dekkan would have Ariel know was lost as an amused voice behind him interrupted.

"Children! Children! Stop your squabbling."

Ariel's Dance

Dekkan groaned and closed his eyes. How could an interstellar contract negotiator with years of experience be caught in so many embarrassing situations within a single standard day? With ill-fated resignation, he waited for Ariel to confirm the identity of the man who'd caught him childishly bickering in the hall.

"Jeccad." Ariel's voice had lost its heat and taken on more subdued tones than Dekkan had yet heard from her. "We were just coming to talk to you."

Drawing on the last of his composure, Dekkan drew himself up to his full height and tried to recover whatever shreds of dignity remained to him. "Gentleperson Jeccad, I give you good day." By refusing to look at Ariel and concentrating fiercely, he managed a Third-Degree Peer Formal Bow without disgracing himself or landing on his nose.

Jeccad was a small man, little resembling his exotic daughter. With his barrel chest and long mane of silver hair, he could have been a range-rider for the stockyards in Amity's South Continent. His long and powerful arms fit oddly on one with such a bandy, bowlegged gait. Despite his unprepossessing appearance, he was richly garbed in loose pants of expensive sarsilk, an elaborately embroidered overshirt of fine linen, and a long, floor-length brocade vest.

After Ariel's terse introductions, Jeccad led them to his study farther down the hall. Ushering them inside, he waved them to chairs in a room that continued the chilly decor of the hall. Dekkan eyed the unpadded marble seats and wondered briefly if the uncomfortable seating was meant to discourage interruptions. He had to admit that such a tactic would probably work well against anyone not so determined as he. He gingerly settled into the most appealing seat of the lot, a double-width backless chair of unyielding marballoy just a few centimeters too low for comfort.

"Well, sir, do you want to tell me why you've inveigled my daughter to introduce you to me?" Jeccad's voice had lost any hint of amusement somewhere between the hall and the study. He perched majestically on a chair that sat higher than the rest, bringing the little man's head to a level just a trace higher than any other seated person's would reach.

It was also, Dekkan noted, the only seat in the room with a comfortably padded cushion. The contrast between the austere frigidity of this room and the exotic warmth of Ariel's home flashed through his mind. No question which of the two environments he preferred.

Ariel didn't bother to sit, but flitted from place to place as restlessly as a butterfly, touching a porcelain bust along one wall, then running her fingers along an abstract metallic sculpture. She offered Dekkan a small, silent wave of her hand as if passing the control of the conversation over to him. Her movements kept her within his line of sight, which made her more of a distraction than he could afford.

For an instant, Dekkan regretted not letting her lead the conversation, then chided himself for such a lack of nerve. He'd conducted hundreds of successful negotiations. No reason to think this one wouldn't conclude with equal success. Besides, surely he would get used to Ariel's presence quickly once the discussion with Jeccad got to the point.

Standing behind her father's chair, Ariel turned then, presenting her profile to Dekkan. When she reached up to pick up a small figurine in an alcove just above her head, the deep armhole of her dress gaped away from her body, leaving him with an unparalleled view of her naked chest in profile. He swallowed heavily. He would have thought it an accident if she hadn't looked over her shoulder at him and given him a hearty wink.

He clenched his hand over his still-aching knee and reminded himself that he was there to negotiate, dammit, not ogle his opponent's daughter.

To make sure that he achieved his aim, he angled his body so Ariel was just out of sight. No sense tempting his own willpower any more than necessary—it had already failed him several times in her presence.

"Gentleperson Jeccad," Dekkan began, only to be interrupted by Jeccad's harsh voice.

"Jeccad will do. So you're Stonnor's son. You have much the look of him. I wondered who he'd send."

The man's unyielding expression did not engender much optimism in Dekkan, but he plowed ahead. "I am glad that you remember my father. It makes my task easier."

"Hah! Who couldn't remember the Amitan fool?"

Dekkan clamped down hard on his anger at such disparagement of his father. In truth, in his own mind he'd called Stonnor that and more in the days since he'd heard of this fiasco.

"Jeccad, I have come to redeem my father's debt. As you know, he left a token as payment for that obligation. I am here to redeem that token."

Jeccad's face had grown progressively darker through Dekkan's careful explanation. "What is this? What token?"

"The ring. My father offered a ring in payment of a debt of . . . of . . ." No matter how he tried, he just couldn't bring himself to say the words that indicted his own father of gambling away the family heritage.

Jeccad burst into sudden, unexpected laughter. "What you mean is Stonnor um Galawan gambled the ring away."

Dekkan inclined his head in silent acknowledgment. He had to shift in his chair again to keep Ariel just at the edge of his vision. If he looked at her too long, she had a tendency to scramble his wits.

"That is what you mean, isn't it, boy?" Jeccad's harsh voice insisted on a verbal response.

Dekkan dragged his concentration back to the discussion. "You may call it so, if you wish. I am not here to argue semantics. I merely wish to repay you for your courtesy in accepting the ring as security for the debt and take it back."

"Take it back? Take it back? Ho, ho, ho!" Jeccad leaned back in his chair, his arms folding over his thick waist while deep laughs shook his frame. "You hear that, Ariel? This boy thinks he can take back an object his father lost at my table."

"Gentlesire, I am not a boy!" Dekkan stood and loomed over the older man's laughing form. "I merely want to buy back the ring my father lost. Is that so difficult to comprehend?"

Dark thunder clouded Jeccad's face as he, too, rose. "And what makes you think I'm willing to sell the ring? Your father lost it fair and square—." Ariel's sudden choking cough distracted Jeccad for a vital moment. He glared at her, but she met his eyes with determined calm. "Fair and square, I say. I'm under no obligation to sell that bauble back to you."

"It's not a bauble! It's an heirloom, and I'm more than willing to pay any fair price—."

"Fair! You talk about fair when you come bearing

Ariel's Dance

lies? Stonnor lost the ring in a game of *shallon*. He didn't wager it as a 'token of payment.' He wagered the ring itself." Jeccad sat back down wearing a smug smile that made Dekkan want to wring the man's neck.

Before he could judge the wisdom of his words, he blurted out, "Which leads me to wonder just how honest that game was. My father is an expert *shallon* player. In fact, he took the championship on Amity three years running."

"Well," Jeccad said with a condescending smile, "one can hardly compare Amity, a backwoods planet full of rubes, to the interstellar gaming center here on Mariposa. Stonnor was simply out of his league in playing for high stakes here."

Dekkan's hands clenched, and he struggled to control his temper. A remote part of him watched in bewilderment as anger flooded through him in an onrushing wave. What was wrong with him? He had never let emotions interfere with his negotiations. Why did he have an insatiable urge to wrap his fingers around this infuriating little man's neck? He had never let himself get distracted during a negotiation either. So why did Ariel's slightest movement send a sizzling heat through his body? Why did every bounce of her breasts remind him of how delicious she tasted on his tongue?

He was losing control of his body and his mind. A quick memory of his discarded patch lying in Ariel's waste disposer brought insight but no comfort.

While Dekkan sought words to calm the situation and convince Jeccad, Ariel took her own action. She moved to stand beside Dekkan and placed a calming hand on his tensed arm. To his astonishment, instead of inspiring instant lust, the touch of her flesh against his sent a soothing flow of warmth throughout his body. He could feel his muscles relax as comfort seeped from her to him. The sensation was so unexpected he almost missed her words.

"Jeccad, I believe Dekkan has not yet told you the other reason we are here."

"Other reason?" The man's tone held a definite wariness, matched by the sudden realization that struck Dekkan.

"Ariel—"

She overrode his interruption. With a gay smile she said, "Of course. Dekkan would have no need to bring me along on such a task. No, I'm here because Dekkan and I—"

"Ariel, don't do—"

"Dekkan and I plan to wed." She finished the statement in a rush before Dekkan could protest more. "We wanted to tell you so you could wish us happy."

"Marry?" Dekkan and Jeccad asked in appalled unison.

For once, he and Jeccad were in total accord. Each viewed the prospect of a union between him and Ariel with equal horror.

Dekkan opened his mouth to deny it all, but not a sound issued. Instead, he watched an astounding transformation occur on Jeccad's face. Where only a moment before hostility and anger had reigned, now his expression showed only pleasure and . . . relief?

Jeccad stared at his daughter as if she were a member of an exotic alien species. "You're going to marry him? You're really going to do it?" The words contained an awestruck quality belied by his incredulous inspection of Dekkan. "You're going to marry . . . *him?*"

Ariel's Dance

Dekkan couldn't even begin to take offense at Jeccad's disbelief. He was too busy glaring at Ariel and mauling the fingers of the hand she still pressed to his arm. He also was fighting down his body's enthusiastic approval. Marriage to Ariel meant the opportunity to hold her, touch her, kiss her.

Make love to her.

With lust raging inside him, Dekkan squeezed her hand in his. "I thought we agreed that you weren't going to say that," he said in an intense whisper. "Remember?"

She smiled through gritted teeth and vainly tried to loosen his grip. "I remember that we didn't come to a conclusion."

"Ariel! This is wonderful news!" Jeccad pressed a button on a small table beside his chair. "I can't believe it's finally happening. You're going to get married." He shook his head in bemused wonder.

Ariel's I-told-you-so look didn't soothe Dekkan's need to salvage something from this fiasco. "Uh, Gentlesire Jeccad . . ."

Jeccad bounced to his feet and strode over to slap Dekkan's back with too-hearty congratulations. "None of that 'gentlesire' business between us, my boy. You're going to be family. I told you to call me Jeccad."

"Uh, Jeccad, then . . ."

Gummy tottered into the study, interrupting Dekkan again. "You wanted something, sire?" His suspicious glance left Dekkan feeling as if he'd been caught with his hands in the family silver chest. "Is this gentleman creating any . . . difficulty?"

"No, no, no. No difficulty. Gummy, our little Ariel's going to marry! Can you believe it? She's going to marry this fellow!" Jeccad again pounded Dekkan, this time almost knocking him over.

"Uh, Jeccad..." Dekkan tried again to stop things from progressing further, despite not quite knowing what he could say to accomplish that.

"Wonderful, sire!" Gummy's toothless grin was painfully evident. "This is excellent news indeed. Shall I announce it for you?"

"No! Wait!" Dekkan's horrified protest went unheeded.

"Good idea. Put it out over the usual channels." Jeccad turned to Ariel and gave her a squashing bear hug that made her eyes roll. "My little girl getting married at last!"

With a spryness that belied Gummy's earlier decrepitude, the old man hustled out the door, ignoring Dekkan's protest.

Dekkan sank into the backless chair, wondering just where in the conversation things had taken a turn for the bizarre. It didn't take long for him to conclude that Ariel's brief contribution had generated the strangeness that now swamped him. Worst of all was the realization that if he were truly given his choice, he wanted the announcement to be true. Galaxy help him, he *wanted* to marry Ariel, no matter how inappropriate the match might be.

"Jeccad." Ariel firmly disentangled herself from Jeccad's embrace. "Don't you think it would be nice if you gave Dekkan a little token of your thanks? For agreeing to marry me, I mean."

"Token?" Jeccad's paternal glee sank behind the shrewdness that surfaced. "What are you talking about?"

"The ring," she said sweetly. "Don't you think it would be a courteous gesture if you let Dekkan redeem the ring? I mean, it is a family heirloom and all." She blushed and lowered her head as if in maidenly shyness. "We'll need it for the engagement, you know."

"Oh, well, why didn't you say so, son?" Jeccad's suspicion changed back to the expansive good humor of before. "You didn't tell me this was your family's traditional engagement ring." His eyes narrowed in shrewd suspicion. "That is what Ariel is trying to tell me, isn't it? That you'll be giving it to her as a betrothal present?"

Dekkan felt his entire world spinning out of control. The ring was in truth the traditional wedding present from the heir of Misthaven Keep to his bride. The only problem was that he was expected to give the ring to Sebella as soon as he returned to Amity.

Carefully choosing his words, he said, "Once I redeem the ring, I do intend to give it to my fiancée at our wedding." He ignored Ariel's gasp and the flash of anger that sparked in her eyes. "It is a tradition in all marriages in my family."

"Good, good." Jeccad relaxed again, returning to his seat. "Ah, life is good today."

Ariel settled beside Dekkan on the uncomfortable backless chair. She clasped his hand as if she couldn't bear to part with him. Dekkan suspected her true motive was to ensure he didn't push her off the chair. "So, Jeccad," she said persuasively, "if you'll give Dekkan the ring, he'll be happy to give you its worth in credits." After a quick glance at Dekkan's face, she added, "Plus a gratuity to thank you for your help."

Dekkan nodded once in acceptance of the terms Ariel had presented. The situation seemed to be returning to normal, and he began to relax a little. No for harm seemed to have been done by Ariel's outrageous story. Jeccad's mood had certainly changed dramatically with her announcement.

So what if his expectations were raised for a wedding that would never be? After a little time, Ariel could announce that the betrothal was off, and everything would return to normal. In the meantime, Dekkan would get the ring back. Quickly he buried the regret that the marriage would never be. Sebella. He had to think of Sebella.

Everything seemed to be going well.

Jeccad's pudgy fingers drummed on the arm of his chair, and for the first time his gaze refused to meet either Ariel's or Dekkan's. "What's the hurry?" His eyes flickered around the room. "We can take care of those little details later."

The door hissed open and Gummy came back in. "It has gone out, sire."

With palpable relief, Jeccad leaped on the change of subject. "It's done then?"

Gummy nodded, then wandered over to give Ariel a pat on the head. "All the media have been informed. I think if you'll check your news 'porter it should already be hitting the headlines."

"Headlines?" Dekkan's voice weakened as he realized that perhaps this "engagement" wouldn't be quite so easy to get out of as he'd supposed. He asked again, "Did you say . . . headlines?"

Jeccad fiddled with a control, and a screen swooped out of the ceiling. Another twist brought the current holo-news video onto the screen. Before Dekkan's horrified eyes, he saw the huge headlines screaming across the wall.

WEDDING OF THE YEAR: MARIPOSA'S MOST ADMIRED DANCER TO MARRY AMITAN HEIR.

ARIEL TO WED AT LAST! WILL SHE RETIRE?

Ariel's Dance

JECCAD SNARES AMITY'S MISTHAVEN KEEP HEIR FOR DAUGHTER.

"SETTLEMENTS WILL BE PROFITABLE," JECCAD PROMISES.

"What—what's going on?" The question was not one of his wittier comments, Dekkan knew, but it was the best he could offer. Not that anyone paid any attention to his weak protest. After all, not many men had been so bludgeoned into matrimony—no, it was only an engagement! The relief he expected from that thought didn't come. Somehow, the notion of being married to the luscious Ariel didn't seem so bad.

Especially when compared to being married to Sebella.

Immediately, he buried that guilty thought. How could he even consider Ariel as wife material? Someday soon he'd have to give up his interstellar travel and settle down to be a staid and sedate farmer. When that happened, he'd need a wife who'd been brought up to help him manage Misthaven's diverse and profitable interests. He certainly didn't need a frivolous butterfly who flaunted her too-exotic looks in front of any man willing to plunk down a credit or two.

He glanced at Ariel, caught another glimpse of the side curve of her breast, and groaned. His mind might know that she was all wrong for him, but his body knew equally well that she was perfection itself.

Ariel's dangerous tone interrupted his none-too-coherent thoughts. "Jeccad," she asked. "What have you done?"

"Done, my dear?" Even a six-year-old would have known a guilty secret lay behind that question. "Whatever do you mean?"

"Turn off that holo-news and answer me," she insisted.

Reluctance in every move, Jeccad slowly turned off the projector. Before that instant, Dekkan would have sworn that nothing short of a nine-foot-tall Huattl giant from Panjobab III could have intimidated Jeccad. But there he sat, clearly nervous addressing his slip of a daughter. Dekkan eyed Ariel with a new respect.

"Jeccad, tell me what you've done." Her voice brooked no argument.

"Why . . . nothing."

"Ha!" She watched Jeccad carefully, and Dekkan could see the wheels turning in her mind.

He decided that the faster they concluded their business, the better—before things got any worse. "Ahem. Jeccad. Perhaps you could just get the ring and allow me to redeem it? I can do that in cash, of course."

Jeccad's eyes again refused to meet Dekkan's. "Well, son, I can't exactly do that."

"*Daddy*, what have you done?" Ariel's voice held all the danger of a striking viper. It was the first time she'd used such a familiar address to her father, and Dekkan devoutly prayed she never addressed *him* in such a tone.

After a bit of hemming and hawing, Jeccad admitted, "Well, you see, I don't exactly have the ring to give you."

"What does 'I don't exactly have the ring' mean?"

"Uh, I sort of gave it to someone."

"Someone?" The threat in Ariel's voice reached a point where even Dekkan would have thought twice about crossing her. "Who, Daddy? Who did you give the ring to?" A sudden thought struck her and she said, "You didn't give it to . . ."

Ariel's Dance

"Who?" Dekkan asked, not quite understanding the reason for her consternation. "Who did he give the ring to?"

Jeccad ignored the interruption. He nodded mournfully. "I'm afraid so. I gave the ring to . . ."

A thick swallow interrupted Jeccad's final words, and Dekkan opened his mouth to ask his question again.

Ariel forestalled him. She completed Jeccad's admission in a voice of doom. "Floribunda. He gave it to Floribunda."

Chapter Six

Stonnor glanced furtively around the Mariposa landing terminal. Had Sebella spotted him? No. With a mental wipe of his brow, he hastened his steps out to the ground transport center. Two days in Sebella and Brolla's company aboard ship made him wonder one more time whether Dekkan had imbibed a little too much home brew the day he had proposed to the woman. The thought that she might soon rule the Misthaven Keep home brought shudders to his strong frame.

He had just lifted his hand to hail the next groundcar when he heard a commotion behind him. *Damn!* Just when he thought he'd gotten away.

"Stonnor! There you are. I feared you'd gotten lost." Sebella's tone implied that he couldn't be trusted even to take himself to the sanitary facilities without help. As usual, Brolla stood slightly behind and to one side of Sebella, silently carrying her three valises and two smaller cases.

"Ah. Sebella. I was, uh, just hailing a groundcar for us." He hoped the gods of Mariposa would forgive the lie.

A small vehicle hummed to a stop in front of them, and its doors opened automatically. "Where to?" the driver asked with a laconic, Mariposan drawl.

"I'm staying at the Mariposa Grand," Stonnor said quickly before turning to Sebella. "I don't suppose you're planning to stay somewhere so expensive?" Try as he might, he couldn't entirely keep the hope out of his voice.

"The Grand will be fine," Sebella said as she directed Brolla to place her bags in the small car's interior. "I had my parents' secretary check with yours to find where you stayed on your vacation here earlier this year. Brolla and I have a reservation, er, reservations."

Stonnor's heart sank like the springs on the little car as the three of them crammed themselves and their bags into the small passenger space. He should have known; he really should have. With a stern warning, he reminded himself that Sebella was his son's choice of wife and would soon become his daughter-in-law. It took all his self-discipline, but he managed not to groan aloud at the thought.

With Brolla's elbow mining holes in his rib cage, he winced in earnest as he listened stoically to Sebella's comments about the "vice and degradation" on the streets they passed on their way to the Grand. By the time they arrived, he was more than pleased to be able to unfold himself from his cramped position. He courteously held the door for the overburdened Brolla—Sebella didn't trust the looks of the hotel's baggage handlers—and herded the pair toward the registration kiosk. Gravely, he stepped aside and permitted Sebella to register first.

"I need a room with a view of the countryside, not the evil businesses here in the city," Sebella commanded.

"Gentlelady, all our rooms have your choice of holo-views," the deferent clerk assured her. "You may select any view you wish."

Sebella flushed and inclined her head to a yet more regal angle. Probably doesn't like having her parochialism revealed, Stonnor thought. To his knowledge, not a single inn on Amity had the technology to permit guests to dial their own views.

A second clerk became available and Stonnor moved up to speak in a low voice. "My name is Stonnor um Galawan, from Amity. I have a reservation."

To his left, Sebella was demanding a copy of the latest holo-vid news to take to her room. "I have to keep up on interstellar affairs, you know. Our family keep depends on my knowledge of the galaxy's business," she explained with a sniff.

The clerk bowed and assured her he would print one out on the instant.

"Yes, gentlesire. I have your reservation here." The clerk in front of Stonnor recalled his attention to the matters at hand.

"You see that lady registering to my left?" Stonnor kept his voice to just above a whisper. The clerk's eyes glistened with sympathy for his co-worker, who was still dealing with Sebella's complaint about the slowness of the registration printer.

Ariel's Dance

"Yes, gentlesire." The clerk eyed Stonnor speculatively. "You wish to be positioned near her?"

"Galactic spirits, no! I want my suite as far from hers as possible. Preferably in another building, if you have one." Stonnor slid a hundred-credit note surreptitiously across the counter. "You understand?"

Gentle comprehension lit the clerk's eyes. "I understand perfectly," he said as he bent his head in a vain attempt to hide his smile. The credit note disappeared as if it had never been. A few taps at the reservation system caused a three-dimensional display to appear between them.

"Your suite, gentlesire, is here in the northern tower complex." The clerk pointed to a glowing area at one extreme end of the image.

"And where is the lady's?" Stonnor asked suspiciously. A second area lit up diagonally opposite the image.

"Her reservation is for this suite. Unfortunately, unlike you, she made her reservation too late to get one of our better accommodations."

Stonnor smiled and met the clerk's gaze in silent masculine communication. "Thank you. I won't forget your kindness."

"Have a pleasant stay with us." The clerk winced as Sebella snatched the printout from the other clerk's hand and turned to stalk toward the liftgates leading to the guest suites.

Stonnor walked over to where Sebella and Brolla were waiting for a lift to their suite. "I'm sorry, my dear," he told her. "I take the other lifts to my suite. I hope you enjoy your stay." He nodded at Brolla and started to move away when he heard a shriek that turned every head in the bustling lobby. The commotion centered on Sebella, who released yet another shriek of rage.

Sebella stood, holding the printout and pointing a shaking finger at the headline emblazoned across the page.

WEDDING OF THE YEAR: MARIPOSA'S MOST ADMIRED DANCER TO MARRY HEIR TO AMITY'S MISTHAVEN KEEP

Beneath the lurid headlines, a respectably good still image of Dekkan sat in intimate proximity to a beautiful publicity holo-vid of Ariel in midperformance of her butterfly dance. While the holo-vid shimmered and twirled through a ten-second loop of the dance, Sebella's mouth opened and closed silently in time to Ariel's graceful moves.

And, of course, Ariel was gloriously naked.

Stonnor groaned and tried to ignore Brolla's avid interest in the holovid. The headline seemed clear enough. Somehow, Dekkan seemed to have acquired a second fiancée without bothering to divest himself of the first. Stonnor could only applaud his son's superior taste in women with his most recent selection, but what had gotten into the boy to so ignore the honor of his upbringing?

And what the hell was Jeccad thinking of to allow this match to be aired so publicly?

Jeccad's astounding efficiency in announcing the supposed engagement between Ariel and Dekkan had left even Ariel gasping in bewilderment. Of course, she'd known he'd be pleased with the fact that she at last planned to give in to his desires and take a mate—but this was utterly ridiculous. Something odd was going on here, and for once Ariel didn't have any idea what that something could be.

Which didn't help her deal with the large, extremely irate male who stalked by her side with all the good humor of an enraged Fansonian devil-cat.

At the moment, she counted herself lucky in merely having extracted him from Jeccad's home before he expressed his mood by tearing something—or someone—apart. Any further concessions would be hard-won indeed. She also knew she owed him some explanation for the situation they now found themselves in, but what those explanations could be and whether they would cool his temper, she didn't have the slightest idea.

She could tell him the truth, she supposed, but when she glanced at his heavy frown and noted the furious clenching and unclenching of his fists, she realized that the truth might not be something he could appreciate at the moment.

Deciding that she might as well face up to the argument now, she subtly guided him to a quiet corner of a small local park. Mariposa's visitors rarely spent much time outdoors in this neighborhood of high-stakes casinos and exotic entertainment, so she figured they'd have the place pretty much to themselves. She was right. Only a few children playing a couple of hundred meters away broke the privacy of the stone table and benches under shaded fern-palms. Although she sat cross-legged on the warm sandstone bench, Dekkan paced back and forth with long, angry strides.

He moves like a cat. Even when he's mad as hell, he moves like a cat. The sudden thought flustered her slightly. She had no business thinking about him that way. Instead, she'd better concentrate on how she was going to explain her way out of this mess.

At last he stopped directly in front of her, fists planted firmly on his hips. "Would you care to explain what that little farce was about?" The silken tone of his voice didn't fool her for a moment. She knew a dangerous man when she saw one.

Ariel propped her chin on her hand and asked with a nonchalance she didn't feel, "Do you want the long version or the short version?"

"How about giving it to me straight? First"—he ticked off the number on a finger—"how in screaming banshees did Jeccad get the word out so fast? Second, *why* did he get it out that fast? And third . . ." He paused for a deep breath. "Why the hell is he so anxious to get rid of his only daughter? What's wrong with you?"

The final question, pitched as softly as the others, nevertheless made Ariel wince. It wasn't exactly the most tactful of queries, but then, she didn't think Dekkan was in the mood to consider her feelings to any great extent.

She held up one finger. "Okay, you asked for it. First, Jeccad's brother is the publisher of the major holo-news system on Mariposa. It's a simple thing for him to get anything published he wants. And since the holo-news is updated every five minutes or so throughout the day, our, um, situation got into the news almost immediately."

"It's updated every five minutes?" he asked blankly. "Why?"

She cocked her head to one side. "We're a tourist planet, and a lot of our visitors are businessmen who don't like to be out of touch with what's going on in the galaxy. Mariposa has the most efficient news-dispersal system of any planet in the Federation—or at least that's what Uncle Liall says." She cocked her head to one side in inquiry. "How often is the holo-news updated on Amity?"

"A couple of times a day, I suppose," Dekkan said blankly.

Ariel's Dance

Ariel was shocked. She couldn't even imagine what it must be like to be so out of touch with important events.

But Dekkan had other things on his mind. "Wait a second. What did you say about Mariposa's holo-news?"

"I said, Uncle Liall claims we have the most efficient system in the Federation."

He groaned and rubbed his hand over his face. "Do you mean that Mariposan holo-news is efficiently distributed here on Mariposa, or—"

"All over the Federation, I guess. I know several of the big interstellar news organizations have their headquarters here and monitor all the latest releases." She looked at him anxiously when he groaned again. "What's wrong?"

Dekkan sank down onto the bench beside her and stared at her, horror in his eyes. "So the report of our so-called engagement might at this very moment be winging its way through subspace all over the Federation."

She shrugged. "Sure, I suppose so. But I wouldn't think many other worlds would bother to pick it up."

"I don't care about just any world, only one. Amity." His gaze bored holes right through her as she at last realized why he seemed so appalled.

"You mean the Amitan holo-news service might . . ."

He nodded his head.

"Oh, damn." All his friends and relatives could be reading about their mock engagement—perhaps even his fiancée, the patient Sebella. "I'm sorry, Dekkan," she said sincerely. "I never meant for this to happen."

He ignored her, lost for the moment in his own

calculations of the likely extent of the disaster. "The good thing is that Amitan holo-news channels don't have the technology to run that holo-vid of your dance," he said, more to himself than to her. "And they wouldn't take a still frame from it because it would be considered too lewd." He brightened for a moment; then realization struck him again. "On the other hand, no way would they not report what you are, and what you do for a living."

"What do you mean, 'what I am'? What's wrong with what I am?"

He ignored that question, too, to prop his forehead on his hand. "Amity's foremost contracts negotiator caught in a scandal with, with . . ."

"With what exactly?" She was plenty tired of hearing him say nasty things about her.

"With a nude dancer, for goodness' sake. Though I don't suppose 'goodness' has much to do with it," he added nastily.

She leaped to her feet. "All right. That does it. I've just about had it with you insulting me all the time. My job is perfectly respectable here on Mariposa. No one here thinks I'm lower than a swamp-crawler's belly except you. So I think it's time you had your attitude adjusted."

"There's nothing wrong with my attitude!"

"Is that so? Then how come you're the only person on the whole planet who thinks there's something wrong with my dance? Didn't you even look at that profile of me in the paper? I'm one of the most popular dancers on Mariposa. People come from all over the galaxy to watch me perform."

"If you will put it in the shop window for all to see, you can't expect men not to look, now, can you? I doubt if too many men bothered to read the 'profile,' as you call it; they're all too busy leering over

Ariel's Dance

the 'profile' you present in that holo-vid clip!"

His snide response sent a flush of rage pouring through Ariel. She leaned closer in an attempt to tower over his seated figure. "I sure noticed you doing plenty of looking when you came to my dressing room. You didn't seem to have any problem checking out every detail."

He glared up at her, fists tightening to white-knuckled tension at his side. "That's different."

"Ha! What's so different about your leers from other men's?"

"I didn't leer!"

"Well, I certainly couldn't tell the difference." She rested her right elbow in her left palm and tapped her chin with mocking thoughtfulness. "No, there was one difference. You were practically salivating. Most of the men I meet have a little more class!"

"Why, you . . ."

Whatever he planned to call her, she never knew, because in a swift motion he scooped her up and plunked her flat on her back on the herb-scented grass, following her down and pinning her body under his. His mouth rammed into hers in violent possession.

She started to fight him, then stopped when she suddenly realized that for all his fury, he was taking exquisite care not to hurt her in any way. Even the forceful pressure of his mouth on hers owed nothing at all to pain and everything to a deep well of heat and pleasure. She gave an instinctive wriggle and smiled under his lips when he settled himself more firmly against her.

She moaned and fought to get her arms free. Once she'd pulled them out from under the weight of his body, she hesitated, hands beside her head in the grass. Her eyes opened to stare into his. He pulled back slightly, freeing her kiss-swollen lips and asking an ageless, wordless question with his lambent gaze.

She could detect no sign of the rage that had triggered his attack on her. Deliberately, she ran her tongue around her lips. His eyes focused on the movement, and she felt his body sink harder against her own. He wanted her. She knew that. The question was, did she want him?

He propped his weight on one elbow and gently raked her hair out of her face. His eyes were dark, like her favorite bitter chocolate, with pupils that swallowed the light and gave her only her own reflection. He studied every centimeter of her face while his fingers teased her hair with gentle strokes. He didn't release the silken mass, but ran his fingers through it over and over.

"You have the most fabulous hair," he whispered. "I've never seen such a color before. It's vibrant, alive." He brought a handful up to his mouth and inhaled deeply of her scent.

"Dekkan . . ."

"Ariel." His gentle mockery of her unexpressed query brought a quivering smile.

Immediately, his finger traced the outline of her curving lips, tormenting them into trying to capture that fickle touch. Her gaze never left his face: the shape of his nose, the arch of his brow, the curve of his ear, the sensual tilt of his lips. The tiniest detail gave her more pleasure than she'd ever experienced with any other man.

Without giving herself time to fret over her decision, she lifted her arms around his neck, stroking his skin while she allowed her fingers to trace the path her gaze had followed.

"Ah, Ariel, that feels so good." He shut his eyes

Ariel's Dance

like a cat being caressed in just the right place. She was sure he'd begin to purr at any moment.

"Yes," she told him quietly. "You do feel good."

"I meant you." His lips curved into a slight smile.

Her fingers badly wanted to trace that intriguing new shape. "I know. But you feel wonderful, too." She wriggled her hips slightly against him and felt his immediate, uncontrollable reaction. A deep flush stained his cheeks, and he shifted as if to move away.

"I'm sorry—"

"No!" Ariel locked her arms around his hips and pulled him back into the cradle of her thighs. She wanted him nearer, not farther away. "Don't go." Her breasts expanded into a heavy, achy fullness in reaction to his sensual appeal.

"But . . ."

She felt his body harden still more, his manhood a heavy shaft that pressed against her intimately. Instinctively, she spread her legs wider and pulled him still closer against her. The thin silk of her shift pushed up her legs and allowed her to feel every centimeter of him. Only his trousers offered a significant barrier to the penetration she was beginning to need as she needed air to breathe.

Another wriggle drew a groan from him, and she opened her eyes to see him staring down at her in a confusing mixture of desire, uncertainty, and . . . shame?

Shame?

Desire fled as rapidly as it had arrived. "What's wrong?" She heard the huskiness in her voice and tried again. "What's wrong, Dekkan?"

Dekkan buried his face in her neck, sending exquisite shivers up and down her spine. "I can't believe I'm doing this—with you."

More hurt than she possibly could have imagined, she shoved him to one side and pulled herself to her feet. The effort needed for that simple task dismayed her. With her dance training, it should have been simple to rise from the ground. Instead, it felt like the hardest thing she'd ever done.

But it didn't compare with the difficulty of leaving him forever when their time together came to an end and he returned to his lucky, lucky fiancée.

She turned away so he couldn't see the agony she knew must be etched on her face. He still lay on the ground, dealing with whatever guilt and shame he felt. She hugged herself in a vain effort at comfort and wished she'd never started this. It was out of control—*she* was out of control.

For the first time in her life she fought raging feelings of jealousy. She resented Sebella. No, she hated the woman. How could she have been engaged to Dekkan for half a dozen years and not succumbed to the wild desire that now pulsed through Ariel's veins? If Ariel had been truly Dekkan's betrothed, she didn't think she'd have lasted six days!

At the rate she was going, she might not last another six hours.

Behind her, she heard Dekkan slowly get to his feet. He moved to her side and reached out as if to place his arm around her shoulders. Ariel flinched. If he touched her now, she'd go up in flames; she knew she would.

Dekkan's arm dropped back to his side in a futile gesture. "I'm . . . sorry, Ariel. I didn't mean for that to happen. I did not plan to become another of your . . ."

His words sliced through Ariel's mental fog. Her eyes narrowed and the remnants of her desire dissolved like smoke on a windy day. *How dare he!*

Ariel's Dance

How dare *he!* Despite all that had happened between them, he still thought of her as some kind of—of offal, beneath his touch. No, she corrected herself, not beneath his touch, merely beneath his respect.

Ruthlessly, she stomped on all the tender feelings that had begun to sprout inside her for him. He didn't deserve them. No, he deserved the lesson she'd originally planned for him, the one about not judging other people's sins. It merely remained for her to serve him with the instruction he so richly deserved.

She considered her possible tactics and chose the one most likely to have the strongest effect. Taking a breath to fortify herself, she slowly turned to face him.

Dekkan saw the pain in her eyes and mentally blasted himself for the damage he'd done. She hadn't deserved any of it. Not his scorn. Not his anger. Not even his kiss.

But, oh, galaxy, how much he wanted to kiss her again!

With the discipline of years of experience of difficult contract negotiations, he forced the thought away. It helped if he didn't look closely at her. Her soft lips, sweetly curved, tempted a man to taste them. Her fabulous hair curled and crackled as if alive. That luscious body made his teeth ache with the power of its attraction.

How the hell was he going to work with her to get the ring back? Could he restrain himself around her without the help of the patch? He didn't have answers to any of the questions spinning around in his brain.

He only knew it was going to be the hardest thing he'd ever done.

A sudden thought intruded. Never had he experienced anything like this, and certainly not with Sebella. How could he contemplate marriage to a woman who didn't inspire even a modicum of desire within him? Had the now-useless patch suppressed all these feelings? If he met Sebella now, with no patch to block his natural feelings, would he feel the same for her as he did for Ariel?

A more horrifying thought struck. Perhaps he was some kind of sexual pervert who had been held in check only by the patch. Now that he was free of its rein, would he find that his desires spilled past the normal boundaries of acceptability?

How could he ever be sure?

Questions and confusion filled his mind, making him barely aware that Ariel had quietly moved away from him to sit primly on the bench. Just as well, he supposed, though his memory insisted on replaying the pleasure of her hands gripping his buttocks, pulling him closer and closer to the feminine heat that scorched him to his toenails.

Okay, calm down. You don't have to act like an uncivilized brute around her. Show her you can be just as classy as any other man she's known.

Ignoring the shaft of pain that speared through him at the thought, he walked back to the table and sat down, this time carefully taking a seat on the bench across from Ariel. On the one hand, it kept him away from her. On the other, it offered an unparalleled view of the top of her bowed head.

Bowed head?

"Ariel, I'm sorry. I didn't mean to attack you."

At first he didn't think she'd answer him. Then he heard a low "I see."

He cleared his throat. "Do you feel like talking now?"

Ariel's Dance

She lifted her head and nodded. For the first time, her face held an expressionless quality that made it impossible to read what she thought and felt. Somewhere inside, he grieved for the loss of the spontaneity and vivacious spirit that had plagued and charmed him in equal parts since their first meeting.

"Can we talk about this engagement? What are we to do about it?"

She shrugged. "Ignore it, I suppose. We'll have to do something to make sure your . . . fiancée isn't hurt by it. Other than that, there's nothing to be done."

"Sebella will listen when I explain it's all a mistake. She's a very, uh, rational person."

"Rational? Is that what you want in a wife? Someone who'll listen when you explain about an engagement to another woman?"

Her head cocked to one side in what he was beginning to recognize as a typical pose. He thought she looked cute, like a curious little butterfly trying to decide whether to sip the nectar of a particular flower. *I'd love her to sip my nectar,* he thought, then caught his breath at the sheer exhilaration of the thought.

Yes, he was a pervert after all.

Forcefully, he dragged his mind back to her question. "I need a wife who will help me with the keep. Soon enough I'll have to retire from being a negotiator and settle down at Misthaven." Even he heard the reluctance in his voice, so he injected a bit more enthusiasm. "Sebella will be a good helpmeet. She's very knowledgeable about keep affairs."

"I see." One finger picked at a slight smudge of the delicate nail tint on her other hand. "What's she like? Sebella, I mean."

How could he describe a woman he hardly knew? The realization appalled him almost as much as everything else that had happened today. "She's tall. Like most Amitan women, she's tall and blond like me, with brown eyes. She's . . . suitable."

"I see."

The thought of the "suitable" bride waiting for him back at home didn't warm his heart nearly as much as the small, highly unsuitable woman across from him.

It's just hormones, he assured himself. *Once I get back to Amity, everything will be fine.*

"Will you tell me now why Jeccad so badly wants you to marry?"

She glanced up at him from under her brows, then straightened her back and looked away. A breeze flipped her hair over her face and she shrugged it behind her shoulders. "It has to do with my mother. She died when I was a little girl, but she left me with an inheritance. Her will had some provisions about my marriage in it."

"What kind of an inheritance?" His confusion made the question more urgent than he'd intended. Did this have anything to do with her unexpected desire to go to an academy?

She shifted uncomfortably on the bench, and her gaze skidded away from his. "Well, it's sort of a property thing."

Her evasiveness made him suspicious. "What kind of 'property thing'?"

"Well . . ." She was back to picking at her nail tint.

He put his hand over hers to still her busy fingers and draw her attention back to the discussion. "What is your inheritance?"

She drew a deep breath, then looked him in the eye. "Jeccad's casino and house. I own them."

He released her hand and leaned back, stunned. "No wonder you don't need any money to finance your education."

"It's not like that. I own the building, but Jeccad owns the business. That's why I dance. The credits are very good. It pays me enough to let me save up for my education."

Looking into her eyes, for the first time he really believed she was serious about wanting to continue her training. "I think I owe you an apology—another one, I mean."

She gave him a small smile but didn't reply.

"So," he continued, "when you marry, you take control of the property. Presumably he's administering it in trust for the day you marry." He thought that over. "But that doesn't make any sense. Why should Jeccad be so eager for you to take ownership of the property? I'd think he'd prefer you not to marry so he could keep control of it."

For a moment he didn't think she was going to answer. Again her gaze drifted away from him. "You don't understand. I don't take over the property when I marry. I told you, I already own it."

He frowned. "I'm confused, then. What were the marriage terms in your mother's will?"

She smiled slightly. "It's the property. I don't take it over on my marriage. Just the opposite. When I marry, I have to give it back to Jeccad."

Chapter Seven

"You have to give it back?" Dekkan couldn't conceive of an inheritance with such restrictions.

Ariel shrugged. "Come on. Let's go home." She tugged his arm and he automatically rose to accompany her.

They walked in silence through the streets while Dekkan struggled to comprehend the situation she'd described.

"I don't understand," he said as soon as they arrived at her bungalow. "Why would your mother do such a thing?"

Although he'd managed to restrain his curiosity while they were in public, once the door to Ariel's house closed behind them, the questions bubbled out. "Why would a parent grant an inheritance, yet place such strings on it? Didn't she want you to marry?"

"That's not it at all." Ariel's protest sounded a little weak. "She just wanted to make sure. . . ."

Dekkan thought he knew what Ariel was about to say, but he wanted her to confirm it. "Make sure of what?"

Ariel's glance was an apology. "She wanted to make sure no one married me for my money. By taking the property away at the marriage ceremony, she made sure no man could have a claim to it."

"What happens if you don't marry at all? Do you get to keep your inheritance then?"

"If I don't marry, I come into permanent ownership of the building at the age of fifty-five. After that, it doesn't matter if I marry or not. I still get to keep the property."

"But if you wed before then the property goes to Jeccad! That puts it under control of a man." This entire situation was rapidly degenerating into the bizarre.

"That's different. Besides, he doesn't actually get ownership of the building—just a ninety-nine-standard-year lease."

Suspicion reared its head. "If he won't own the building, who will?"

Again she shrugged. "It reverts to my mother's family. She was one of the Am'Zophias."

Dekkan's eyes narrowed in thought. "Your mother was one of the female supremacy clan?" He inspected Ariel's exotically colored hair, skin, and eyes. "Of course. I should have recognized the look."

"You don't have to make it sound like I've got some kind of horrible skin disease!"

He grinned, pleased to have at last punctured her composure. "Why not? You definitely have the look of an Am'Zophian. The only thing is that you're a little short. Aren't they generally bred for height?"

She glared at him. "A more courteous person wouldn't have pointed that out."

"A thousand pardons, lady." His formal Fifth-Degree Bow for Ceremonial Courtesy displayed his gentle irony with elegant ease.

She took his teasing with an ill humor he could tell was three-parts show. "There's no talking to you, is there?" she complained. "I'm going to get some exercise." She stalked toward the door leading to the lush private courtyard at the back of her house.

"Wait a minute! I thought we were going to go visit this Floribunda and try to convince her to let me purchase the ring."

She levered open the door to the patio and glanced over her shoulder at him. "We will. But we have to wait at least until early afternoon. Floribunda prides herself on never rising until the afternoon is well under way. If we were to call or visit now, we'd only spend several hours cooling our heels in her lobby waiting for her to awaken."

"Oh." He thought about that. No doubt Ariel was right. "What should I do while you're exercising?"

She paused at the door and gestured grandly. "Whatever you want. Listen to music. Watch a holovid. Sleep. You can even come join me, if you like. A little exercise might be good for you."

Her careless invitation sent his entire body into red-alert mode. Suddenly he wanted nothing more than to do some calisthenics alongside Ariel. He could watch her stretch and move, see the sweat glisten against her skin. *What harm could merely watching her move do?* The devilish thought tempted him beyond endurance. As long as he only looked, no one would be hurt.

With a smile he couldn't suppress, he nodded. "I

Ariel's Dance

think I will join you. I'll just change into something a little more appropriate and be right with you, all right?"

He barely saw her answering nod and smile before he headed for his sleeping alcove to dig some comfortable shorts out of his luggage.

A few minutes later, dressed in well-used exershorts and singlet, he opened the door and stepped out onto the patio. Tall, lush plants and the tinkling of water gave the private area the air of a tropical paradise. An occasional flash of color betrayed the passing of a nectar-eating hoverwing. Bright little geckos skittered along the path in front of him.

Although the total area wasn't large, it gave the impression of a substantial space through the winding graveled path that led into it. It was less a patio than a garden, he saw now; the air was filled with the damp, fecund scents of a blossoming jungle. In an odd way, the heavy aroma of fertile earth reminded him of home, despite the exotic plants and animals that flourished here.

He followed the twisting path, brushing aside the large fern palms until he reached an open area at the far side of the garden. There he could see the tall adobe brick wall surrounding the garden, a wall that rose at least five meters high.

No doubt about it, Ariel liked her privacy. At first he didn't see her in the glade, and thought he might have taken a wrong turn somewhere. But just as he was about to retrace his path, a shimmer of color caught his eye. He walked over to a low bench and picked up the delicate swath of material.

It was her dress.

A boulder lodged in his throat and his heart leaped into triple-time at the thought of what she might—or might not—be wearing, given that her dress was most certainly not covering her anymore. Surely she hadn't . . . she wasn't . . .

Unable to complete that thought, he felt his fingers tighten on the cloth. By concentrating heavily, he managed to keep his breathing and his speculations more or less under control.

"Hi! I'm up here!" Ariel's voice floated down from somewhere above him.

Nothing could have stopped his gaze from homing in on the naked sprite perched on a fern-palm some four meters above the ground. Nothing could have stopped the inevitable tightness in his groin when he saw that she indeed *had* . . .

"Hi." He had to swallow twice before the word stumbled past his thickened tongue. Never once did he take his gaze from her slim beauty, even for a blink. He wasn't any too sure that if he glanced away for even an instant, she wouldn't disappear.

"Come on up," she invited.

"I'm, uh, not good with heights," he said. In fact, he'd never experienced vertigo. But if he tried to balance on that limb next to her while she was wearing only a smile, well, he simply preferred not to risk his neck so rashly.

"Oh. Sorry." She gave him a flirty grin. "I guess I'll have to come down to you. Catch me!"

"No! Wait!"

But she didn't wait. With a reckless disregard for life and limb, she dove headfirst toward the ground. Panicked, he stepped forward under her, determined to break her fall if he possibly could. Absently, he noted an odd, tingling sensation in his feet and legs, but he kept his attention on her falling form. Her body flattened into the delicate arc of a swan dive, and he braced himself for her impact against him—only to realize that her headlong dive had slowed to a gentle downward drift.

Only after several eternity-long seconds while he waited for her to reach him did he realize that he was standing in a low-grav area. She'd obviously installed a system similar to the one on the stage where she danced so that she could practice her routines. Maintaining the graceful arch of her dive, she settled horizontally into his outstretched arms with utter assurance, letting him guide her to a secure hold.

"Oof!" Unexpectedly, he staggered under her impact against him. He'd expected her to settle with little effort from him, once he'd realized they were in a low-grav environment. Instead, he was all too aware he'd caught perhaps forty-five or fifty kilos of slim female.

Still caught in his arms, Ariel twisted around so her feet touched the ground, but made no move to step away from him. Unfortunately for Dekkan, the motion resulted in her entire body rubbing itself down the front of his lightly clad torso.

"Are you all right?" she asked.

"Fine. I wasn't quite prepared for you, though," How had he kept his voice so calm?

"It's my mass. It's one of the hardest things to remember when you're working in low-grav. Your weight may be less, but you still have the same mass."

"I see." He didn't, of course. How could he concentrate on the physics of moving in low-grav fields when he held an armful of naked woman against his body? Ravishing naked woman. Sexy naked woman.

He could no more have kept his hands from straying to her hips than he could have flown. They cupped the twin globes of her derriere and kept her pressed against an arousal that was becoming more painfully obvious by the moment.

She stood in his arms, either oblivious to his reaction or politely ignoring it. A quick glance revealed no discomfort in her face at his intimate hold, nor any modesty about her lack of attire. Why should she feel either? he realized. She was used to having hundreds, even thousands of men see her naked. Why should she fret over his lustful stare?

"You're ogling my breasts again," she told him.

Embarrassed, he jerked his gaze back to her face. *Damn her!* She found the situation *amusing!* "Sorry," he said curtly. He ordered his hands to let her go and took half a step away from her.

At least that was what he'd meant to do. His hands, however, had a will of their own. They slid gently from her hips to her waist before slipping upward slightly to just under her breasts. And the half step away from her somehow translated into a half step closer, as he felt himself letting his knee nudge its way between her legs.

"What are you doing to me?" he asked when he realized what he'd done. "I try to move away and instead move closer. I try to let you go and instead . . ." His hands moved again, this time cupping the breasts that had fascinated him for so long.

"Aaahh." He closed his eyes and let the sigh seep out of him. "That feels so good. You feel so good." His palms caressed her hardening nipples and transmitted the sensation in waves of excitement all over his body. He breathed in the rich jungle odors and the woman-smell that was Ariel's alone.

Her arms trailed around his neck, and he opened his eyes to see her move even closer, her face lifted to his.

"Dekkan," she said softly, her breath washing

Ariel's Dance

over his face like a caress. "Why don't you kiss me?"

His grip on her breasts tightened in stunned reaction to her invitation. She wanted him to kiss her! His hands slipped away from the delicate mounds and returned to her hips, where they tugged her closer to the straining manhood beneath his shorts. Her eyes glistened with sultry enticement. He bent his head and let his lips stray over her brow and cheek while his hands kneading her hips like a kitten kneading its mother's breast.

Even the light touch of her skin against his mouth sent electric shocks surging through him, and he had to lean back to catch his breath. When he did so, she arched her back, leaning away from him and presenting her breasts, to his delight.

"You have the most beautiful breasts," he whispered, inspecting every subtle curve and sway. "They're just perfect."

"Why don't you kiss them, then?" Her hands curved toward the back of his head and guided his mouth toward the rosy-tipped peaks that cried out for the touch of his mouth.

Or his tongue. Eagerly he licked and tasted the warm, slightly salty, slightly spicy flavor of her nipples. He lifted her hips and she curled her legs around him, letting him take her whole weight. In the low-grav field, she was no burden at all. The hot, damp pressure of her femininity grinding against his heavy manhood urged him to do more. With the sense of coming home, he took one entire nipple into his mouth and suckled.

Her molten reaction rippled through her body, encouraging him to greater efforts. She arched upward, forcing her breast farther inside his mouth. He licked and kissed and suckled until the nipple turned rosy red and engorged. Then he transferred his attention to the other one, letting the subtle reactions of her body guide him to bring her the greatest pleasure.

Only when both breasts had been satisfied did he lift his head and press his forehead against hers. "I can't believe what you're doing to me," he told her. He sucked air into his lungs with shaky breaths and tried to calm himself.

Her fingers stroked through his hair, and her legs loosened their grip around him slightly. "What I'm doing to you? Don't you have that backward?"

"No. Somehow, every time you get within arm's reach, I want to . . ."

"Kiss me?"

"That, too," he acknowledged with a rueful grin. "And other things."

She looked interested. "Other things? Anything you want to tell me about?"

With a great effort of will, he shook his head and let his grip on her relax. Her legs uncurled from around him and drifted downward in the minimal gravity field. "I don't think so. We came here for exercise, remember?"

She grinned. "And you don't think your other ideas would involve any exercise?"

"Not the kind I had in mind, I'm afraid," he said. His heart had stopped thundering and had settled down to an almost normal cadence.

She slipped from his grasp and sauntered over to the bench. "Then I guess playtime is over."

Playtime? Uncomfortable with having their encounter so blandly described, he studied her morosely. How could she treat their reactions so casually? How could she walk away from him as if nothing of import had happened?

"Do you always get your exercise naked?" It was

Ariel's Dance

the only thing he could think of to say. His voice sounded harsh, even to his own ears.

She glanced over her shoulder and picked up the dress from the ground. Tsking over a smudge of soil on the fabric, she shrugged. "What would you suggest I wear? A formal gown?"

"Well, you could put on exercise garments."

"Why? Then I'd just have to wash them. This way, a quick step into the cleanser and I'm done."

He gave up. It wasn't the point anyway. He stepped out of the low-grav field, barely keeping from tripping as his muscles overcompensated for the sudden return of most of his weight. Standing over her as she sat on the bench—she still hadn't bothered to put the garment on, damn her—he wondered how he was going to cool his reaction to her. Struggling to bring his traitorous body under control, he tried to remind himself of all the reasons he should not get involved with Ariel.

Nothing worked. She was just as alluring as ever, with that faint smile that tempted and taunted him, her exotic coloring, and, most of all, her utterly perfect body. He could no more keep from wanting her than he could stop breathing. Which didn't change the fact that she was not—could never be—the right woman for him.

With a frustrated growl he muttered, "I'm going inside. I've had enough." Turning on his heel, he stalked away.

"Enough exercise?" her voice called in slightly too innocent tones.

The question made him stop. He looked back over his shoulder at her and invested his voice with as much discipline and command as he could muster. "Just . . . enough." He shook his head and started moving away again. "Let me know when it's time to leave to see Floribunda. I'll be in my sleeping alcove."

He didn't have to look at her to know that she badly wanted to ask what he'd be doing there. He increased his pace to get out of speaking range before she could ask. He didn't want to tell her he'd be meditating on his many sins.

Mistress Floribunda d'Amatorio's House of Joy squatted smack in the middle of Mariposa City. Holding firmly on to his hard-won control, Dekkan spent a moment trying to decide what the huge marble tower resembled. Brilliant laser signs announced it as THE MOST JOYOUS OF JOYFUL JOYS in flashing fluorescent purples and pinks that were so bright even Mariposa's afternoon sun couldn't dim the display. The signs, inscribed in the seven most common languages in the Federation, were accompanied by graphic animated displays fully three stories tall that illustrated dozens of erotic experiences from all seventeen species that populated the Federated Planets.

Dekkan could only shudder at the monumentally bad taste that had led someone to erect such a building, and the even worse judgment of the local Mariposan government that hadn't razed it immediately upon completion.

Ariel must have seen him wince. "It's not so bad," she told him as they walked across the street toward the entrance. She hadn't mentioned their brief foray into "exercise," and he hadn't known what to say either. He'd merely been relieved to notice that when she told him it was time to leave, she'd garbed herself in a reasonably modest dress that covered her from neck to ankles in iridescent green and gold. Of course, at certain angles the fabric briefly and abruptly shifted from opaque to totally transparent, but he figured it was as close to a modest garment as he'd seen her wear yet, so he shouldn't criticize.

Besides, it kept his gaze firmly locked on her, just to catch those brief glimpses of coppery skin and alluring curves.

"I don't see how it could be worse," he said, referring to the building they approached.

"Well . . ." She shot an impish grin at him. "When Floribunda bought the place, the walls weren't marble but magniglass."

"You mean—?" He stopped dead in the middle of the street, and Ariel tugged hard on his arm to get him out of the darting traffic's way. "All of them?"

"Yup," she told him, as she towed him toward the portal. "The patrons' activities were magnified for the passersby." Her grin invited him to share her amusement. "It was quite an attraction. Stopped traffic for blocks."

"I can imagine."

"It would have lasted longer," she explained, "except the Mariposa City manager was participating in an unfortunate, uh, celebration when his wife happened to pass by. The resulting commotion could be heard out in the suburbs."

"He was in there with someone other than his wife?" Dekkan had thought he was sophisticated, but he couldn't keep the shock from his voice.

She pressed the announcement stud. "Several someones, actually. And all of them a whole lot younger than Mrs. City Manager." She chuckled. "As you might imagine, she was not amused. Within hours the previous owner was shut down, and a day or so later Floribunda's offer to buy it was accepted. She got the building for a ridiculously low price, too."

Dekkan had no time to reply because the door slid aside and a cadaverous porter ushered them inside to a large lobby. The man's long, almost gray face held an expression that would have doused even the most cheerful person's joy. His formal demeanor intimidated rather than welcomed.

"He's not exactly what I expected as official greeter for a place like this," Dekkan whispered.

"I know. Floribunda loves to disconcert people." In a louder tone, she told the porter, "We're here to meet with Mistress Floribunda. She should be expecting us."

The man bowed formally, escorted them to two comfortable seats, and disappeared through a doorway at one side of the lobby, all without uttering a single sound.

Dekkan used the time to inspect the lobby. He considered it an exercise in discipline to turn his attention away from Ariel to something more neutral, less distracting. To his surprise, the large lobby was decorated with exquisite taste. Leather banquettes and plush upholstered seats dotted the room in pleasant groupings suitable for conversations. A few small groups of people clustered in low-toned, private discussions, each well separated from the others. Charming, accent-lighted artwork, none of it explicit or even questionable in taste, provided focal points for the eye. Even the lush plants, most of them the purple and slate blue flora of Regulus IV, offered soothing counterpoint to the garish exterior.

"It's quite different inside, isn't it?" Dekkan remarked. "Not at all what I expected."

Ariel nodded. Her smile was almost more of a

smirk. "Uh-huh. Floribunda always says the outside is what draws people in, but once here they get cold feet unless something reassures them."

"So behind the insanely risqué exterior is a perfectly respectable interior."

She stared him straight in the eyes as she answered. "A lot of Mariposa is like that, you know. What people see on the surface isn't at all what we're really like." She shrugged and looked away. "Just be careful not to judge too quickly from appearances. They can be deceiving."

He knew what she meant, but didn't wholly accept her claim. Before he could refute it, however, the cadaverous porter returned and gestured for them to accompany him. "Doesn't he ever speak?" Dekkan asked Ariel in a whisper.

"How should I know?" She stopped dead in her tracks to glare at him. "You think I come here a lot?"

He grabbed her arm and urged her forward. "Hush, *dear*. We'll discuss this later," he said in a strained voice.

She continued with obvious reluctance but muttered under her breath, "You bet we'll discuss it. I'm getting tired of your insults."

"Later!" Dekkan told her again.

Their silent escort led them down a long corridor to a large, ornately carved double door at the far end. With a flourish that would have done justice to a peerless prestidigitator, he flung open the doors to a simply furnished salon. He announced in a deep, resonant voice, "Mistress Floribunda! Your guests, Ariel and Dekkan um Stonnor!"

Dekkan swallowed hard to contain his chuckle and forced his face into the courteous expressionlessness of the professional negotiator. His dignified bearing was lost on his intended audience, however. Mistress Floribunda had her eyes closed. She lay on an armless couch in an artless sprawl that revealed her ample charms, from the arch of her foot to her carelessly draped arm. Dekkan recognized her too-casual pose as an attempt to gain the upper hand in a meeting not of her choosing. Despite its blatant studiedness, he had to admit she made quite a sight.

Carefully disarrayed hair in an unusual shade of lavender curled over the end of the couch and pooled on the floor. Layers of sarsilk in a rainbow of colors floated over her body, alternately clinging and drifting free, so it was difficult to assess just like what the lady's figure really looked like. The only thing Dekkan could determine was that she strongly resembled the sofa on which she lay: plushly padded and overstuffed in all the right places.

Courteously, he waited for his hostess to acknowledge his presence.

Ariel, however, wasn't nearly so restrained. "Oh, do give it over, Floribunda. It's just me—Ariel."

One languid eyelid snapped open, and the lady jerked erect with a thunderous frown. "Oh. You're that Ariel," she snapped, sending several hard puffs of air upward to displace a few stray curls from in front of her face. "Gianvers said a gentlesire—Well, hello there, handsome." As suddenly as the indolent pose had disappeared, a coquettish smile reappeared, and she extended a languid arm to Dekkan.

Obediently, he accepted her fingers and bowed to brush his lips across the back of her hand. "My pleasure, gentlelady. I am Dekkan um Stonnor."

"Oooh. What a courteous gentlesire you are!" Black eyelashes more than four centimeters long batted furiously at Dekkan. She flipped a curl back over her shoulder, got her hand tangled in her hair's thick length, and struggled briefly to free it. When the small victory was achieved, Dekkan had to cough to cover a smile, for the battle had knocked the lady's wig slightly askew, allowing another strand to cascade over her face and into her eyes.

He glared at Ariel in rebuke for her barely stifled giggle. "Gentlelady, I am most pleased to make your acquaintance. Ariel has told me much about you."

"Well!" Floribunda cast a suspicious glare Ariel's way. "And you came anyway. No doubt to see if I am as—."

"As charming and gracious as Ariel told me." Dekkan's deft interruption generated a skeptical look from his hostess and another gasp from Ariel. He ignored both. "And I see that Ariel was wrong. You are far more charming than I had heard."

Floribunda sent a triumphant smirk Ariel's way and straightened on her couch to pat the seat next to her. "Come. Sit by me. You can tell me all about how Ariel slighted me."

Ariel rolled her eyes and sat firmly in a nearby chair, while Dekkan took the seat Floribunda had indicated. The soft surface sloped toward Floribunda's generous hips, forcing him to arch away slightly to keep from listing into her side. While he unobtrusively struggled to remain upright and apart, her right arm promptly tugged him closer until his chest was squashed firmly against her generous bosom. He saw Ariel's eyes roll again as he floundered for a more proper posture.

Floribunda's soft hands stroked over his hair and brow and down his cheek. "I hadn't realized Amitan men were so charming. Are they all as sweet as you?"

"Uh . . ." Dekkan's voice became muffled as she pressed his face against her upper chest. He felt as though he were drowning in duck fluff pillows. In desperation, he managed to lean back a bit and gasp in a mouthful of air.

"Floribunda, I think Dekkan wanted to talk to you about something."

Dekkan barely repressed a sigh of annoyance at the irritation in Ariel's voice. Didn't she know better than to interrupt at a time like this? He had everything under control—or at least he would once he freed himself from this blasted wig.

"Oooh. Is that it, sweetie?" Floribunda's voice dropped to a purr that Dekkan could feel vibrating in his toes—which also seemed to be the only part of his body that wasn't pressed tightly to her overwhelming mass. "Did you want to say something to me, cutie-pie?"

Dekkan twisted his head against her puffy flesh until he could see Ariel with one eye through the tangle of lavender hair that ensnared him. Both of Floribunda's hands held his head now, and her fingers ran along his scalp and down his neck. He freed his mouth from her hair and flesh and took another gasping breath. "Yes, I mmmpfh—"

Smothered again, he flopped against her, reluctant to forcibly extract himself from Floribunda's snare. At this stage, he didn't want to risk hurting or insulting the woman who could determine the success or failure of his mission. He managed to meet Ariel's eyes through a mass of lavender hair. This was getting ridiculous; yet . . . did he dare risk the Misthaven ring's fate by protesting too strongly?

Obviously, Ariel understood his dilemma. "Floribunda! Cut that out! The man's trying to talk to you." If she could rescue him from this mountain

Ariel's Dance

of a woman, Dekkan was willing to do anything Ariel asked. Anything at all, he vowed silently, as his captor snuggled him closer still.

"I don't want to talk," Floribunda insisted. "And neither does he. See? He's perfectly happy."

She relaxed her grip for an instant to prove her point, and Dekkan surged to free himself. It almost worked. He at least was able to get his arms between his chest and hers and lever his torso away from her.

"See? He wants to play!"

Floribunda's smug announcement came simultaneously with Ariel's horrified "Dekkan!"

He looked down and felt an instant wave of heat roll up his neck and over his face. His hands maintained a firm grip on Floribunda's enormous breasts. A sudden recollection of holding Ariel's breasts in a similar grip sent another wave of heat over him and threw him off balance.

He released Floribunda instantly and felt his elbows begin to buckle as his leverage failed. With a manful effort, he pushed himself away from her, rolling away on the couch. In the process, one hand accidentally tangled in the thick wig, pulling it even further askew. The woman squealed and gave him a hard shove. Unprepared for her push, Dekkan hit the floor with a painful thump just as he felt a mass of hair settle over his face in a ticklish blanket.

Ariel broke into chortles of laughter.

Irritated and embarrassed beyond belief, Dekkan glared up at her through a furry lavender screen. "That's enough, Ariel!" The effect of his command was ruined by the mouthful of hair he had to spit out halfway through it.

Ariel's chuckles dissolved into choked giggles as she helped him disentangle himself from both wig and woman while Floribunda maintained a continuous stream of muttered curses. At last he staggered to his feet, with a hand from Ariel. He tugged his waist-length jacket into some semblance of order and struggled to recover his composure. Nothing like this had ever happened in any negotiation in his life!

Floribunda sat erect on that death trap of a couch and glared at him with untempered dislike. Ariel held on to his arm as if she needed support to stay on her feet. Maybe she did, at that. Certainly if the snickers she muffled against his sleeve were any guide, she was in grave danger of collapsing onto the floor in laughter.

A glare in her direction served no purpose except to initiate another round of snickers. Her breasts, unbound beneath that peekaboo dress, pressed against his arm, and he had to force his mind away from the recollection of the taste of her nipples on his tongue, the feel of her legs clamped around his waist.

He gave up any attempt to control Ariel. In the meantime, he still had to accomplish his mission with Floribunda.

Perhaps an apology would sweeten her mood? "My pardon, gentlelady," he offered tentatively. "I am a clumsy oaf." Forcing his mind away from Ariel, he gave Floribunda his most respectful bow, the one he usually saved for Tenth-Degree Most Esteemed Honorifics. "Are you all right? Has my ineptitude harmed you?"

Despite his humble words, he carefully maintained his focus on the wall just behind the lady's left shoulder. If he looked at her too closely, he'd notice too many details—such as the fact that the wig now drooped in sad splendor off the right side of her head, leaving her own straggly pink hair to creep out from the left.

"Why'd you do that?" Floribunda demanded. "We were just starting to have a little fun!"

"Ah, gentlelady, er . . ."

While Dekkan fumbled for a reply, Ariel interceded. "Floribunda, stop it! You grabbed him, not the other way around. He isn't here for fun and games."

Settling herself more firmly on the couch, Floribunda protested. "Then why'd he grab my boo—"

"It was an accident, dear lady," Dekkan interrupted. "I assure you I meant no disrespect. I just, er . . ." Floundering again, he tossed a helpless look at Ariel.

She stamped one delicate foot. "Enough! Floribunda, forget what happened on the couch. Dekkan needs to talk to you. Right, Dekkan?"

With great relief, he agreed. "Right. I am most sorry, but I do need to discuss something with you."

Floribunda ran her hands through her hair. With irritated jerks she settled the wig more firmly on her head, sending another wave of hair cascading in front of her face. Dekkan heard Ariel's breath catch.

He sent her a commanding glare and gave a warning press to the hand that still clutched his sleeve. He didn't want her erupting into laughter and further irritating Floribunda. He clamped Ariel to his side and hoped she understood she was to interfere no more. Even now, frantically trying to salvage the shreds of his mission, he felt his body react to her nearness.

"Well?" Floribunda asked. "What is it you want?"

Dekkan took a deep breath and gathered the tatters of his thoughts. As diplomatically as possible, he described his father's unfortunate experience at Jeccad's gaming tables.

"You see, gentlelady, the ring has profound sentimental meaning for my family," he concluded. "I would consider it a great favor if you would allow me to redeem the ring—at its full value, of course—and take it home to Amity with me."

During his explanation, Floribunda's brown eyes had narrowed in concentration, but otherwise she showed little reaction to his words. Despite his negotiating skills, he hadn't the faintest idea how she would respond.

Dekkan's words faded into silence, and for a long moment only the faint hiss of their breathing disturbed the quiet. Then Floribunda heaved herself to her feet. Standing, she barely reached his shoulder, being a little taller than Ariel, though she weighed probably three times as much. Arranging her ample clothing around her, Floribunda walked over to a wall and pressed a small stud. Immediately the entire wall became a reflective surface. She frowned and began straightening her off-kilter wig.

The silence stretched for extended heartbeats. Just as Dekkan was about to break his number seven rule in negotiating—Never let your opponent force you to end a silence—Floribunda spoke.

"Do you like my dress, Dekkan? You don't mind if I call you Dekkan, do you?" A smile lit her face, and a little of her earlier coquettish behavior returned.

"I am honored, gentlelady. You may indeed call me Dekkan. And your dress is, uh, very flattering on you." Groping for another compliment, he blurted, "The color is especially good for your delicate complexion."

Ariel's Dance

She preened harder. "Really? Which color exactly, do you think?" A careless flip of her hand indicated the rainbow of hues in the flimsy garment.

Helpless again with such a topic, Dekkan cast a pleading look at Ariel. She shrugged. "Don't ask me," she told him softly. A wicked smile curved her lips as she added in a whisper, "I'm not much on dresses myself—as you might remember." A slight flick of her wrist ballooned her dress away from her body in such a way as to make it almost completely transparent for a heartbeat of time.

An instant recollection of her casual nudity before him filled his brain. No, Ariel didn't chain herself to fashionable attire. But then, she needed no adornment. In fact, she didn't have to be naked to raise a reaction in him; just the memory of her was enough to affect his body with alarming power. He shifted uncomfortably and tried to remember why he had his mouth open as if about to speak.

"Well?" Floribunda's suspicious glare met his gaze in the mirror. "What color?"

Dekkan ran the finger of his free hand around his collar and swallowed hard. *Oh, yes. Something about a color.* "Uh, blue! Yes, that's it. The blue looks absolutely beautiful on you, gentle—"

"Floribunda, dearie. Call me Floribunda." A girlish giggle escaped as she returned to her preening. "In fact, you can call me Flossie, if you like."

"Flossie, then." Too relieved at the recovery of his wits to care what he called her, he smiled expansively. "It was hard to choose for a moment because all the colors look so good with your wi—I mean, hair."

Ariel's elbow nudged his side, and he leaned down. She murmured, "You think I'd look good in that wig, too? It'd go so well with my stage costume, don't you think?"

Another surge of pure lust raced through his body as he remembered that her stage costume had included no fabric at all, but only a few dabs of paint and powder. The damnable part was that she indeed would look terrific wearing that wig and her costume. Or better yet, nothing at all. An anguished groan almost escaped his tight lips. He glared down at her. Why would she bring up such a subject now? Couldn't she see what her comments did to his concentration?

Her impish look confirmed his worst fears. She'd done it on purpose! His Ariel had a vicious streak in her that he'd have to work hard to overcome. But he was tenacious. He'd persevere. He'd—

Wait a second . . . *his* Ariel?

One part of his mind toyed with that concept while he maintained what he hoped was a courteous, superficial conversation with the bizarre Floribunda. He spoke as if in a trance, not really paying attention while he considered the mind-numbing possibilities. Him . . . and Ariel? She certainly bore no resemblance to the practical person he needed as a wife. Her negative points made up a list almost as long as his arm, starting with her outrageous lack of modesty, her disconcertingly exotic looks, her wicked sense of humor, and her ability to provoke passionate responses from him without even trying. Of course, she had a few good points, too, starting with that same outrageous lack of modesty, her disconcertingly exotic looks, her wicked sense of humor, and her ability to provoke passionate responses from him without even trying.

But what about Sebella?

"So you think that's a reasonable request?" Flo-

Ariel's Dance

ribunda's triumphant query brought Dekkan crashing into the present.

He couldn't believe he'd drifted off in the middle of a negotiation. It just went to show that being around Ariel too long would certainly rot his brain. Another negative point to add to his list. "Could you clarify that . . . uh, Flossie?"

In the few moments he'd been otherwise mentally engaged, Floribunda had come close to him and grasped his other arm. He felt hemmed in between a silently frowning Ariel on one side and a triumphant Floribunda on the other.

One lavender-tipped nail raked up his neck and around his ear. "Why, you just admitted you understood that in the time I've had the ring, it's become a great favorite of mine. You know how we women are with such things. Terribly sentimental and all that."

"Of course." *Damn.* Getting the ring back was going to cost him a whole lot more than he'd planned. Well, he might as well hear the bad news. "So can you tell me how much money it will take to soothe those sensibilities? Approximately speaking, of course. In round numbers."

"Oh." Floribunda purred like a devil-cat about to pounce. "I'm not talking *money*, you know. Sentiments can't really be assuaged with cash." She leaned around Dekkan to address Ariel. "Don't you agree, Ariel? Money isn't the issue at all."

A puzzled expression on her face, Ariel nodded. "You're absolutely right. But—"

"Sentimental tokens shouldn't be bought and sold," Floribunda insisted with a pious smirk. "They must be given . . . with love and affection."

"You mean you'll give me the ring?" Dekkan

couldn't contain his astonishment. "You'll just . . . give it to me?"

Floribunda smiled with all the success of one who had completed a masterly negotiation. "Of course I'll give it to you. Didn't I just say so?"

Dekkan exchanged a bewildered look with Ariel. Could it really be this easy? Floribunda seemed perfectly sincere. He took a deep breath for the first time since being ushered into her presence. "I cannot thank you enough, gent—I mean, Flossie. But I feel very bad about giving you nothing in return. Won't you let me present you with a gift as a reflection of your kindness to me?" He'd just give her the purchase price in another piece of jewelry, and his conscience would be soothed.

Floribunda squealed and clapped her hands in eager—too eager?—delight. "A present! How delightful! And I know just what I want. In fact, why don't we make a little ceremony of it—you give me your present and then I'll give you mine. What do you think about that? Two friends—two loving friends—honoring each other with their gifts."

No matter how Dekkan turned it over in his mind, he couldn't see anything wrong with her suggestion. Sure, it was obvious she wanted to cloak the purchase of the ring as an exchange of gifts, but that was no problem. He could deal with that. Slowly, he nodded his assent to the plan. "That sounds like a good suggestion." The flare of triumph in her eyes prodded his wariness awake again. "Perhaps we could have this ceremony on the morrow? I would like some time to prepare my gift to you."

"Oh, there's no need for you to *prepare* exactly, Dekkan," Floribunda assured him. "I know exactly what I want you to give me. But I do agree that tomorrow morning will be an excellent time. You give me your gift tonight, and tomorrow morning I'll give you back your family ring."

"Tonight?"

He heard Ariel's breath escape in a sharp gasp, but he couldn't spare the time to worry about her reaction; he was too busy wondering just what outrageous present he'd agreed to give Floribunda—and just when *had* he agreed to give whatever it was to her?

Floribunda nudged Ariel aside with a rigid elbow and looped her hands around Dekkan's neck. "Why, yes, lover, tonight. You give me . . ." She snuggled heavily against him, making him stagger back a step.

"I give you what exactly?" The words came out in a choked gasp as her mouth nibbled slowly along the base of his neck. His hands started to pry hers from his nape, but fell limp in shock at her next words.

"You. You give me yourself tonight, and then—if you please me well enough—tomorrow I give you the ring. That's what it is, isn't it? A ring for lovers?"

Chapter Eight

"*No!*" Ariel's angry protest surprised even her. Even more surprising, a wave of possessiveness surged through her.

She couldn't remember ever being possessive about a man, couldn't even remember ever caring whether a particular man came or went. With her job, men were easy to come by and easy to replace—if she cared to bother.

In truth, she'd spent her whole life so focused on her goal of getting a professional education and doing something important with her life, that the few personal relationships she'd indulged in had taken a dim second place. Mostly, men were more trouble and aggravation than they were worth.

But somehow Dekkan had rearranged her personal priority list. It had been hard enough watching Floribunda paw Dekkan. Floribunda's overtures irritated Ariel in a way that was as un-

Ariel's Dance

expected as it was unwelcome. Ariel had gritted her teeth and made suggestive remarks to remind him that he didn't need the other woman to generate a flare of passion.

This proposition of Floribunda's, however, was totally outside the realm of possibility. No way would Ariel let that woman get her hands on Dekkan—he was hers!

While Dekkan and Floribunda still gaped at her in shock, Ariel stalked over to them and forcibly ripped the other woman's hands from around Dekkan's neck. "That's not an acceptable deal," she informed them. She didn't dare meet Dekkan's eyes, so she held her gaze firmly on Floribunda.

"Ariel—"

Floribunda didn't let Dekkan finish whatever he wanted to say. "Don't you think Dekkan here is old enough to make such a decision for himself?" She smugly traced her nails against her overendowed bosom. "The deal is between him and me, you see. You have nothing to say about it."

"Ariel—"

"Of course I have something to say about it! His father sent him to *me* to help get the ring back. That gives me a whole lot to say about it."

"Really, my dear?" Floribunda drawled. "Why don't we ask Dekkan whether he appreciates being led around like a child still in dampies? Hmmm?"

"I don't lead him around!"

"It certainly appears that way to me. A real man makes his own decisions about who he beds. He doesn't let a little skin-dancer tell him what to do."

They glared at each other, totally ignoring Dekkan. Only after long moments did Ariel drop her gaze. She knew in her heart that Floribunda had a point. Ariel had manipulated and teased Dekkan since the moment she'd met him. She'd intended no insult to him or his masculinity, but . . . would others see it that way?

Would Dekkan?

With fearful eyes she met Dekkan's gaze at last. She could read nothing in his eyes, nothing at all. Quivers of disappointment flickered through her.

"Are you ladies finished?"

Ariel winced at the sardonic note in Dekkan's voice. Floribunda's open triumph didn't settle her nerves any better.

"Certainly, sweetie," Floribunda said in a purr.

Dekkan spoke slowly, obviously choosing his words with care. "Mistress Floribunda, I am of course honored at the exchange you offer. But I can't help wondering why you suggest something of such little, uh, monetary worth. The ring I seek is not valueless, and I'm willing to give you its true price."

Floribunda practically rubbed her hands with glee. "Valueless? Valueless, you say? Of course not! I plan to prize every moment you spend in my bed."

"But . . ." Dekkan gestured to indicate the entire edifice around them. "Surely you can find other lovers than I. Why should you want to bed a stranger?"

"Yes, why is that exactly, Floribunda?" Ariel asked with sudden suspicion. "Why are you so determined to have Dekkan in your bed?"

"You mean you truly don't know?" Floribunda shook her head in blatant disbelief. "You are an Amitan, are you not, Dekkan? Raised in the Amitan tradition?"

He nodded.

"Then you're perfect! Don't you know what I could charge for your services here on Mariposa? Women would flock to my house from all over the

Ariel's Dance

planet. You could take your pick of the most beautiful women anywhere—after I've sampled you, of course!" Her expression changed to that of a shrewd bargainer. "What say you? I could make you richer than your wildest dreams within a moon-phase or two."

Dekkan raked his hand through his hair. "I don't understand. Why should you think I'd . . . ? Blast! I don't even know how to phrase the question!" He turned away and stalked to the far side of the salon, where he poured himself a drink from a crystal decanter on a small table.

Ariel was beginning to have her suspicions, but she wanted Floribunda to confirm them. "What's so special about the fact that Dekkan is Amitan?"

"Why, it's because of how they live. Don't you know that they don't indulge in the more, um, erotic pleasures until they marry?"

"Well, sure, but—."

"Ariel, my dear, just think of it. A fully grown, drop-dead-gorgeous male who's also a *virgin*. Do you have the slightest idea how rare that is in the universe? I could make a fortune with him." A broad wink invited Ariel to share the delicious prospect of a merchant making a killing from a gullible public.

Ariel's mouth opened and closed silently. In truth, she'd never really thought of Dekkan as a virgin. Sure, she knew about the patches Amitans wore, but she'd never extrapolated that to understand that Dekkan had never . . . had never actually had . . . Her mental meanderings broke down at that point.

"You *are* a virgin aren't you, Dekkan?" Floribunda's voice carried all the greed of a merchant who knew she could corner the market.

Chloe Hall

He propped his shoulder against the wall and sipped his drink meditatively. "Sure," he confirmed matter-of-factly. "Almost all unmarried Amitans are." Ariel stared at him in awe, not just because of his admission, but at the casual way he made it.

Floribunda positively slithered her bulky body over to him and fingered the lapel of Dekkan's jacket. "Don't you want to know just what you've been missing, lover? No one can teach you better than I."

Ariel's disgusted snort didn't have any effect on him, as far as she could see. Instead, he reached out and smoothed his hand over Floribunda's collar, toying with a slim chain circling her neck. "You think you've got some lessons I should learn?" His voice had the husky purr of a stalking leopard.

Across the room, Ariel clenched her fists in impotent fury. She had no right to interfere. As Floribunda had so rightly pointed out, Dekkan was a big boy now and fully capable of making his own mistakes. Surely even a half-wit ought to be able to see that the woman just wanted to use him.

Of course, Ariel had never been too sure that the average male mind ever achieved the mental capabilities of a half-wit.

"Count on it, loverboy," Floribunda promised.

"But I don't have time to stay here with you. I have to return to my home on Amity. It would just be for tonight, you know." One strong male finger lifted the sparkling chain and began working it free of Floribunda's gauzy garment. Ariel could feel his gesture as if he caressed her own skin instead of Floribunda's. The imaginary touch maddened her so that she had to shut her eyes.

Yet shutting her eyes didn't help. She could still

hear the soft murmurs of the couple across the room.

"That's terrible, sweeting," Floribunda was saying. "But at least I'd have the chance to show you the basics."

"And tomorrow morning you'll give me the ring?"

"Of course, honeycakes. Ooohhhh . . ."

Ariel's eyes popped open just in time to see Dekkan lean down and brush his lips over the skin beneath Floribunda's ear while his hand continued tugging at that ridiculous chain. He was going to do it! He was really going to do it with Floribunda just to get that stupid ring back! Rage and something else—surely not grief?—rushed through her, making her quiver, yet rooting her to the spot. She couldn't have spoken or moved if her life depended on it.

"Ah. I thought so." Ariel felt Dekkan's satisfied sigh as a rasp along nerve endings strained far too tightly. One of his hands cupped something dangling on the chain that circled Floribunda's neck.

"You thought what, baby doll?" Floribunda's eyes were still squeezed shut. "That's it, darlin', right there. Maybe a bit lower." She arched into the firm male hand that caressed her shoulder.

"What—" Ariel had to clear her throat before the word could come out as more than a squeak. "What are you holding, Dekkan?" His possible misinterpretation of that question inspired a rare blush. "In your hand, I mean." That didn't seem much better. "On the chain."

Dekkan's concentration shifted from the abundant flesh of the woman in his arms to something cupped in his hand. For the first time, Ariel began to hope that he didn't plan to make love to Floribunda after all. She also tried not to contemplate why she felt such relief at the realization.

"Pull me closer, sweetcheeks. Don't stop!" Both Dekkan and Ariel ignored Floribunda's husky command as the woman continued arching into Dekkan's other hand.

Dekkan pulled the chain farther from Floribunda's ample cleavage and opened his cupped fingers to display the object to Ariel. "It's the Misthaven ring. See?"

Ariel moved closer. She'd never really taken a good look at the ring during Stonnor's visit. As she moved over to Dekkan's side, she could see that the ring's central gemstone was one of the legendary heartfire gems of Cantiphur III held in an ornate gold setting. A living opaline flame flickered with turquoise light inside the auburn stone. A century or so ago the legendary gemstone had been one of the rarest and most precious in the Federation, until modern synthesizers began to produce artificial versions of flawless quality.

"It's beautiful," she said softly. "I never paid much attention to it when Stonnor had it, but I don't remember it being so colorful. I thought it was paler somehow—more yellow than red."

Dekkan cast a sharp glance her way before returning his attention to the ring. "This ring is more than two hundred and fifty years old. Sometimes the genuine heartfires change color. It's one of the reasons they were replaced by synthetics." Dekkan studied the stone and did not meet her eyes. "Do you know much about heartfire gems?" For some reason the too-casual question seemed of great importance to him.

She shrugged. "Just that they used to be a lot more expensive than they are now."

She thought a look of relief flitted over Dekkan's

Ariel's Dance

face, but Floribunda interrupted. The woman had obviously just figured out that Dekkan's attention had strayed. "What's going on?" Floribunda asked.

Dekkan dropped the ring and it settled on its chain back between Floribunda's breasts. He offered the lady a charming smile as he pulled his arm from around her. "Sorry, my dear, but I'm afraid I'll have to decline your invitation."

"Decline? *Decline!* Don't you know what you're passing up here?" Floribunda's face, flushed with rage, took on a pugnacious look. She pulled away from him to flounce across the room. "Well, in that case, forget about ever getting your precious ring back." Her hand came up to cover the ring protectively. "I'll never let you have it!"

"I'm sorry to hear you say that, Flossie—"

"You can call me Gentlelady D'Amatorio, if you please!"

"I'm sorry, gentlelady. It was not my intention to anger you. It's just that we Amitans feel very strongly that such intimacies must be reserved for a man and his wife, and not treated lightly." Dekkan kept his voice low and conciliatory, but even Ariel could hear the duranum steel in his decision.

I ought to be jubilant at his decision. Ariel couldn't understand why the thought of Dekkan sharing such pleasures with the worthy Sebella depressed her so much.

"Well, I don't know why you Amitans think you're so much better than the rest of us," Floribunda whined. "We could have made a lot of money, you and I."

"Ah, but money isn't my primary goal, you see," Dekkan assured her. "Are you positive that you will not let me purchase the ring from you? I'm still willing to give you an excellent price for it."

"No!" Floribunda's pugnacious look degenerated into pure obstinacy. "I'll never let you have it. I wear it all the time, twenty-five hours a day, so don't think you can take it either."

"I see." Dekkan placed a small card on a nearby table and bowed formally to Floribunda. "Then I must accept my failure with good grace, I suppose. If you change your decision, you may contact me at any time. I will always be willing to redeem the ring." He grabbed Ariel's hand and urged her toward the door.

Floribunda wouldn't let them leave without one last jab. "You'll be sorry, you know. When you're freezing in bed with your stupid little bride, you'll be sorry you passed up the chance to learn from a real woman!"

In her heart of hearts, Ariel could only wish that Dekkan did want to learn about love from a "real woman." She herself would be more than pleased to introduce him to whatever pleasures he aspired to.

But the chance of that seemed so remote as to approach impossibility.

Dekkan's mood remained distracted and withdrawn for the rest of the afternoon. Ariel took him to her favorite restaurant, where they ordered meals of exotic salads and spiced-meat rolls. Despite her best efforts, all attempts at conversation dwindled into nothing, and they finished eating in silence.

Finally, she had to ask. "Are you going to give up?"

He looked up from stirring his after-dinner mug of tea and frowned. "Why would you think that?"

She shrugged. "You haven't said much. I just wondered."

"It was just a surprise seeing her with the ring around her neck. I hadn't anticipated that. I'm so used to thinking of the Misthaven ring as being worn by family members that it was a shock, I suppose."

It was her turn to stir her tea with studied care. "I see."

Dekkan put his hand over hers. "I haven't thanked you for helping me with this, have I? I do appreciate all you've done."

The warmth of his skin touching hers made her long for things she could never have. She pulled her hand from under his and laughed with too-casual unconcern. "It was nothing. You still don't have your ring back. Besides, you're going to pay me handsomely, remember?"

He straightened in his chair as if prodded with a sharp stick, and his voice took on a remote quality. "Yes. I remember. You needn't worry that I won't live up to my promise. You'll get admitted into school, if it's within my power."

"Dekkan, I didn't mean—" She honestly hadn't meant him to think that was the only reason she helped him.

"Never mind. Don't you think we ought to leave? The manager has been eyeing this table for a good ten minutes."

Distressed, but not knowing how to make things right between them, she nodded silently. "Where to now?"

"Back to your place, I think," he answered as they exited onto a street at dusk. "I have something I want to discuss with you in private."

"Privacy?"

He nodded and urged her toward the nearest hire-car stand. "I don't think we should talk about it here. Let's go home."

Let's go home.

The simple words echoed in Ariel's mind throughout the ride to her bungalow. Did he think of her place as home? No, of course not, she chided herself. It was just an expression. He didn't mean it literally. How foolish she was even to consider that he might be attached enough to her to think of her residence as home.

By the time they arrived, Ariel's mood had slipped over the edge of regret and into depression. Morosely she unlocked the door and led the way into what had once been a cozy retreat. Now she could only think about how lonely it would seem once Dekkan left for Amity.

To shake off her mood, she moved to the kitchen area and prepared a large pot of tea, then as an afterthought added a slug of Denebian drakka brew to the pot. She figured she'd need a little fortification for the private discussion Dekkan had requested.

When she carried a tray with tea and mugs into the salon area, she found him settled comfortably in the middle of her couch. She couldn't resist the opportunity to sit beside him, but she did manage to keep a comfortable half meter away. She had to take her personal victories where she could find them.

"What did you want to talk about?" she asked when it seemed obvious that Dekkan wasn't going to open the conversation.

He cupped his mug in strong hands and took a large swallow of tea. "Do you think Floribunda will change her mind and sell me the ring?"

"No," she told him bluntly. "I think she was mightily offended when you refused her offer." A deep swallow of the spiked tea burned its way down her throat. "I think she'd sooner see you in the bowels of a flame lizard than give you the time of day."

He nodded in confirmation. "That's what I think, too. I wasn't exactly at my best in negotiating with her, was I?"

"Well . . . it's difficult to deal with her. She's pretty hardheaded."

"So I found out." He twisted his mug in his hands. "Did your father really have her as his mistress?"

"Of course. She collects men. It's no big thing." Her matter-of-fact tone hid the regret she felt. Much as she'd always been on the outs with Jeccad, he surely deserved better than Floribunda. "He's been a devoted admirer of hers for years, you know."

"I see." He drank again from his mug, emptying it.

Silently, she offered him a refill from the pot. The drakka brew didn't taste half-bad—though it felt like having one's esophagus burned by acid. Dekkan hadn't commented on the tea, so she didn't know how it affected him.

"Ariel . . ."

"Yes?"

"I was wondering. Would you be willing to do me a favor?"

"What favor?" She never made open-ended promises. Nevertheless, several ideas for personal services popped into her mind before she forcibly suppressed them.

"I think I need your help to get the ring back."

She sighed. "Look, Dekkan, why don't you face it? Floribunda is never going to sell you that ring, and she apparently wears it all the time. You'll never get it back." She had to swallow hard before she could say the rest of the words, despite knowing she had no right to hold them back. "Why don't you go home and forget about the ring. Go home and marry your . . . marry Sebella."

He shifted to face her on the sofa, one knee bending as he angled toward her. "Go home? Without the ring? Are you serious?"

She, too, finished her tea and thumped the mug onto the table. With a lowered head, so she didn't have to meet his eyes, she said, "Yes! Stonnor wouldn't blame you. You've done your best. Go home and—"

"And what?" His voice deepened and one hand brushed back a strand of hair from her face. When she didn't immediately respond, he tipped her head back with a firm finger under her chin. "Is that what you truly think I should do?"

Yes! Anything to stop the temptation I feel to snatch you for myself! Swallowing hard, she nodded.

His eyes searched hers, but she managed to meet his gaze. "Well," he said, "I won't do it. I'm going to get that ring back no matter what."

Ariel's eyes closed and she slumped slightly. Until this instant, she hadn't realized just how badly she wanted him to stay. "How—how are you going to do that?"

He didn't answer for a long moment until she opened her eyes and met his gaze again. With a determination she could only admire, he explained his plan.

"I thought I'd follow my father's plan. I'll steal it."

Chapter Nine

"Steal it?" Of all the things he might have said, *steal it* had to be the most bizarre.

"Sure." Dekkan leaned forward and refilled both their mugs. "It's a good idea. Obviously my father thought the idea was sound."

"But . . . what about all that Amitan virtue you're so proud of? How can you justify stealing?" The conversation's strange twist had knocked all the misery out of her.

"It won't exactly be a theft, will it, if I leave the value of the ring in cash?"

"You're going to steal the ring and then pay for it, too?" She shook her head and took another gulp of the drakka brew. "I can't wait to hear this."

"I would never knowingly be the cause of another person's financial loss," he told her stiffly. "But I have no objection to redeeming an object that rightfully belongs in my family."

"Stonnor lost that ring by gambling, you know."

"But the game was not a fair one, was it?" His piercing gaze demanded an answer.

"No," she admitted. "It wasn't fair. Jeccad always cheats at *shallon* when he starts losing. It's why I didn't want to take Stonnor there."

"I thought as much. So by taking the ring back, I'm merely restoring an object that was unfairly taken from my family."

"Uh-huh. Right. And Floribunda will agree with that all the way to the constabulary."

"Hmmm." Dekkan's frown made him look like an adorable little boy. "You have a point. She's bound to notice the ring is missing, and she'll certainly report it."

"Yes," she added. "And since you're the only person around here who's made an effort to get the ring, you're the first person they'll suspect."

He drummed his fingers against his knee while he sipped his tea. "We'll just have to keep Floribunda from finding out that the ring has been taken, then. Any ideas?"

She was silent for a long moment while her thoughts whirled around her head in an alcoholic haze. She hadn't had that much tea—had she? She wasn't used to strong spirits: a dancer couldn't afford to indulge too much, but surely even a couple of large mugs of the spiked tea couldn't make her drunk.

Or could it?

The drakka brew was the only explanation for the insane idea that had popped into her head. It had also popped out of her mouth before she could have second—and wiser—thoughts. "Why don't you replace it with a fake?"

"A fake?"

Ariel's Dance

Defensiveness for her dumb idea warmed her voice more than she really felt. "Sure. Why don't you substitute a copy of the ring? See, you can sneak in . . . somehow . . . take your ring, and replace it with the fake one. You get the original to take home with you and Floribunda keeps the duplicate. Everybody wins."

A heavy frown pleated his brow. "Only one problem. I don't have one to substitute."

She waved that objection aside. "Details. So you get a copy made—"

"How?" he interrupted. "I don't even have a good holo-image of the ring."

"Oh." She thought about that for a moment. "Well, then, I guess you have to sneak in, take the ring, get it to a jeweler to have a copy made, then sneak back in and substitute the copy."

"And do all this without having Floribunda discover that the ring—which she wears around her neck at all times, remember—is missing for a couple of days while I get a duplicate made?"

She drummed her fingers against her knee as she thought about this latest objection. Like him, she'd twisted around and now faced him on the sofa, their bent knees almost touching. His warmth distracted her from their conversation, and she had to concentrate fiercely to come up with a plan. "Maybe I could help you out there," she offered at last.

"You help me out all the time." In a sudden shift, his husky voice deepened a pitch and his thumb smoothed across her cheek in a path that sent fiery tongues of flame roaring along her nerve endings. "You have a smudge here," he pointed out.

Involuntarily, she closed her eyes and arched her neck toward that roaming thumb while she desperately snatched at her composure. "I know someone

. . . oooh . . . who might be able to help. . . ."

"Help?" His head bent as his hand tipped up her chin. Warm lips teased at her temple, first the left, then the right.

"Uh . . . to make the . . . the copy." Triumphant at having uttered a complete thought in only two or three attempts, she made the mistake of opening her eyes.

His brown eyes burned with amber fire from mere centimeters away. How had he moved so close? For the first time she realized that his arms now enclosed her. Even as the realization seeped into her consciousness, he drew her body closer, closer, until the tips of her breasts hovered just a whisper away from his chest. Every hair on her body stood at attention while streams of sensation arced between them.

"What are you doing?" Was that breathy voice really hers?

"I just thought you might be willing to help me out." The deep tones vibrated along every nerve of her body.

"He-help you?"

"Yes." One warm thumb started a circling path at her nape. "I think Floribunda might have had a point. I should learn something about pleasing a woman, don't you think?"

"Pleasing . . . a woman?" Driven practically incoherent by the massaging pressure of the thumb that probed behind her ear, tugged on her earlobes, and soothed her scalp, Ariel hardly knew what she was saying. "Oh, you do please . . ." Her whole body strained forward, aching, needing to feel the pressure of his body against hers.

Alarm bells clanged belatedly in her mind when he shifted yet closer. Fighting herself more than

A Special Offer For Love Spell Romance Readers Only!

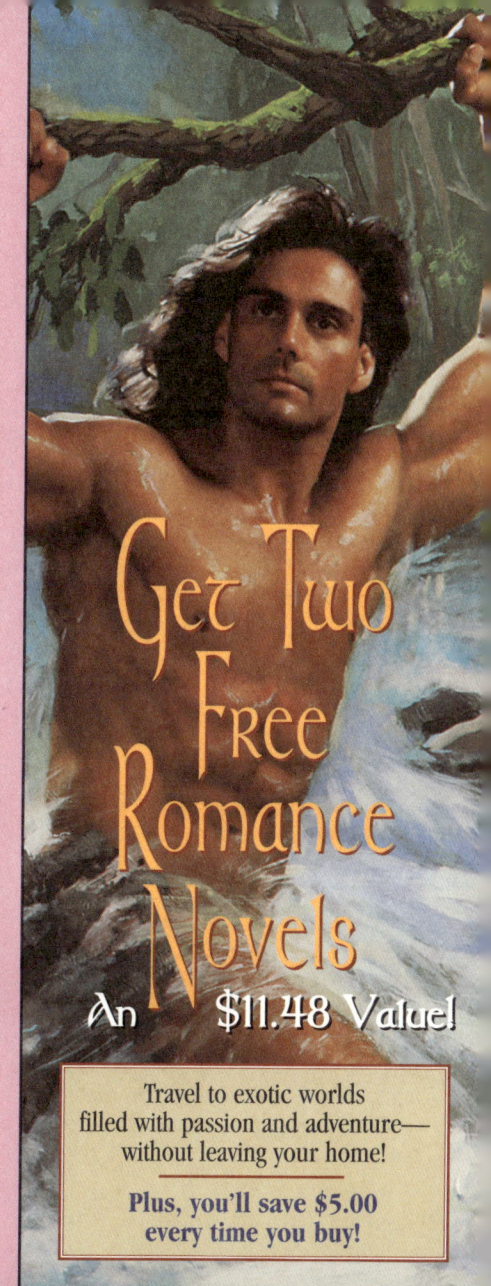

Get Two Free Romance Novels

An $11.48 Value!

Travel to exotic worlds
filled with passion and adventure—
without leaving your home!

**Plus, you'll save $5.00
every time you buy!**

Thrill to the most sensual, adventure-filled Romances on the market today...

FROM ✦ LOVE SPELL BOOKS

As a home subscriber to the Love Spell Romance Book Club, you'll enjoy the best in today's BRAND-NEW Time Travel, Futuristic, Legendary Lovers, Perfect Heroes and other genre romance fiction. For five years, Love Spell has brought you the award-winning, high-quality authors you know and love to read. Each Love Spell romance will sweep you away to a world of high adventure...and intimate romance. Discover for yourself all the passion and excitement millions of readers thrill to each and every month.

Save $5.00 Each Time You Buy!

Every other month, the Love Spell Romance Book Club brings you four brand-new titles from Love Spell Books. EACH PACKAGE WILL SAVE YOU AT LEAST $5.00 FROM THE BOOKSTORE PRICE! And you'll never miss a new title with our convenient home delivery service.

Here's how we do it: Each package will carry a FREE 10-DAY EXAMINATION privilege. At the end of that time, if you decide to keep your books, simply pay the low invoice price of $17.96, no shipping or handling charges added. HOME DELIVERY IS ALWAYS FREE. With today's top romance novels selling for $5.99 and higher, our price SAVES YOU AT LEAST $5.00 with each shipment.

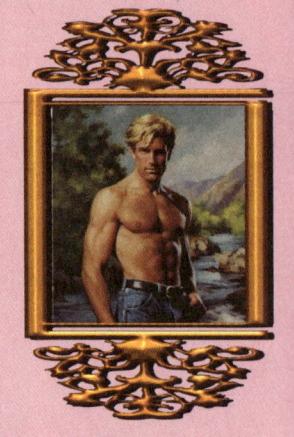

AND YOUR FIRST TWO-BOOK SHIPMENT IS TOTALLY FREE!

IT'S A BARGAIN YOU CAN'T BEAT! A SUPER $11.48 Value!

Love Spell ✦ A Division of Dorchester Publishing Co., Inc.

GET YOUR 2 FREE BOOKS NOW–AN $11.48 VALUE!

Mail the Free Book Certificate Today!

Free Books Certificate

YES! I want to subscribe to the Love Spell Romance Book Club. Please send me my 2 FREE BOOKS. Then every other month I'll receive the four newest Love Spell selections to Preview FREE for 10 days. If I decide to keep them, I will pay the Special Member's Only discounted price of just $4.49 each, a total of $17.96. This is a SAVINGS of at least $5.00 off the bookstore price. There are no shipping, handling, or other charges. There is no minimum number of books I must buy and I may cancel the program at any time. In any case, the 2 FREE BOOKS are mine to keep—A BIG $11.48 Value!

Offer valid only in the U.S.A.

Name _____

Address _____

City _____

State _____ Zip _____

Telephone _____

Signature _____

If under 18, Parent or Guardian must sign. Terms, prices and conditions subject to change. Subscription subject to acceptance. Leisure Books reserves the right to reject any order or cancel any subscription.

TWO FREE BOOKS

A $11.48 VALUE

Get Two Books Totally **FREE —** An $11.48 Value!

▼ Tear Here and Mail Your FREE Book Card Today! ▼

PLEASE RUSH MY TWO FREE BOOKS TO ME RIGHT AWAY!

Love Spell Romance Book Club
P.O. Box 6613
Edison, NJ 08818-6613

AFFIX STAMP HERE

him, she struggled to get her arms into position to push him away. Using every ounce of her fading strength, she managed to distance her face a few centimeters from the lips that sizzled along her temple. "What are you doing?"

His smile was purely predatory. "Don't you know?"

"But . . ." Surely there was a reason she hadn't expected this sudden action. Sluggishly she forced herself to think. "How can you . . . ? What about the . . ." She gasped as his mouth found a particularly sensitive spot behind her left ear. ". . . the patch?"

As if scalded, he jerked his face away from her, his brow frowning in suspicion. "Patch? What do you know about . . . Ah, I see. Stonnor." Obviously he'd correctly concluded how she knew about something few Amitans spoke of.

Now that he'd withdrawn his fiery teasing, she found herself able to think more coherently. "Stonnor told me about them, and that they make men unable to—to—" She was sinking in deep water, so she brought the subject back to more immediate concerns. "He said you wore yours religiously."

His frown grew deeper. "So?"

"So how can you kiss me like this, when you know you can't, I mean . . ." The words trailed into a woeful wail, and she wished with all her heart that she could call them back. She didn't really want him to know how much she wanted him to be able to finish what he'd started . . . did she?

His frown disappeared and he gathered her closer. "Is that what's bothering you, sweet?" Without waiting for a reply, he nuzzled behind her ear, sending jolts of sensation flooding through her veins and destroying her train of thought. "No problem. My patch ran out yesterday."

What patch? she wondered fuzzily as she chased his lips with her own. Who cared about some stupid patch anyway? She looped her arms around his neck and pulled him closer.

He answered her silent pleas with a mouth that traced a roving path down the side of her face, under her jaw, and back to her ear. His tongue and teeth teased the sensitive lobe, making her whimper restlessly. She grasped his head with her hands to try to force him to continue the sensuous torment, but he moved away, leaving only the musky scent and the sweet aftertaste of him to console her own seeking lips.

"Ariel?" Only when her eyes opened and gazed into his through the blur of passion did he continue. "Ariel, I want you."

"I want you, too, Dekkan." It felt so good to say the words out loud. "I want you to touch me . . . please."

She stared into his eyes, willing him to yield to her demands. She didn't care about a single thing in the universe except him. Nothing mattered to her at all, not him, not the ring, not even his fiancée. . . .

His fiancée! Dammit, the man was engaged to be married. To someone else.

Abruptly, she pulled back again. Her breath hissed between her teeth as she struggled for a control she longed to ignore. "Haven't you forgotten something? Or someone?" It took every trace of willpower in her to make her voice strong and cold.

Dekkan drew back, too. He ran his hand through his hair, mussing it into a tangle her fingers itched to straighten. "Forgotten?"

"Sebella, remember? Your fiancée?" Each syllable sent knives of jealousy slicing through her.

His other hand dropped away from her in what felt like abandonment, and she mourned the loss. "What am I doing?" The mutter hardly seemed meant for her ears.

"I don't know," she answered anyway. "What are you doing?"

With obvious effort, he pushed himself to his feet and stalked away from her to the window. Outside, the deepening twilight cast a shadowy mantle over the garden in the enclosed patio. The glow of Mariposa City's evening lights lit the sky. Dekkan stared out for long moments before turning to face her with a scowl.

"This is all your fault," he accused.

"*My* fault?" She jumped to her feet, passion melting into fury at his outrageous claim. "How can you say that? I was sitting there, helping you make a plan to get that stupid ring back—"

"It's not a stupid ring! It's a family heirloom."

"It's a *stupid* ring," she insisted. "And I was just helping you figure out how to get the thing back, when you jumped me."

"Ha!" He paced forward until they stood toe-to-toe, nose-to-nose. "I didn't jump you. All I did was wipe away a smudge of dirt. That's all."

"That's all? That's all?" All but incoherent, she grabbed the lapels of his jacket to pull him down to her level. "What you did had nothing to do with a smudge of dirt. And you know it." A crushing memory returned, and she backed away from him. "You said you thought you ought to learn about pleasing a woman. That's what this was all about, wasn't it?" Her hoarse whisper revealed just how badly that notion hurt her.

"What in the twenty-six dimensions of hyperspace are you talking about?"

"You were using me, weren't you?" she accused, nearly choking. "You want me to teach you to be a good lover so when you marry . . ."

A look of pure obstinacy crossed his face and stuck there. "I'm telling you, I just wiped away the smudge, and the next thing I knew you were practically wrapping yourself around me, like you needed a man more than your next breath." He drew a harsh breath. "Come to think of it, maybe I've interfered with your usual activities."

A confusing mixture of despair and rage deprived her of any hope of regaining control. She battered him with her fists in frustration, making no noticeable impact upon his muscled frame. "That's not true! I did *not!* I'm not like Floribunda! Take that back!"

He fought back, obviously trying to grab her hands to keep her from beating him any more, but even through her anger she sensed he was taking care not to hurt her. She squirmed and wriggled, trying to get her hands or legs free enough to make him unsay those cruel, hurtful words. When he finally gathered both her fists in his in an unbreakable grip, she gave up and stood frozen, panting hard from the exertion of their fight.

Hesitantly, she lifted her gaze to his. Bewilderment clashed with arousal, and she realized the physical skirmish had done nothing but rekindle his desire for her. It had ignited her own desire, too, and for an instant she hesitated, not sure she was willing to take the biggest risk of her life with this man.

His grip on her hands loosened, and she freed one to reach up and touch his face just beside his mouth. "I'm sorry," she whispered. "I wasn't really trying . . . I didn't mean to hurt you." Did she dare risk everything for him? Did she dare risk . . . ?

"I know," he told her in an equally soft voice. "I shouldn't have said such things. I know they're not true. But Ariel—"

"What?"

He took a deep, shuddering breath that she felt all the way to her toes. "I'm not sorry I kissed you."

For one moment she hesitated, and then her lips curved upward. Her question was answered. She would dare all to have this man, even if only for this brief instant. She would risk her body, her passion. She would even risk her heart.

Her fingers trembled as she smoothed her hands up his shoulders and around his neck, pressing herself against his body and luxuriating in his warm male strength. "You know what?" she confessed just before her lips touched his. "I'm not sorry either."

His arms tightened their grip on her as their mouths met and clung, met and clung again. Willingly, she surrendered herself to the dangerous risk of loving this man.

Stonnor knew this visit was going to end in disaster. Every bone in his body ached with the knowledge that it was not a good idea. Unfortunately, Sebella had taken charge and demanded an audience with "this Jeccad person," and Stonnor found himself carried along on the tide of Sebella's outrage.

Uncomfortably ensconced in a painful chair in Jeccad's stark home, all Stonnor could do was pray that Jeccad's management of Sebella would prove more effective than his own. In the background, the latest holo-news release about the upcoming nuptials played in a silent loop. Brolla's gaze had trouble unlocking itself from the loop of Ariel's dance, Stonnor noticed. If Sebella saw the same thing, Brolla would regret his lapse of discipline, Stonnor was sure.

"My dear gentlelady, it's obvious you've been misinformed." Jeccad's genial manner failed to disguise his growing irritation.

"Misinformed! Misinformed!" Sebella paused to take a long, shaky breath. "It's you who're misinformed. My fiancé, Dekkan um Stonnor of Amity, is not going to marry your—your—" Her mouth opened to say something that Stonnor knew would cause untold disaster. Jeccad's growing glower must have warned her. She took a deep breath before continuing in a more moderate tone. "Your . . . daughter. I will try to explain it in simple terms. Dekkan is engaged to me. He has been engaged to me for quite some time. It is impossible for him to marry your daughter when he has made a binding commitment to me!"

"Hmmm." Despite the clarity of Sebella's explanation, Jeccad didn't look convinced. "And how long has this . . . understanding . . . been in place?"

"It is not an 'understanding'! It's a firm, binding commitment!" Sebella's voice rose toward a shriek, and she again paused for breath and control. "Dekkan has no right to even think of marrying anyone but me! He's been betrothed to me for six years."

"Six years, eh?" Jeccad asked. He eyed Sebella's sturdy but unbeautiful form up and down before making an obvious comparison to the lissome Ariel shimmying in the holo-news image. "I can understand why."

Sebella looked ready to murder him on the spot.

Ariel's Dance

She wildly cast a glance around the room, looking for support. Brolla became the unhappy recipient of her attention. "Tell him, Brolla!"

The hapless young man dragged his attention back to Sebella. "Uh. That's right, gentlesire. Made a commitment. Has to keep it." Brolla's patent relief at having successfully strung together four whole words into a single sentence almost sent Stonnor into a choking fit. Meanwhile, the younger man subsided into a relieved silence, still sneaking darting glances at Ariel's image.

"What are you laughing at?"

Sebella's glare and ill-tempered question quelled Stonnor's cough more effectively than his favorite hot rum toddies. "Nothing! Nothing!" he assured her. "I just, uh . . ."

"Yes, what do you have to say for your son, Gentlesire Stonnor?" Jeccad's question made Stonnor the focus of everyone's attention.

He struggled for something—anything—to say that might either absolve Dekkan of wrongdoing or at least remove the burden of an explanation from his own shoulders. Before he could do more than open his mouth, a loud *ding!* captured everyone's attention.

Jeccad pressed a small stud on the wall, and a holo-image appeared in the middle of the room. It showed a small man, dressed a bit shabbily, with scuffed shoes and drooping shoulders. "Gentlesire Jeccad? I've got the information you asked for." The man's voice sounded as soft as two leatherskins rubbing against each other.

"Do you, Weeven? A moment, please." Pensively, Jeccad, flexed his fingers until the knuckles cracked loudly. "Excuse me, gentlelady and gentlesires. I must speak with this person in private, if you don't mind."

"Well, I do mind!" Sebella proclaimed. "Does he know anything about Dekkan?"

"Sebella!" Stonnor's reprimand sent a flush up her cheeks, but she didn't back down.

"I want to know! This man and his daughter are perpetrating some . . . some hoax on me, and I think I'm within my rights to demand to hear whatever information he's found out about my fiancé."

"Gentlesire Jeccad," Stonnor began, turning to his host. "I can only apologize for—"

"Never mind. I understand that the, er, lady is upset. I always consider the source of rudenesses."

Sebella's flush turned scarlet, but she stood her ground. "Insult me, if you wish, but I still wish to hear what this . . . this . . . person has to say."

Jeccad eyed her as dispassionately as a farmer would a cow to the slaughter before shrugging. "Very well, then." He turned back to the holo-image of Weeven. "You heard the lady. Tell me what you've discovered."

The man pulled off a soft cap and twisted it around and around in his hands as he spoke. "I followed 'em like you said. He stayed with her—"

"Who?" Sebella demanded. "Who is he talking about?"

"Hush!" To Stonnor's surprise, the command came from the usually silent Brolla. "Listen." To Stonnor's greater surprise, Sebella hushed. And listened.

"—overnight, Gentlesire Jeccad." Weeven hadn't missed a beat in his report despite Sebella's interruption. He followed with mundane details about the unnamed *they* and their activities throughout the day, including a visit to this very house. His whispery voice made the report about as interesting as daily rya-grain prices to a fisherman.

Stonnor had to fight a yawn as the report droned on. Nothing interesting here. Even Sebella looked faintly bored at the mundane details of each meal eaten, and precisely how long each of the pair had spoken in every conversation. Since Weeven's observation post had obviously been out of earshot of the speakers, little could be gleaned by such trivia. Maybe Dekkan could get over this whole thing after all.

That hasty assessment crashed around Stonnor's ears when Weeven hesitated. His image seemed to shrink into himself as he gave a hunted look at Sebella. "Uh, at forty-three minutes past the midday hour, they approached an address on Heaven's Gateway."

"An address? What address?" Sebella had obviously been paying more attention than Stonnor had thought.

Was that a faint flush on Jeccad's face? Stonnor's curiosity rose when the other man waved Weeven on. "Never mind. It's not important what the address was," Jeccad commanded. "Continue."

The too-hasty words shrieked of dissembling. "What was the address?" Sebella insisted.

Weeven shifted uneasily and tried to ignore her question. His gaze skittered away from Jeccad and down to the cap in his hands. "Uh, they entered the establishment at—"

"What establishment?"

"—at forty-seven minutes after midday and stayed inside for two hours and twenty-five minutes—"

"*What establishment?*" Sebella's roar could not be

ignored. Weeven fell silent, a pleading look on his face.

Jeccad urgently shook his head, but Sebella's will was stronger. Weeven literally quailed at the Valkyrie who stalked over to stand nose-to-nose with his holo-image. "Tell me what establishment they entered. *Now!*"

An uneasy feeling crawled along Stonnor's spine. Suddenly, he himself did not want to know. He half rose from his chair, but it was too late to stop the words from tumbling from Weeven's lips.

"Mistress Floribunda d'Amatorio's House of Joy." With a gasp of relief, the little man shrank yet further inside himself like a messenger who fully expected his head to be the next to roll.

He had no need to worry, however. With an enraged shriek, Sebella fell into a dead faint and was saved from hitting the floor only by Brolla's quick reaction.

Stonnor felt like fainting, himself. What in the galaxy was Dekkan thinking of? A notorious house of love? *Dekkan?* He shook his head in stunned disbelief over his suddenly wayward son's actions while Brolla fussed over Sebella. Only when she began to rouse did Stonnor try to figure out what should be done next.

Jeccad sat silent and hunched on the only comfortable chair in the room. The holo-image of Weeven had disappeared. It was a good thing, too. Stonnor figured the last thing Sebella needed when she recovered from her faint was going to be any reminder of the news she'd just heard.

Stonnor walked quietly over to Jeccad. "What in blazes is going on, Jeccad? Why did Dekkan and Ariel go to Floribunda's?"

Ariel's Dance

Jeccad recovered enough to raise his head and glare. "Because she's got your ring!"

"Hush!" Stonnor urged. "Do you want them to hear you?" A vague wave of his hand indicated Brolla, still fussing over the prone Sebella.

Jeccad planted his hands firmly on the arms of his chair and stood. When he was fully erect, the top of his head reached Stonnor's nose. "Don't hush me! I'll have you know this is all your fault. If you hadn't—"

"Never mind!" Stonnor raked a hand through his thinning hair, desperately seeking a way out. "It's a mess, though. How are we going to straighten this out?"

"We?"

Jeccad's icy question didn't faze Stonnor. "Yes, 'we.' We're the ones who caused it, aren't we?"

Jeccad hesitated, but finally nodded once in acceptance.

"So how are we going to fix it?" Stonnor pressed. "We've got to get Dekkan out of this."

"Why? He's the one who—"

Stonnor's sharp glare shut Jeccad up. Again Stonnor raked his hand through his hair. "I sure could use some of Dekkan's negotiation expertise about now," he muttered. Across the room Sebella was sitting up with Brolla's devoted assistance.

The light of an idea settled in both his and Jeccad's minds simultaneously.

"Dekkan!" Stonnor breathed

"He can—" Jeccad added.

"—negotiate anything!" they finished together. Smiling broadly, they turned together to face the now-standing Sebella, who clung to Brolla's arm. Stonnor glanced at Jeccad, who nudged him back with a discreet elbow.

"Sebella," Stonnor began, "it's obvious that some terrible misunderstanding has occurred. The Dekkan we know is honorable and fully aware of his duties to you and to Misthaven Keep. Are we agreed about that?"

She gave a grudging nod.

"Well, then, it seems clear that the only way to resolve this is to go to the source of the problem. We need to discuss this with Dekkan himself." At Jeccad's prodding elbow, Stonnor added hastily, "And Ariel, of course."

"That's the first sensible thing you've said since we left Amity," Sebella said. "Did that Weeven person say where they are now?"

Jeccad nodded. "They have returned to my daughter's home." His dislike of Sebella was apparent in every syllable.

"Good," Stonnor declared with all the heartiness he could muster. He rubbed his hands together with all the joy of someone about to dump a serious problem in someone else's lap. "I will be pleased to escort you there, Sebella. Brolla can return to the hotel and await us there."

"No, Keepsire," Brolla insisted. "I go, too. Sebella needs protection." A mulish expression settled on his face. "I protect her. From Dekkan, too."

The aspersion against his son riled Stonnor, but he refused to let his anger show. It was too unimportant an issue to worry about now that things were almost back on track.

"And I'm going, too. My daughter's rights need to be protected."

Jeccad's announcement did surprise Stonnor. His questioning look was met with a blank adamance that countenanced no disagreement. Stonnor shrugged. What was one more person at this stage?

Ariel's Dance

With a little confusion, the group managed to leave Jeccad's home and snag a hire-car. Jeccad had of course usurped the seat by the driver, leaving Sebella, Stonnor, and Brolla to squeeze into the inadequate backseat. As the electric engine whined up to speed, Stonnor prayed the trip wouldn't take long.

It didn't. The last wisps of twilight still gave the sky a dusky glow when the car whirred to a near-silent stop. When Brolla opened the door, the three rear-seat passengers popped out in relief. Stonnor dusted himself off and took the lead up the walkway to the bungalow. With a quick glance over his shoulder to ensure that everyone was ready, he confidently pressed the announcement stud on the door.

No one answered.

Lights shone through the windows, so unless Ariel commonly left her house lit at night while she was away, someone was inside. He pressed the stud again.

Still no answer.

A third press netted the same result. Sebella shifted restlessly behind him. He was about to try a fourth time when Jeccad elbowed his way to the front.

"Never mind that," Jeccad said. "She . . . they may have just stepped out. I'm keyed for entry, so I'll let us in, and we can wait for them to return." He pressed his palm to the announcment panel and the door clicked open. A simple push opened it completely, and everyone crowded inside.

Only to stop in horror as they saw what an enraptured Dekkan and Ariel were doing on the couch.

Chapter Ten

Dekkan had never felt so out of control. Somehow, Ariel smashed all his restraints. Had he really said, "I want you"? Had he actually told her he wasn't sorry he'd kissed her?

When she smiled up at him and said, "I'm not sorry either," his heart pounded in his chest. She didn't regret his kiss! She didn't regret the taste of passion they'd sampled. Her arms looped around his neck, tugged his willing mouth lower, and when their lips touched, a great barrier collapsed in his mind. Just this once, he'd follow his own wishes. Just this once, he'd do something that wasn't carefully thought out.

Closing his mind to all the "oughtn'ts" and "shouldn'ts," he pulled Ariel closer into his embrace. "Ah, Ariel, you make me so happy."

Her lips traced the curve of his jaw, while her

Ariel's Dance

hands delved into the opening of his shirt. "That's what this is all about."

Her clever fingers found a sensitive nub buried in the hair on his chest, and a gasp hissed between his teeth. He inhaled deeply, savoring every nuance of her touch, her honey-spice taste, her scent. "I can't believe I've actually captured a butterfly for my own." He guided her back down to the sofa, and stretched beside her. "I thought I'd go crazy before I figured out how to snare you."

Her head tipped back, and he saw the amusement brimming in her turquoise eyes. "I'm only a butterfly onstage," she assured him. "In your arms, I'm a woman." Her eyes darkened to a shimmering, iridescent blue.

"No. You're a butterfly—my butterfly." He dipped his head to sip delicately from her mouth and stop further argument. "Now, butterfly," he muttered, a whisper away from her lips, "give me your nectar." His mouth demanded entrance to hers.

The world spun wildly around him. Every touch, every taste, every scent beckoned him farther from the security of the world he'd known. "You're the most beautiful thing that's ever happened to me." His voice sounded husky, foreign to his ears.

He regretted the words instantly, because she pulled away to look up into his face. Her hands framed his cheeks. "You've got that backward, you know," she told him.

Drowning in the seductive hunger that flickered in her eyes, Dekkan barely managed to mumble, "Backward?"

Her rosy lips curved upward. "You're the beautiful one. You make me feel special—as if you care about only me."

"Ah, Ariel, I can't even think about anyone or anything except you." He pulled her closer into his arms and bent his head to snare her lips again.

He never intended for things to go quite so far. He only knew that he couldn't bear another moment without the shimmering excitement he felt only when he held her close. He'd done nothing all day except want her. Every action, every word had led up to this one single moment when his mouth could explore her face and his hands were free to roam her body.

She seemed to take equal pleasure in her own explorations. Her hands smoothed down his chest in a caress that aroused him even more. His breath came in shallow gasps as she accurately located every singing nerve end.

Her hands smoothed over his abdomen. Surely she'd notice his missing patch. She'd remember they had to exercise self-restraint and stop this intimacy. *Please, not yet.* He had to have one more moment, just one minute of exploring each other before they stopped. Just one moment more . . .

His mouth found hers again, shared the passion of a woman who truly wanted him—not his keep, not his money, not his social status. An instinct buried deep inside him knew that Ariel didn't care about those things. She responded to him, to his body making love to hers. He wrapped his arms around her and tugged her closer.

She struggled against him, and he reluctantly loosened his grip. She pulled away and sat up. They should stop this; she was right. Yet . . .

Slowly, seductively, Ariel loosened the long copper-colored scarf from around her neck. The filmy drapery drifted free, revealing the low-cut top of her dress. With a casual gesture, she flicked the

Ariel's Dance

scarf away, letting it drift to the floor in a sensual heap. Dekkan's gaze became riveted on her hands as they ever so slowly worked at the tie on the shoulder of her dress. He forgot to breathe as he watched her. She didn't plan to . . . she wouldn't . . . would she?

His erotic speculations ended as the top of her dress dropped to her waist, revealing breasts ripe enough to fuel any man's fantasies. With a quick shimmy of her hips, she slipped the garment over her buttocks and tossed it to the floor. Another move stripped off her panties and left her naked before him, with a surprisingly vulnerable look in her eyes.

Dekkan took in every detail with a hunger he didn't bother to disguise. "You're beautiful," he said huskily. "So beautiful." With reverent awe, he skimmed his hands over her coppery skin, tracing every curve. The contrast between his tanned flesh and her exotic coloring enthralled him. Her silky skin seemed too delicate for hands more used to the rough exercise of running a keep. He'd never seen a woman so beautiful, never believed such loveliness could belong to him. Her hands explored his body, leaving trails of fire on his flesh.

He couldn't stand it any longer. His groin throbbed so tightly that he was sure he would explode at any second. He shifted position to lie flat on the sofa, tugging her with him so she lay full-length on top of him. His hands caressed her back and drifted down to clutch the luscious curves of her naked hips. Dekkan's mouth closed over hers in a kiss that quickly grew so carnal that every cell in his body felt ready to merge with hers.

The opening door went unnoticed until he heard a chorus of gasped protests.

"Dekkan!"
"What are you doing?"
"Harrumph!"
"Hey, buddy!"

Bemused from the kisses of the woman who still seemed oblivious to the intruders, Dekkan lifted his head and cleared a fistful of silky auburn curls from his face. Ariel's lips roved down his chin and neck with single-minded determination, but Dekkan's ardor drained away like water in an emptying tub when he saw the foursome gaping at him and Ariel.

Ariel! She's naked!

Hurriedly, Dekkan tried to stop Ariel's kisses, while at the same time groping around on the floor for something to cover her with. Despite her incoherent protests, he managed to free his mouth. "Ariel—mmmph—we've—stop for a minute—mmmph—got—mmmph—visitors."

"Visitors?" Her distracted, dreamy voice made it clear that she hadn't taken in what he'd said.

"Yes. People! Here!" With a surge of strength, he managed to sit upright while at the same time snatching the first thing his fingers touched. He draped the garment over her, trying to cover as much of her as possible. Only when he had the thing in place did he realize he'd picked up the filmy scarf. It didn't cover much, but at least it hid her round buttocks from Brolla's lustful gaze.

"Dekkan! What's going on here? What are you doing with this—" Sebella's voice screeched like fingernails on a slate.

"Sebella!" Dekkan managed to sit up and push Ariel into a sitting position beside him. Hurriedly, he redraped the scarf to cover her again, while frantically searching the floor for her dress. "It's such a . . . a surprise to see you! You didn't tell me you planned a trip to Mariposa."

"Surprise is right, you worm! Is this the way you conduct negotiations when you're off-planet?"

Dekkan flushed, feeling as guilty as Sebella could have desired. He spotted Ariel's dress and tried to snare it, but it was just out of reach. If he let go of the scarf it would fall, yet he couldn't hold on to it and still reach her dress. "Now, Sebella . . ."

Jeccad patted Sebella ineffectually on the arm. "You see? Your friend is clearly engaged to my daughter, not to you. You must have misinterpreted him."

"Uh, gentlesire . . ." Dekkan had no idea what he was going to say, but his own father interrupted him.

"Dekkan, I'm shocked! This is not the behavior I expect of my son!"

"I know, Father. I just . . . she just . . . it just . . ." Beside him, Ariel stirred. He adjusted her scarf again. Maybe he could reach her dress with his toe and drag it a bit closer? He nudged her behind him, trying to move her further out of view.

"She just what?" Sebella accused. "Forced you down? Tripped you onto the couch? What?"

"Yes, son, if you've got an explanation for this scene"—Stonnor waved his hand to encompass the rumpled cushions, the scattered garments—"now would be a good time to share that explanation."

"I—"

Before Dekkan could formulate an answer to the unanswerable, Brolla picked up Ariel's discarded dress and held it out. "Want this?"

"Yes!" Dekkan snatched it from his friend's hand and pushed it toward Ariel. She didn't take it. "Why don't you put this back on?" he suggested quietly.

Silent until now, Ariel stared at him with deep suspicion shadowing her eyes. Dekkan found he couldn't maintain eye contact with her.

"I'm waiting!" Sebella's foot tapped with impatient demand.

"Please, Ariel." Again he pushed the garment toward her, ignoring the increasingly deafening conversation of the others. "Go put it on." Again his eyes met hers, but this time suspicion had given way to a simmering anger that made her turquoise eyes practically glow. Just what he needed, yet another outraged female. Silently he continued to hold out the garment.

He wasn't sure she'd do as he asked until she snatched the garment from his hand and stalked unceremoniously away toward the relative privacy of the bath. Unfortunately, the scarf draped across her hips lent a seductive twitch to her walk that Dekkan couldn't help but notice.

Nor could Brolla, Dekkan saw with a scowl.

Reluctantly he turned back to face the gathered fury of his father, his best friend, and his fiancée. An explanation was due them, he knew.

He just wished he had one to offer.

Ariel slammed the bathing room door. *Damn him!* She'd been so lost in passion, she'd barely noticed when the door had opened. Yet he'd been alert enough to notice the interruption immediately. How could that man do this to her? She was hardly promiscuous, but she'd had enough experience with lovemaking to know that sex wasn't something that swept her away. At least not normally.

So why was it different with this man?

She tossed away the scarf and stared into the mirror. Her whole body still tingled with the memory of his hands on her. Somehow, she expected to see some sign of his caresses. Even now, she could feel every stroke of his fingers. How had his touch not branded her skin?

She pressed the button to activate the cleanser and stepped inside the compact booth. Maybe the stinging spray of water would erase the memory of his touch.

It didn't work. Even after she'd given herself a deliberately brisk rubdown with an exfoliant that left her skin darkly flushed, the memories remained. She applied her favorite skin cream, then tugged open a drawer to get a clean set of undergarments. She might as well go back and join the now-rumbling conversation.

A quick peek into the clothes chamber produced a fairly conservative catsuit. At least it covered her from neck to toe, even if it did fit rather tightly. No doubt the all-too-perfect Sebella would sniff no matter what she wore.

Ariel fussed with her hair and cosmetics, consciously avoiding the moment she'd have to face her unwelcome visitors. Something precious had been tainted by the interruption, and she didn't want to face the reality that Dekkan belonged with another woman.

"This is ridiculous!" she told her reflection. "It's not as if anything really happened."

Not for lack of trying, her conscience told her with a sneer. *Given a few minutes more and they might have seen something a lot more interesting than your bare bottom sprawled on top of the man.*

"It wouldn't have gone that far."

No? Says who? You didn't plan to stop and neither did he.

A flush heated her cheeks. She gathered her courage and opened the door, only to hear Dekkan say, "I do apologize for my lapse in conduct, Sebella. I assure you it has not happened before, nor will it—"

Before he could complete the promise, a blinding fury overtook Ariel, and she stormed into the main room, stalked up to Dekkan, and pulled him around to face her. "Lapse? *Lapse?* Did you just call me a lapse?"

Dekkan's mouth opened, but Sebella interrupted, jerking his arm until he faced her again. "My fiancé was explaining how he came to be found in such unsavory circumstances."

"Oh, galaxy," Stonnor muttered. "I wish she hadn't said that."

"Unsavory circumstances?" Ariel repeated in her most dangerous tone. She pulled Dekkan back around to face her. "Did *you* say that? Did you say unsavory?"

Once more Dekkan tried to speak, but Sebella cut him off, again tugging him away from Ariel.

"How else could this . . . this . . . situation"—Sebella gestured broadly to indicate the room, the still-strewn articles of clothing, and the rumpled depression in the cushions of the sofa—"be described? Unsavory is the least of it, I would say!"

Ariel's attention turned back to Dekkan, pulling him around once more. "Did you say unsavory?" she demanded.

He pulled free and stomped away from both women, crossing his arms over his chest. "Enough!" he roared. "You will both cease pulling me about like a lapdog. Sebella, stop tormenting Ariel. Ariel, calm down and listen for a moment."

"Listen to what? You insulting me one more time? Calling me a lapse?" Ariel folded her arms across her chest in blatant imitation of his gesture,

Ariel's Dance

and stood still, tapping her toe in irritation.

"Well, if the girdle fits . . ." Sebella's snide tone drew a snarl from Dekkan, but hardly a glance from Ariel.

"Ariel, I was explaining that we . . . that *I* intended no harm here. We, uh, *I* simply got carried away—"

Before he could finish, Jeccad stalked up to him and thrust his chin at Dekkan's chest. "Are you telling me you've been trifling with my daughter? That you don't mean to follow through on the promise you made to her?"

"Jeccad—" Ariel shifted uncomfortably. She'd never really intended Dekkan to be caught in her lie—had she? A memory of her overriding Dekkan's explicit instruction not to announce the bogus engagement sent a trickle of remorse through her. What trouble had she caused with her stubborness? It seemed that Dekkan was going to pay the price for her actions.

Sebella didn't give Ariel a chance to finish her protest. "What about the promises he made to me? I'm the injured party here—not some tawdry dancer in a cheap peep show! What about *me?*"

"We all know more than we care to about you, madam," Jeccad said. "what's at stake here is whether this man will live up to the promises he made my little Ariel." Every word was punctuated by a hard poke to Dekkan's chest.

Dekkan caught Jeccad's hand and forced it away. "You made your point. There's no need to become physically abusive."

"Abusive? I'll show you abusive, you young sneak-peeker!" Jeccad put up his hands in an exaggerated version of the stance of an Aldebaran *kojo* fighter.

Dekkan waved off Brolla, who had silently stepped forward, obviously intending to restrain Jeccad. Dekkan clearly itched to take some form of physical action. He took up a classic defensive kick-stance in preparation for Jeccad's opening attack.

Despite Dekkan's age and height advantage, Ariel feared Jeccad would win any confrontation. She knew all too well that Jeccad never fought fair.

"Dekkan! Jeccad—*Daddy!*" Ariel's protest went unheeded by all. She appealed to Stonnor. "Can't you stop this?"

"Let them fight it out!" Sebella demanded. "It would serve the cad right to take a beating after what he's done to me."

Ariel didn't bother guessing whether Sebella relished Dekkan or Jeccad as the possible loser. "Stonnor, *please.*"

With obvious reluctance, Stonnor waded into the fray. "Now listen, everyone. This is enough. We need to settle this in a more civilized fashion."

"He's not going to get away with twiddling with my daughter and not make things right. No, sir!"

Dekkan choked. "Uh, 'twiddling'?"

Jeccad glared at him. "Yes, *twiddling.* I saw you. You were twiddling with my little Ariel." His too-pious expression and pugnacious stance slipped as he overbalanced slightly and had to hurriedly regroup to keep from falling over. Like a cub who'd misjudged a jump and ended up clinging awkwardly by one paw, Jeccad tried to cover his mistake by sending an I-meant-to-do-that glare around the room.

"Jeccad, I'm an adult now. You've never cared about any other man I got involved with." Ariel felt bound to defend her independence.

"Yes, but those men weren't your promised hus-

Ariel's Dance

bands, now, were they?" Jeccad pointed out with confusing illogic.

Dekkan's head swiveled around, and he glared at Ariel with a ferocious gleam that made her step back a pace. "*Other* men? What other men?"

Sebella's face was as red as the crimson honey-blooms in the garden. "I demand restitution! I demand that he make things up to me!"

"There's no need for anyone to become violent here." Stonnor's measured, gravelly voice cut through the rising hubbub. "We're all civilized people. We can settle things calmly and quietly."

For an instant, Ariel and everyone else paused to stare at Stonnor in sheer disbelief. Then they all exchanged a what-planet-did-he-come-from look before resuming their shouting. Only the silent Brolla, still hovering protectively near Sebella's shoulder, didn't contribute to the increasing din.

"Now, Dekkan, I was just speaking, uh, hypothetically," Ariel said.

"You keep out of this! You're nothing!" Sebella insisted to Ariel. "Dekkan, tell her that you've arranged to marry me just as soon as we get home."

Dekkan shook off Sebella's grasping hand on his arm. "I want to know about those other men."

"I'm not letting you mess with my daughter and not make things right. You're not getting away with this, you young jackanapes!"

"Forget the other men. They're not important." Ariel brushed her hair back off her forehead.

"And who says so?" Dekkan asked. "Would you expect me to believe that you would feel so sanguine about my past experiences with other women?"

"Other women!" Sebella shrieked. "You've done this with other women, too? Oh, mercy, mercy,

mercy!" She fell back into the conveniently waiting arms of the hovering Brolla.

"What other women?" Ariel asked, sensing her temper flaring upward toward the danger zone.

A smug grin curled Dekkan's lips. "Forget them. They're not important."

"That does it!" Jeccad snapped. "You're obviously a cad who has preyed upon innocent young misses for years. But you've come to the end of your preying now." He waggled a finger in Dekkan's face. "I'm going to make sure you never get the chance to abuse another father's hospitality."

Jeccad had often called Ariel the most stubborn of Chimosian chockwallabulls, but for the first time she recognized the accusation's truth. With firm determination, she stuck to her topic. "What other women have you done this with?"

"Have you worried now, do I?" Dekkan asked, clearly enjoying his ability to fluster her.

Unfortunately, their not-so-private conversation had also triggered Stonnor's worries. "Dekkan, am I to believe that you have made a practice of exceeding the bounds of propriety with women while you've been off Amity?" The old man seemed to have aged many years in only moments. "I can't believe that my son could have been so . . ."

A dark flush of shame flowed over Dekkan's neck and face. He turned to Stonnor. "No, Keepsire, no. I promise you, I have done nothing . . . shameful before. You need not fear—"

"*Shameful!*" Ariel's fury mounted again. "Shameful! First I'm a lapse, and then I'm unsavory, and now I'm shameful." She stalked over to him and deliberately stomped hard on his foot, relishing his gasp of pain. "That'll teach you to call me shameful!"

Ariel's Dance

Dekkan bowed his head in ironic courtesy. "Are you finished with your abuse, madam? I acknowledge your right to punish me for going beyond the bounds of courtesy." He lowered his head until his nose practically touched hers. "But don't do it again!"

Stonnor, obviously relieved at Dekkan's assurance, again tried to soothe the troubled waters. "Well, then, gentlepeople. Let's all sit down and see if we can make some sense of what's to be done."

"I'll tell you what's to be done. He's to marry my little Ariel, that's what's to be done." Jeccad's persistence confirmed to Ariel where she got her own stubborn determination.

"He is not going to marry that... that... *person*," Sebella said. "He's going to marry *me* just as soon as we get back to Amity."

The roar of voices grew louder and louder until Stonnor's shrill whistle cut through the noise, creating a frozen silence.

"Enough!" Stonnor glared at each person in the room, daring them to utter so much as a squeak. "At last, some quiet. I don't know how you expect to settle this dispute when you're making enough noise to shatter the viewports of a star liner." One more glare sufficed to douse any remaining rebellion.

"Keepsire, I believe that a simple explanation will settle this issue." Dekkan's modulated tones sent a shiver down Ariel's back. Did he plan to expose her lie to her father?

"No!" she interrupted. When Dekkan and Stonnor turned toward her in equal amazement, she felt heat rush up her cheeks. "I mean, what's the problem? Everything's perfectly clear, isn't it?" The ridiculousness of her claim sent the heat flowing down her neck as well.

Stonnor's frown creased his brow. "Not to me, Ariel. My son was found in an, uh, embarrassing position with you, when he is committed—"

"To me!" Sebella insisted.

"To my daughter!"

"Enough!" Stonnor commanded. "It seems to me that we need to deal with the reality of the situation, the facts as they exist, rather than as we would like them to be. Dekkan, you were clearly behaving improperly with Ariel, is this not true?"

Stiffly, Dekkan's head nodded his head once in acknowledgment. "To my regret, yes, Keepsire. It is true."

"See! I told you he couldn't be trusted here!" Sebella's so-there expression brought a silencing glare from Stonnor.

"To your *regret!*" Ariel huffed. She refused to acknowledge the hurt that lodged inside her with his admission.

"Quiet, daughter!" Jeccad bellowed. "Let the Amitan explain how he's going to correct the situation."

"So," Stonnor pronounced with measured care. "We see the problem. Dekkan has compromised his integrity by becoming intimate—"

"He did not become intimate with me!" Ariel insisted.

Sebella destroyed that argument. "Only because we interrupted you!"

Stonnor ignored her. "—becoming intimate with Ariel without a formal marriage contract between them. On the other hand, such an arrangement has been publicly announced here on Mariposa, which would itself ameliorate the situation. After all, even on Amity, a few engaged couples have occasionally exceeded the bounds of propriety."

Ariel's Dance

"*I* certainly don't engage in such pursuits!" Sebella announced.

"Yes, I can see that." Jeccad's assessment of Sebella sent a wave of color up her cheeks. "You have my sympathies, Dekkan um Stonnor."

"May we return to the issue?" Stonnor asked, again ignoring the interruption. "I cannot allow Dekkan um Stonnor's reputation for honesty and integrity to become besmirched by one sordid incident. His entire future and position with the Amitan negotiating team would be compromised if it were discovered that he has fallen short of our ideals in such a way. So the key to this situation is that the engagement to Ariel—which would make Dekkan's liberties understandable if not fully acceptable—conflicts with his prior commitment to marry Sebella." Stonnor stared at each person in turn, gathering consensus as he went. "Is this agreed?"

Nods, ranging from Jeccad's vigorous up-and-down shake to Ariel's hesitant acceptance and Dekkan's terse inclination, greeted his survey.

"What we need to do is to find a way to salvage Dekkan's honor by enabling him to meet both commitments," Stonnor continued, generating a unified gasp.

"Bigamy isn't usually allowed on Mariposa," Jeccad offered. "Besides, why would a man marry *her* when he could have my Ariel?"

"My husband will come to me pure or not at all!" Sebella demanded.

Ariel, noticing the light of a plan in Stonnor's eyes, asked, "What are you talking about, Stonnor?"

"Yes, Keepsire, tell me what you propose." Dekkan's voice sounded rusty, as if breaking his silence had startled it out of hiding.

Stonnor rubbed his hands together in a gesture

that matched Ariel's mental image of the glee of a farmer measuring a bumper crop of prizewinning rya wheat. "It's very simple. Dekkan must marry Ariel to make things right with her. He must also marry Sebella to honor his commitment to her. So . . . he has to make a choice as to which wrong to redress."

"And that means, Father?" Dekkan definitely sounded wary now.

Stonnor's finger stabbed the air. "You marry the woman you've wronged the most—Ariel—and you do it now. Tonight. Then there can be no question that your honor has been upheld."

Chapter Eleven

Dekkan heard his father pronounce his fate with a sense of profound relief. Even Sebella's resumed screeching didn't dispel his incredible sensation of a man who had avoided the executioner's ax by the merest stroke of fortune. Marry Ariel! The idea hadn't seemed a realistic possibility to him—at least not seriously—but now that his father insisted on it . . . yes, the plan had a strange merit.

He turned it over in his mind. To wed Ariel. That would give him the right to explore those new feelings that swamped him whenever she was within arm's reach. He could relax and enjoy his new wife, without worrying about his duty or obligations to his fiancée.

Galaxy! His *fiancée!*

With a sudden swivel he turned to face Sebella. Surely after six years of betrothal, he should feel something more at the dissolution of that arrangement than relief? She had worked herself into a frenzy, her face flushed and her eyes spitting rage. Was this what it would be like to be married to her? With an effort, he suppressed a shudder.

A quick glance brought Ariel into view. She stood quietly, not meeting anyone's eyes, head lowered and hands clasped together, in clear contrast to the unrestrained fury of Sebella. He had no idea what triumph she felt, if any, at having brought the Misthaven heir to heel. Yet he could not find reason to blame her entirely for this situation.

"I won't have it!" Sebella's strident protest snapped his attention back to the argument still going on. "Dekkan is promised to me. He has an obligation to wed me!"

"Now, Sebella. Don't be like that. Let me finish explaining—"

Stonnor's soothing tones didn't survive Sebella's continued protest. "No! I can't believe you'd welcome to your keep such a lowborn, base—"

"*What* are you calling my daughter?" Jeccad's booming question shut Sebella up for a moment of blessed relief.

Dekkan decided to use the moment of silence to ask his own question. "Father, how will such a marriage restore my honor? It seems to me that I will still have failed in my obligation to Sebella."

"Ah, Dekkan, that's the beauty of my plan!" Again Stonnor's expression could only be called smug. "You see, you'll wed Ariel with a pro tem mating license. That's valid only until you leave Mariposa. Then when you return to Amity you can still wed Sebella. You see how simple it is?"

Dekkan glanced at Jeccad, who nodded in agreement. "That will satisfy me, my boy." The man's immediate assent to the plan puzzled Dekkan, until he realized that Jeccad probably didn't need Ariel to make a permanent marriage to receive control of her inheritance. Any wedding would do, even one destined to last only a few days.

He refused to express the instant regret that followed that thought.

"Simple?" Sebella said. "You mean simple-minded! You think I would take a husband who'd allied himself with that—"

"Watch what you say about my daughter, missy!" Jeccad warned.

Ariel opened her mouth and took a shaky breath. Suddenly, Dekkan realized that there was another party whose opinion mattered in all this. He noticed that she seemed to be building her courage up to say something—what, he wasn't sure, but he also wasn't sure he wanted to hear her say she didn't want to be tied to him even for the short time he'd be on Mariposa.

It didn't matter. Stonnor gave her no chance to speak. Instead, he commandeered everyone else into organizing the event.

"Jeccad, get on the holo-vid and find us a cleric to seal the ceremony. Sebella, stop your screeching. Brolla, move some of these sofas out if the way. We need some space here. We've got a mating ceremony to arrange!"

To Dekkan's amazement, Ariel hesitated, then swallowed whatever she was going to say. Within a bare ten minutes, the arrangements were complete, despite Sebella's continued mutterings and Ariel's unnatural silence. He wished he had even a clue what she might be thinking or feeling. He hoped she didn't resent being bludgeoned into this situation. He wished . . . He didn't know what he wished.

Except for a moment of privacy with his too-silent bride-to-be.

But privacy was nowhere to be found. All too soon, Jeccad had a holo-image of one of the city's leading clerics projected into the middle of Ariel's salon. The man looked disheveled and slightly bewildered, but he was there, ready to perform the ceremony.

"Uh," the man stammered, "are we all ready?"

Dekkan tried to conceal just how ready he was as he obediently moved into position according to Jeccad's direction. Ariel hesitated a long moment, but she too moved to stand beside him.

Sebella, however, had more to say about the subject. She walked directly to Dekkan's other side and tugged on his arm.

He looked down at her. "What is it?"

"Before you do this, I want to get a few things straight with you." Her voice held little of the modest decorum he was used to hearing from her.

"We're here to unite, pro tem, this man and this woman." The cleric looked puzzled for a moment. "Uh, Jeccad?"

"What is it?" Jeccad's impatience was all too obvious.

"Uh, this man and *which* woman, exactly?" the man asked, gesturing at Ariel, on Dekkan's left, and Sebella, on Dekkan's right.

"Me!" Sebella inserted.

Brolla frowned and grunted.

"Now, Sebella," Stonnor chided. "You know we decided Dekkan was to wed Ariel for now."

Dekkan collected Ariel's hand with firm assurance. "This woman, gentlesire. I am wedding Ariel, daughter of Jeccad." To his surprise, her hand was

Ariel's Dance

cool and slightly damp. Nerves? In his superconfident Ariel?

"Well, if he had to ask . . ." Sebella said, with a pout. "Now, Dekkan. I want to get some things straight before we begin this ceremony."

"Get on with it, man!" Jeccad said to the holo-image of the clerk, who hastily stuffed a flask back into the dangling sleeve of his robes.

"We are uniting this man and this woman in Mariposan pro tem matrimony. Dekkan um Stonnor, do you take this woman as your own, to have and to hold as long as you are on this planet?"

"Yes," he announced firmly. No vow had ever felt so right.

Sebella demanded his attention again. "Dekkan, remember this mating is only temporary. I don't want you consorting with her."

He choked back a laugh. "Um, 'consorting,' Sebella?"

Impatiently she gestured toward the couch, which still bore the crumpled imprint of his and Ariel's bodies. "Consorting," she confirmed. "I don't want you doing with her what you were doing with her when we came in."

"Ariel Calistara, daughter of Jeccad, do you take this man as your own, to have and to hold as long as you are on this planet?"

Silence. Dekkan's head whipped around and he fixed a stare on Ariel. Surprisingly, she looked not at him, nor at her father, but at his father. "Stonnor, do I really need to do this? Are you sure this is the right thing to do? Are you *sure*?"

"Ariel—" Dekkan began, not sure he knew how to finish that sentence.

"See?" Sebella said. "I told you! Dekkan, you don't want to waste your time with this . . . this *floozy*."

"Who are you calling a floozy?" Jeccad demanded. "That's my daughter you're talking about."

"Well, if you kept better track of what she was doing, maybe she wouldn't go around stealing other women's men!"

"She did not steal me!" Dekkan protested. He resented the implication that he wasn't man enough to make his own choices. What did Sebella think he was, anyway? A frightened ground grubber?

"Say yes, Ariel," Stonnor urged.

The cleric repeated his question. "Ariel Calistara, daughter of Jeccad, do you take this man as your own, to have and to hold as long as you are on this planet?"

"But Stonnor, I never knew helping you would come to this." Ariel's gesture encompassed the still-squabbling Sebella, the looming Brolla, and the overeager Jeccad.

Sebella addressed the cleric. "Gentlesire, if this *floozy* doesn't want Dekkan, I'll take him."

"Jeccad, are you sure you indicated the right woman?" the cleric asked.

"Yes," Ariel whispered while Sebella was insisting that the cleric's question was valid and he should indeed be marrying her to Dekkan rather than some two-credit woman Dekkan had picked up in a dive somewhere.

The cleric's bewilderment grew. He opened his mouth to ask another question, but Jeccad cut him off. "She said yes, man, so get on with it."

"I didn't hear her," the cleric insisted. Sweat glistened on the man's brow.

Dekkan saw him wipe the beads off. "She said it," he confirmed.

"She didn't mean it!" Sebella insisted. Apparently seeing that she was losing this argument, she re-

Ariel's Dance

turned her attention to Dekkan. "Now listen, Dekkan, you're not to mess with her. Just because of this temporary situation, you're not to—"

He brushed her hand away. Even though he knew she was right, it hurt to realize that this mating was strictly for show. He wanted—ah, what he wanted didn't matter. He had to think what was best for Ariel. For Sebella. For his father. For his keep. But, ah, what he might have had . . .

The cleric had progressed further through the ceremony. "If there be any person with valid objection to—"

"Yes!" Sebella interrupted. "*I* object! This isn't—mmmppphhh!"

Dekkan was astonished to realize that Brolla's hand had smothered Sebella's protest.

"No objections," Brolla stated firmly in a voice deeper than Dekkan had ever heard from his friend. "Go on."

The cleric stared hard at Brolla's determined countenance, gulped, and continued. "So since there are no objections, I now pronounce you husband and wife. Pro tem. You can kiss your wife now." The sentences came out in one long, relieved breath.

Dekkan bent his head, more than happy to experience again the pleasure of his lips touching Ariel's, but before he could make contact, Jeccad pounded him hard on the back, making Dekkan's forehead bump against Ariel's. "Ouch!"

"Congratulations, my boy! Welcome to the family!" Jeccad reached into his overtunic and pulled out a rolled-up paper. "Here, Ariel, you need to sign this while the cleric is still here to witness it." He shoved the paper in front of Ariel and thrust a permastylus into her hand.

"Don't get too confident, Dekkan," Sebella demanded. "Remember that I'll be watching you. You have no business doing any 'business' with that woman!"

"She's my wife now, Sebella." Dekkan said. "You'll speak of her with respect."

"Hmmph!" Sebella gave a strong sniff. "Respect is for those who deserve it."

Dekkan lowered his head to glare at Sebella, then caught sight of Ariel obediently bending to sign the document. "Ariel, don't you think you should read what that says before you sign it?"

She looked up in surprise. "I know what it says."

"But don't you think you ought to read it just to be sure?"

Jeccad pushed between them. "No need. No need. She knows what it says. Right, daughter?"

Ariel cast a cynical glance at Jeccad. "Sure I do." She signed the paper with a flourish.

Jeccad snatched it almost before the stylus left the paper. "Here, cleric. Witness it."

The holo-image floundered. "Uh, Jeccad. I can't sign it. I'm not there."

"I know that!" Jeccad's bluster betrayed his error. "I'll put it in the holo-fax. Attach your seal."

"Well, you know I'm supposed to be there in person before I put my seal to such a signature. . . ." Jeccad's fierce frown had the cleric backing down immediately. "I'll just put my seal on it through the fax. Is that all right?"

"Good, good."

Dekkan observed the byplay almost peripherally. His attention was locked firmly onto his brand-new wife. Despite his best efforts to control his emotions, to recognize that his status as husband was strictly temporary, all he could think of was that he now had the perfect right to enjoy his wife's attention. From the excitement surging through his veins, he knew *enjoy* was definitely the right word.

It wasn't until his father clapped him on the shoulder that Dekkan remembered he was not supposed to be luxuriating in a wife he would leave behind in only a few days.

Reluctantly, he admitted that his excitement would have to give way to the duty that lay in wait for him back on Amity.

His duty—and Sebella.

After the ceremony, Ariel found herself sitting in a chair in the corner of her own salon, sipping warily from the drink Dekkan's friend had handed her. He stood silently beside her, much like an ancient megalith statue. What did he think about all this hubbub?

"Brolla, you're a friend of Dekkan's, aren't you?" She grimaced at the inanity of her comment. *Go ahead. Confirm to the man that you haven't the brains of a shadow-thrush.*

"Yes. And Sebella."

She thought about that for a moment. Across the room, Dekkan listened with pained courtesy to Sebella, who was lecturing him severely about something. "Does it seem to you that Dekkan and Sebella are a little, uh, mismatched?"

Brolla was silent for so long that she didn't think he'd answer. "No," he said at last. "It's a good match."

Something in the man's deep voice made Ariel look sharply at him, but his bland, almost characterless face held no expression. "I see." What else could they talk about?

Before she could come up with a new topic of

conversation, Jeccad rolled over, obviously two or three stages past the feeling-no-pain level. "Happy wedding, m'dear. Happy wedding."

"Do you think so, *Daddy?*" Her emphasis was enough to penetrate even Jeccad's euphoric haze. He winced.

"Now, now, m'dear. No need to go on about it. What's done is done. Spilt cormaberry juice and all that."

She took another sip of her drink. It tasted like a hyperstellar strangleblaster, but she hadn't realized the ingredients were in her kitchen. She shrugged. What did it matter anyway? "Well, at least one of us is happy about this wedding."

"Dekkan um Stonnor will do right by you; you just wait and see." The promise sounded vaguely threatening to Ariel.

Something in Jeccad's tone raised her suspicions. "What are you planning?"

His eyes shifted away from hers in a nervous habit she knew better than to ignore. "Why, nothing." Another shift of his eyes reminded her of Brolla's silent, watchful presence.

Whatever Jeccad was up to, this wasn't the time to explore it. A smile as thin as the paper he'd pushed her into signing curved her lips. "We'll talk about it later. Right, Jeccad?"

He shifted uncomfortably, gave a grateful glance at Brolla, and began to edge away. "Sure, Ariel. Later."

Ariel watched Jeccad slink away and wondered again what more was behind this hurried ceremony. The thing had been arranged so quickly and efficiently that it was almost as if . . .

Brolla interrupted her thought. "Why do you address your father thus?"

Ariel's Dance

She swiveled around in her chair to stare up at him. It was the first time she'd heard him string together more than three or four words at a time. "Address him how?"

"By his name. It's disrespectful."

"Disrespectful? How?"

"It's disrespectful to call him by his first name. He should be 'Father' or even 'gentlesire.' Not 'Jeccad.'"

The disapproval in his voice surprised her. She'd have been willing to bet a large amount of someone else's money that he'd taken little notice of her conversation with her father. "I call him Jeccad because he and I are more comfortable when I do so."

"You called him 'Daddy' once," Brolla reminded her.

"Only when I want to irritate him beyond belief." Silently, she dared him to demand a fuller explanation.

Their eyes locked in challenge, each defying the other to pursue the issue further. For the first time, she was aware of Brolla as a person instead of as a silent appendage to the irritating Sebella. He was taller than Dekkan by a centimeter or so, and considerably thicker in the shoulders and neck. Some women would call him handsome, she supposed, with his regular features, shoulder-length, sun-streaked blond hair, and chocolate brown eyes. Still, she preferred the leaner, less overdeveloped physique of Dekkan, her new hus—

No! She had to stop thinking of him in that regard. He might be her mate for the moment, but the instant he got what he wanted from her—help getting that damned betrothal ring back—he'd be off to Amity, and all her wishing and hoping wouldn't change a thing.

Ariel blinked, silently ceding the contest to Brolla. What did it matter what he thought of her? Why should she care? Within a few days' time, he and Dekkan would be gone to Amity, and she'd never see any of them again.

She took a deep swallow of her drink and almost choked on it. Yes, she thought, wiping away tears, definitely a hyperstellar strangleblaster. Brolla's hand thumped hard on her back, almost shoving her out of the chair.

"No need to get violent, Brolla." Dekkan's deep tones made her gasp, causing the strong liquor to sting her throat again. "I can take care of my—of Ariel."

Brolla straightened immediately, and Ariel caught a glimpse of something primitively male passing between them. "See that you do," was all he said before moving away to join the others across the room.

"Were you ever a bouncer?" Ariel asked.

"A bouncer?" Dekkan's brow creased in puzzlement. "What's that?"

She sighed. "Never mind. If you have to ask, you weren't." Cautiously she lifted the glass to her mouth to take another sip. Although she drank liquor rarely, this bizarre wedding night certainly seemed an appropriate occasion on which to indulge herself.

Dekkan's hand snatched the glass away and deposited it on a nearby table. "I'm sure you don't need any more of that."

That's it. I've had all I can stand of people telling me what to do. Ariel jumped out of the chair, prepared to give Dekkan a thorough tongue-lashing, when he deflated her anger as easily as a blow-puff deflated its air sac.

Ariel's Dance

His arm went around her shoulder and collected her into his side. "I'm happy to see you are as ready to retire as I am," he said calmly. He ignored her stiff, unyielding pose and continued with his smooth words. "Shall we send our guests on their way?"

Ariel stared up into his eyes, knowing that his strength more than sufficed to hold her. A patently false smile plastered itself to her lips, and she gritted her teeth so hard her words could barely escape. "Certainly not, *husband.*" She ignored his wince. "They came here to celebrate our marriage. We should give them something more to celebrate."

"Now, Ariel . . ."

But she didn't give him another chance to tell her yet one more time how much he regretting marrying her . . . meeting her . . . setting foot on the same planet with her. She grabbed him around the neck, pulled his head down, and gave him the most carnal kiss she could manage.

Dimly she heard someone—Sebella?—gasp, and someone else—could it be Brolla?—chuckle; then she lost herself in the lava-hot passion of exploring his mouth with hers. Her skin flushed with steamy heat while her tongue indulged in a sensual duel with his. His hands crept around her, pulling her body tight against him and letting her feel the solidity of his manhood against her. Sinuously she began to move in time to the thrumming beat of her pulse.

Her knees were dissolving into puddles of excitement when he pulled abruptly away from her, throwing her instantly from volcanic heat to arctic chill.

"That's enough, Ariel. We have company, remember?" His voice was as husky as she could wish, but held duranum-hard determination.

"What?" She could barely stand. How could he have turned off his passion so quickly? How could he stand there, so calm, so collected, so intense?

So intense?

Still grabbing hard for her elusive control, she took a closer look at Dekkan. His face was flushed, his mouth still curved in a sensual arc, and his eyes still devoured her with unsated hunger. In control he might be—barely—but he was certainly as aroused as she.

And he was also angry.

Around them, a spate of flustered conversation broke out. Sebella sputtered with outrage, while Jeccad and Stonnor conducted a quiet but intense argument. Ariel ignored all the hubbub and tried to figure out what had just happened. All she'd intended to do was demonstrate to Dekkan that she wasn't a nonentity he could ignore. At least that was all she *thought* she'd intended.

She hadn't expected passion to flare again instantly. She'd just yielded to an impulse. Foolish, perhaps. Unwise, almost certainly. But, why was he angry?

While they separated and turned back to their impromptu wedding's guests, Ariel was all too aware that a small war had been declared between her and Dekkan. And though she wasn't at all sure what they were fighting about, she had no doubt as to who would be the winner of their little duel.

No overbearing male was ever going to get the best of her!

Dekkan contemplated the wedding guests still milling around Ariel's home. At the moment, the

Ariel's Dance

last thing he wanted to do was socialize when it was all he could do to conceal the arousal that Ariel's kisses had sparked. He'd escaped her allure, but only barely—and only because he was too conscious of the family and friends still present. In a desperate move, he'd even thought to shelter himself by standing near his fiancée, Sebella—a move that backfired with novalike immensity. His ears now rang with Sebella's repeated commands.

"Don't you dare do anything . . . indiscreet with that loose woman you're tied to," she'd said over and over—was still saying as she hovered by his elbow. "I refuse to let you humiliate me like that."

"Listen, Sebella, I regret that you've been caught in this situation. . . ." Dekkan didn't really know how to apologize to her. Nor did he have a clue how to address the possibility that his betrothal to her now seemed a horrible mistake. Could he walk away from a long-standing commitment for the sake of a woman who was wrong for him in every way?

Perhaps she recognized his ambivalence, because her tone became a hair less accusing. "I'm willing to give you the benefit of the doubt for the moment, Dekkan. But you've got to understand that no Amitan woman wants to know that her man hasn't come to her with his purity intact."

He stiffened. "There'll be no question of that."

Sebella's gaze held more steel than that of any grain negotiator he'd ever faced across the table. "Good." Her finger wagged in his face with added emphasis. "Just you remember that an Amitan woman can always tell when her man has had other women."

The starch in his spine turned to steel. "You need

not be concerned. I assure you that you will not face such distress."

By that time, Dekkan was more than pleased to notice that Ariel seemed in urgent need of rescue from Brolla. He smothered a grin as he realized that his friend's social skills hadn't expanded any while Dekkan had been away. He excused himself with a few words to Sebella, who showed every sign of wanting to continue her lecture. He had to get away from her strictures before his restraint vanished in the gale of her words.

With no regret, he decided it was time that all these people left. Now that he and Ariel had threaded the loop—even if it was only a temporary situation—it was time for everyone to disappear. He still had to work with Ariel to retrieve the Misthaven ring, and he couldn't even plan its recovery while Jeccad, Brolla, or Sebella might hear. If Sebella feared for her reputation should Dekkan's indiscretions become public, it was nothing compared to the scandal that would result if the loss of the ring should become known.

Besides, he really wanted a few minutes alone with his new wife.

Calling on every gram of diplomacy he'd ever possessed to get him through the farewells, Dekkan closed the portal behind Jeccad and viewed with profound satisfaction the room that now held only himself and Ariel.

"Alone at last." He honestly hadn't meant that heartfelt comment to escape, but since it had . . .

Ariel shrugged off his restraining arm and moved across the room to perch on the arm of the sofa. Her eyes didn't quite meet his, and he had little idea what she might be thinking.

He didn't know if the hunger he felt showed in

his face. Not that it mattered, he admitted ruefully. Ariel seemed determined not to look at him in this lifetime.

"I'm sorry you were caught in this, uh, unpleasant situation." Was he sorry? He didn't know, but an apology seemed an appropriate response.

A shaky breath matched her even shakier smile. "It's not exactly how I thought we'd spend the evening."

"No," he admitted. "I'm sorry."

Her hands clenched into tight fists, then abruptly relaxed. With a gaiety that made little sense to him, she jumped up and whirled toward the kitchen nook. "Well, I guess it's a little late to work on our plan, so would you like something to eat?"

"Plan?" His traitorous eyes were too busy watching every move she made for him to concentrate on her words.

"The plan to get that ring back." She enunciated each word with painstaking. "Or doesn't it matter now that it would be given to me instead of Sebella?"

Hot blood rushed up his neck at her barbed question. "The ring will still go to my betrothed at the ceremony when I return to Amity." He'd intended to puncture her flippancy, but found himself hastily suppressing a wince at the reminder.

"Of course," she agreed, far too readily. "Well, we've still got to finish our plans for getting it back. We'd gotten a bit sidetracked when we were interrupted."

Sidetracked? Was that the best description she could come up with? Dekkan remembered the incredible heat that had filled his veins, the excitement and pleasure that had flowed from her slightest touch. In all the nine levels of hell, he'd never have labeled their preoccupation with each other as being *sidetracked*.

He obviously had much to learn about the realities of Mariposan liasons. Time to change the subject to more secure ground. "Yes. Well, perhaps we should discuss how we're going to retrieve the ring." *After I've trained myself not to want you with every breath.* "And no, I'm not especially hungry." Another lie, but one in a good cause. Maybe if he concentrated on his empty belly, he could forget about the other hunger clawing at him.

Being around Ariel was turning him into a magnificent liar.

Ariel glanced at him. "I am. I'm going to fix a snack." She disappeared into the cooking alcove with that peculiar grace that marked all her movements, leaving him to all his if-onlys and what-ifs.

Dekkan thought about the prospects of the long, dismal night ahead, yearning for the prize he had no right to take. Yes, it probably would be better if he and Ariel discussed something that had nothing to do with sleeping or beds.

But no matter what profound plans they discussed or how distracted he was, he was sure of one thing: this night would be as uncomfortable as even Sebella could have wished. No doubt, if she knew, she'd announce that it served him right.

Chapter Twelve

"So, how do you want to do it?"

Dekkan stared as Ariel popped a sweetcheese niblet into her mouth. Her lips closed around the finger-long tidbit with a delicate slurp and sucked it in. They had settled on the couch after she'd collected her late-night snack and changed into her sleep shirt. Now, with her sitting so close that tendrils of her scent tickled his nose, he was having difficulty concentrating. Surely she wasn't asking him to . . .

Stupidly, he echoed, "Do it?"

"You know. How do we get the ring back from Floribunda?"

Only by exerting the greatest willpower did Dekkan refrain from wiping away the beads of sweat that must have popped out on his brow. How could he have imagined she was talking about doing *that* . . . with him? Sternly, he reined in his libido and dragged his attention back to what it was supposed to be focusing on. "We'll have to figure out some way of getting into her apartment," he said slowly, as if he'd been pondering that very problem. "Then we'll have to get the ring away from her without her knowing what we've done. Then we'll—Do you *have* to do that?"

Once again, her pink tongue swiped a moist path around lips too sweetly sensual to be ignored. "Do what?" she asked innocently. When he refused to answer, she pulled a permastylus and holo-pad onto her lap and jotted a few notes. She pressed a stud on the side of the pad, and the list glowed in midair in shimmering tones of brilliant green.

He leaned forward to pick up the mug of tea she'd brought him from the kitchen. Was it his fault that when he settled back onto the couch he was several centimeters closer to her than before? He had to be close enough to read the list hovering just above the hem of her far-too-brief shift—didn't he?

"Okay," she repeated, highlighting the first item on the glowing list. "Step one is getting into Floribunda's apartment, right?"

"Yes," Dekkan said absently, taking another sip. The angle at which she held the pad and permastylus pressed her arms together just enough to give him a view of mounded breasts pushing at the neckline of her shift.

"I know just how we'll do that."

"You do?" Not that he was paying attention. Her little wriggle of satisfaction distracted him again.

A sharp jerk of her head reclaimed his straying gaze. "Yes," she said as if she hadn't noticed his lapse. "I do."

"Okay, how do we get in without Floribunda noticing?" He shifted to ease the uncomfortable tightness between his legs and took another sip to cover the movement.

"Very simple." Her smug smile dared him to find fault with her perfect plan. "We simply sign up as clients for her House of Joy!"

Tea sprayed out of his mouth and dripped onto his shirt.

"*What?*"

But she wasn't paying the least bit of attention. "You do sometimes have a problem with coordination, don't you!" With a chiding *tsk* she popped off the sofa—which relieved Dekkan of one source of tension until she immediately reappeared with a soft cloth. She settled next to him again, this time close enough to press the cloth against his dripping shirt.

He ignored her attempts to dry him off. "What did you say?"

She smiled up at him and continued her drying while she unclasped his shirt. "I said you really do have a coordination problem, don't you?"

Dekkan's head swam with the feminine armful practically sitting in his soggy lap, the exquisitely seductive scent that was three parts sheer woman and all pure Ariel, the incredibly arousing sensation of her hands pressing against his chest. He closed his eyes and took a deep breath, trying to clear his head, only to realize his mistake immediately when her hands hesitated over the pounding throbbing of his heart. He suppressed a moan.

"No," he gritted out, "I meant, what did you say about signing up as clients of Floribunda's House of Joy?"

"Oh." At least she'd stopped patting him, though she was still half-draped across his lap. "It's obvious, isn't it? By signing up as clients we're at least inside the building. All we have to do is sneak into her quarters."

He eyed her with suspicious lust. "And you think she won't notice us there?"

"Of course not. Her House of Joy is one of the busiest in all Mariposa. She can't possibly keep track of all her customers." She shifted position slightly, which arched her back just a little. "Besides, most people go there to, uh, improve their love life. Who'd think a newly married couple would need such stimulation?"

The suspicion grew to out-and-out certainty. "I know I'm going to regret asking this, but what exactly is the House of Joy?"

Before answering, Ariel reached over and snatched another sweetcheese niblet, a movement that resulted in her breast, covered only by her thin shift, rubbing against his still-wet chest. He *could* move away, he supposed. Or get up and sit across the room. No doubt it would be much better for his willpower to step away from the temptation she presented.

But . . . wild *droogs* couldn't drag him away.

Still licking her fingers, Ariel finally began her explanation. "Floribunda's place caters to couples, triads, quads, whatever."

"So it's a brothel?" Somehow, Dekkan was disappointed in that. It certainly hadn't looked like a brothel. Except maybe from the outside.

"Oh, no. Floribunda doesn't supply any, um, personnel. If you know what I mean. She just supplies the extras."

"Extras?"

"Sure. Settings. Holo-images. Props. Music. Stuff like that. You register for the particular, um . . ."

Ariel's Dance

"Fantasy?" Galaxy, but his mind was reeling with fantsies right this moment!

She gave him a repressive glare. "*Situation* is what I was going to say. You're charged according to the needs of that particular scenario. Floribunda keeps one of the biggest scenario selections on Mariposa in her holo-maker. She prides herself on offering more choices than any other house."

A nasty thought settled in his mind. "I suppose you've been there a lot—sampling the possibilities, so to speak."

Despite his carefully neutral tone, she must have picked up on his resentment. She pulled away, which at least relieved the tension of having her pressed against his too-eager body.

"I'll have you know that the only reason I know all this stuff is that she hired me a last year to help her upgrade her holo-maker system." With arms firmly crossed in front of her, she dared him to question her explanation.

Now that the immediate cause of his physical distress had moved at least a few centimeters away, Dekkan was more than willing to grant her a victory. "I didn't know you knew about holo-systems."

"You never asked!"

True. He'd always assumed she was just a beautiful body and hadn't worried much about her brain. Though, now that he thought about it, she obviously had more than her share of business acumen to be able to afford a home as pleasant as this one, and still save up enough to fund a three-year course at a prestigious academy, all on a dancer's salary—even if she was one of the most popular dancers on Mariposa.

"Sorry," he admitted. "So we walk in as clients, hmmm?"

"Yes. And the best part of it is, I know her compusystems inside and out. In fact, I set them up, too. So once we're inside—"

"You can crack her security codes?"

"You bet." With a triumphant smile she uncrossed her arms and reached for the plate of sweetcheeses.

Dekkan's gaze locked onto the front of her shift with laser precision. More precisely, to the virtually transparent wet spot where she'd pressed herself against his sopping shirt—the spot directly over her pouting nipple. A muffled groan leaked out.

"What's the matter?" Ariel caught the direction of his gaze and looked down at herself. "Oh!"

Involuntarily his hand extended, until one finger traced the rosebud peak of her nipple. "I'm sorry," he muttered in a hoarse voice. "I really don't mean to do this. It's rude of me. I just can't stop."

She cupped his hand in hers, then pressed it against her breast. Her other hand moved to his opened shirt and spread it back off his shoulders. "I know. I know."

A shuddering breath rattled through him, and the defenses he'd been so staunchly shoring up all evening collapsed in a heap of useless rubble. "Ah, Ariel. What are you doing to me?"

"Nothing." She slipped his shirt completely off. "I think you're the villain here."

Dekkan froze at her careless words. "Ariel. We—*I* shouldn't be doing this. I am a villain." He worked free the elaborate closure that lay along one shoulder of her shift, then hesitated again.

But Ariel was having none of that. Deliberately, she shrugged, letting her shift fall into her lap. With a quick wriggle of her hips, she scooted completely free of the garment and tossed it away. "We're wed,

Dekkan, remember? I can't think of a single other thing we should be doing right now. Can you?" Gently, she guided his hands back to her body.

With his hands cupping her bare breasts, he couldn't think of anything else as important to do either. He shook his head and lowered it to let his mouth take a drink from the warm bounty he held. He nipped at the delicate bud of her breast, then licked delicately around its rosy crown. When she gasped and he felt her hardening response, he opened his lips wider and took her whole breast into his mouth.

Wildfire flickered through his veins as he finally loosed the arousal he'd been struggling to control. He focused on only one thing—treasuring the pleasure of touching Ariel's body with his own. Impatiently he shed his clothes with her help. Nude at last, he stretched out on the sofa and pulled Ariel on top of him. The sheer glory of feeling her naked body pressed full-length against his made him gasp then gasp again. He wanted to savor the excitement racing through him.

Ariel seemed to sense his desire linger over every sensation. She propped her hands on his chest and supported her chin on them. Wriggling against him with every syllable, she said, "Feels good, doesn't it?"

His hands, unaccountably shaky, traced down her silky back, exploring the dimples just above her buttocks before curving around those globes. "Good? No. I wouldn't call this good," he said seriously. Despite his efforts to keep himself under control, he could hear the two-tones-huskier-than-usual timbre of his voice.

She gave a mock pout, letting her knees drift to the outside of his thighs. The movement brought her dewy femininity into intimate contact with his shaft. "You don't think I feel good? I think I'm insulted."

"Not good. Try . . . try . . ." His voice hoarsened again to a throaty mutter. "I can't think—"

"Then don't think," she commanded. "Just *feel*."

Her lips lowered to trace the line of his collarbone, sending wild shivers down his spine. When she searched over his chest and at last zeroed in on one nipple, he bucked like a moorpony at its first taming. Involuntarily, his hands tightened on her, tremors of excitement quivering through him.

Before he quite realized his own intentions, he'd used his grip on her bottom to guide her into an intimate caress of his sex. Up, down, the movement sent him soaring to levels he'd never explored. His breathing transmuted into harsh pants, and his heart thundered in his chest. Within seconds, he felt the slick moisture of her arousal lubricating the rhythmic rub.

"Dekkan!" Her voice had changed, too. Gasping and urgent, he obeyed her tacit command and pressed her harder against him.

Her head bowed against his chest, her tongue still licked his passion higher. "Ariel, look at me."

She lifted her face toward his. Urgently, he covered her mouth with his own. Their kiss was deeply carnal. Again and again his tongue dueled with hers in frantic mimicry of the bucking rhythm of their hips. The pressure in his groin was now so great he shuddered with each exquisite stroke.

Ariel's breath came in keening pants, and her breasts massaged his chest with growing intensity. Suddenly, her mouth broke from his, and her entire body clenched in a spasm that sizzled through them both. Dekkan watched in wonder as her eyes dilated and her face contorted into a pleasure that seemed only thinly separated from agony. Her nipples, rock-hard with arousal, abraded his chest.

For a long, intense moment, he reveled in her release. He'd done this for her! He'd been the man to give her such pleasure! A combination of pride and humility rushed through him. For the moment, that seemed satisfaction enough, but when she relaxed and collapsed on top of him, his own urgency took charge again. With firm movements, he guided her up his shaft until he hovered just outside the passion-slick entrance to her womb.

"Ariel, look at me again."

He wasn't sure she heard him—wasn't quite sure he'd actually said the words above his own pounding pulse, but she did look up. Her eyes were still glazed with desire, her cheeks and mouth flushed a sweaty, coppery red, her long hair in a sensual tangle around her face; he thought her the most beautiful thing he'd ever laid eyes on.

"Dekkan," she whispered. "Ah, Dekkan."

"Let me in, Ariel. Please."

For an instant she seemed not to understand his words; then her lips curved in a promise so blatantly voluptuous that his heart started another heavy throb. Her hands slid down his chest, past his waist, to the pulsating shaft of his sex. There, while her eyes locked with his, she guided him with slow, lascivious care until the merest tip of him had penetrated her. "Come in, lover," she whispered. "Come in—*now!*"

A moan of pure ecstasy broke from his lips as his body took charge. He squeezed his eyes closed as he pulled her yet closer, delving inside her and feeling for the very first time the utter joy of a woman's moist, velvet passage enfolding him.

Once he'd buried himself fully inside her, he paused, savoring the unbelievable satisfaction of at last being precisely where his body had insisted that he belonged. But even that wasn't enough. He had to experience more! Slowly, he withdrew from her, then surged inside her once again. And again. And again. With each in-and-out passage, he discovered new sensations: the way her most feminine muscles caressed him; the sheen of sweat on her brow when he rotated slightly inside her; the increasing rhythm of her gasps for air; the incredibly arousing scent of her sexuality.

He increased the pace of his strokes and rolled over until she was trapped underneath him. The new position brought new pleasures, and he savored each one as he continued his climb toward climax. He lifted her knee so it wrapped around his waist and continued the rhythm. The new angle allowed him to penetrate still farther inside her until he was almost sure he touched her very womb.

He paused, buried so deeply inside her that he could barely distinguish his body from hers. And then . . . and then he felt the first slight shiver of her convulsion. Stunned, he waited in awe while she dissolved into ecstasy around him. His name keened from her in a soft shriek, and the sound was the final blow to his own restraint. With one final stroke, he spasmed inside her, shouting his rapture while his seed spurted in endless, joyous release.

Eons later, he lifted his head. He was still firmly planted inside her and had no plans to change that status anytime soon. For the first time in a long while, he released her buttocks and cupped her face. A sweaty strand of hair drooped over her brow. He brushed it aside as he tilted her head slightly to the side.

Ariel's Dance

"Ariel," he whispered. "That was . . ." Words failed him. He'd never experienced anything quite so incredible. He'd never dreamed that anything at all could be so ultimately carnal that it seemed totally spiritual in its intensity.

A tired grin tipped the corners of her mouth. Without opening her eyes, she butted her forehead against his in a blatant request for a caress that his lips immediately responded to. "Good?" she suggested sleepily.

"Yes." He sighed, his eyelids drooping in drowsy surrender and his lips lingering to trace one delicate eyebrow. "That was good."

Ariel settled more comfortably underneath Dekkan, savoring the weight of his body above her. He didn't feel heavy. He felt wonderful. His warm breathing tickled her ear. She deliberately recalled every detail of his lovemaking.

Galaxy, but he was a wonderful lover! She could hardly believe that he'd never done this with another woman before her. He'd known instinctively how to give her the greatest possible pleasure. He'd been tender and patient with her, despite his obvious eagerness to satisfy his own needs. And throughout it all, she'd sensed his care and concern for her. He was a generous lover, far more so than any of the few men she'd had sex with before.

And that was what it had been with those others. Sex. Scratching a mutual physical itch, with about as much meaning as the twitch of her wings onstage. No, less so, because her dancing was always carefully choreographed for maximum beauty. Sex with other men, she now understood, had no beauty at all.

Ah, but sex with Dekkan—that was different.

He'd infiltrated her body so thoroughly it seemed she'd never be free of him. And at this moment she couldn't conceive of why she'd ever desire such freedom.

A little wriggle settled him more comfortably on top of her. The movement rasped his flesh within her in a delicious curl of sensation. It was so pleasurable, she repeated the wriggle again. She loved feeling him inside her, she decided. Nothing had ever been this wonderful. Ever.

Idly, she stroked his hair back from his face. How soft and silky it was! It was the only soft thing about him. His body was so firmly muscled she suspected he did quite a bit of physical labor at the family keep.

Learning how to be a good Amitan farmer and husband, no doubt.

The sour tang of that thought disturbed her, so she shoved it away. Far better instead to concentrate on cradling him in her arms now, while she could. For all too soon, he would leave her to return to a life she could have no part of.

A chill shivered down her spine. Involuntarily, her arms tightened around her husband-for-a-while. He wasn't hers to keep. He never had been—never could be. Nor did she aspire to become a keepmistress, decaying away in the middle of a rural Amitan wilderness.

So why did she hate the thought of Dekkan returning to marry his fiancée? Surely Sebella was a far better match for him than she was?

Ariel squeezed her eyes tightly shut and tried to picture her handsome Dekkan threading the loop with the stately Sebella. Physically, they made a depressingly well-matched pair to her mind's eye. Why, she'd bet that Dekkan could even say the word

Ariel's Dance

marriage to Sebella without choking on it. He'd never accomplished that feat with her.

She shifted again under Dekkan's weight, and this time her movements penetrated his sleep. With a husky moan, he rolled sideways, bringing her with him so they lay face-to-face. His eyes, reflecting total contentment, drifted open.

"Hi," he whispered. "You awake?"

She couldn't resist a smile at the silly question. "Mmm-hmmm," she confirmed. "How about you?"

"Nope. I'm having the most wonderful dream."

His sensual smile told her all she needed to know about the type of dream he'd been having. But she couldn't resist a delicate probe to discover who had starred in it with him. "Tell me about it."

"I dreamed I was lying naked on top of you. And that I was still inside you. And that we'd just made love—madly, passionately, wonderfully." His eyes slitted closed and a deep sigh escaped him. "It was a fabulous dream."

It was exactly the right answer. "Are you sure it was only a dream?" she asked. She hooked her leg over his hip to pull him more tightly against her.

His hands drifted slowly over her, pausing to explore in detail her breasts, her waist, her buttocks. "Yes," he said softly. "It was definitely only a dream. Reality could never be so good."

Everywhere his hands lingered, her pulse pounded. She felt herself grow slick and moist. She cupped his cheeks with her hands and let her mouth explore every angle and shape of his face.

"Never?" she said into his ear. Her tongue curled around its whorls before her teeth grabbed his lobe and ever-so-delicately nipped.

Inside her, he hardened, and he took hold of her hips with firm command. "Well," he admitted as they began a slow, sexual dance, "perhaps *sometimes* . . ."

His rhythm increased until they moved with frantic passion. And as she exploded in a riot of falling stars, he whispered into her ear, "Perhaps—with you—always."

Chapter Thirteen

Dekkan woke to bright sunlight and the sound of Ariel humming a gay tune. Warily, he opened his eyes. Sometime during their long, unbelievably passionate night together, they'd drifted from the sofa to Ariel's sleeping niche. The alcove, like the main living quarters of her house, was decorated with a colorful femininity, a cheerful insouciance that totally matched her temperament. From the frilly bedcoverings to the paprika-colored walls splashed with a teal floral print, everything shrieked of his Ariel.

His Ariel.

Damn. When was he going to stop being so ridiculously possessive of a woman he had no hope of holding? An image of Ariel as mistress of Misthaven Keep flashed in his mind, then dissolved as he realized the incongruity of it. Ariel had her own plans for the future—and he was sure they did not include burying herself on a farm on one of the most agrarian planets in the Federation.

Which meant he was going to lose her.

So somehow he had to convince himself—and her—that last night was a onetime lapse they must not repeat.

He heard a clatter and decided he'd better get up. With a stretch and a yawn he rose, then felt the fire of a blush rise up his neck and face. He was completely nude.

Of course you're naked, dummy. You just spent hours and hours being intimate with Ariel. What did you expect?

The thing was, Amitans were generally a modest people. And while he'd had no trouble following local convention on the naturist world of Bareness, nudity there had been a matter of universal consensus. It wasn't . . . sexual.

But his nakedness this morning had everything to do with sex and nothing at all to do with convention.

His clothes were nowhere in sight—no great surprise, since he had a distinct memory of flinging them away on the sofa last night. Wrapping a small coverlet around his waist, he tentatively walked out of the sleeping niche. Ariel was puttering about in the kitchen area, standing with her back to him. He was thankful she'd donned a light turquoise sarsilk robe that covered her from nape to knee. After last night, Dekkan wasn't sure what he'd have done if she'd been as bare as he.

"Good morning." At least his voice sounded okay—not nearly as uncertain as he felt.

Ariel whirled, smiled, and launched herself at him. He caught her with an "oof!" and suffered

Ariel's Dance

through her covering his face and neck and chest with kisses.

Suffered? his conscience asked sarcastically.

Apparently such greetings were the proper way to deal with mornings-after on Mariposa, he assured that pesky inner voice. He was only being, well, courteous. Yes, courtesy was all when one was a negotiator. One should always try to participate in the host world's customs, he reminded himself piously. It was required—sort of.

Sure. It's a case of pure altruism on your part, right?

Right.

Purely—one might even say *solely*—in the spirit of establishing a basis for future interstellar cooperation, his lips took control of Ariel's kiss, deepening it to a passionate level. Her robe somehow fell open, and his hands naturally continued their explorations from last night.

Ariel's sarsilk robe dropped to the floor with a simple push from his hands, and suddenly every hormone in his body zinged into full alert. Only when she grabbed his shoulders to push him away did he pause.

"Dekkan, if this is the way you say good morning . . ."

Suddenly aware he might have overstepped the bounds of common morning-after civility, he froze. "Uh, did I do something wrong?"

She smiled. "No. But if you want to eat breakfast, you have to let me go."

He knew he sent the command to his hands to release her. Well, he was pretty sure he intended to let her go. Sooner or later. Eventually.

"Dekkan?" she prodded. "Breakfast?"

"I'm thinking," he said.

"Devouring me with your eyes will do nothing to satisfy your stomach."

"Maybe not, but—" His stomach inserted its own perspective with an embarrassingly loud growl. "Maybe you're right," he conceded, at last getting cooperation from his rebellious fingers.

He even stooped to gather her robe and give it back to her, though the sigh he gave as she covered herself again had as much regret as victory in it.

"Why don't you use the refresher while I finish putting the food out?" Ariel's none-too-subtle rasp of her hand across his morning beard reminded him of his lack of proper attire.

With a nod, he finally stepped away from her. Something about the woman befuddled his mind, he admitted. But . . . sometimes being befuddled wasn't the worst fate in the world.

Hot water had a way of clearing one's head, and as he let the water stream over him, reality—and his irritating conscience—intruded its ugly head.

What in the depths of the galaxy's black holes had he been thinking?

Of course, thinking had virtually nothing to do with it, he admitted ruefully. He couldn't recall having had a single coherent thought last night from the moment his gaze had locked onto Ariel's breast exposed by her wetly transparent shift. Instead, he only remembered sinking into a sensual quicksand that had pulled him under before he could offer a single whimper of protest.

Or before you wanted to offer a protest?

Probably that was a bit more accurate, he acknowledged. But still . . . to be intimate with Ariel on the basis of a temporary marriage as flimsy as the holographic image that conducted the ceremony! How could he face his fiancée and admit to what he'd done?

And he'd have to do so. Honor demanded that he admit to his moral failings and let Sebella decide whether she wanted to tie herself to a man such as he. Based on her arguments yesterday—had it been only yesterday?—he had little doubt that his shame would negate their marital agreement—no doubt only after she demanded a huge breach-of-trust settlement in the process.

With sneaky satisfaction he considered that with his betrothal to Sebella formally ended, there might well be an honorable way he could continue to enjoy the benefits of his married status. After all, it would not be honorable to leave his wife one night into his marriage—would it?

The complexities of maintaining his honor had never loomed so large. He was used to having a clear vision of the honorable path. But now—was it more honorable to admit his failings to his betrothed, or less so? And, should that tie come to an end, was his honor compromised if he continued a physical relationship with a woman who was, after all, his wife, no matter how temporarily?

A wry smile curled his lips as he realized one person would be at least partially satisfied if Sebella ended their engagement. His father had never fully approved of her as future keepmistress for the family holdings.

His father!

Dekkan jerked the water controls to shut off the refresher and collapsed onto a bench. How could he have forgotten that Ariel, the woman he'd spent last night having wild sex with three—no, four—times, had also been his father's lover?

He'd made love to his father's mistress.

He'd *married* his father's mistress, even if only temporarily!

He bowed his head and clutched his hair with hands that shook. How could he have done that? His father, too, had known the unbelievable joy of merging his body with Ariel's. How could he follow so intimately in his father's path?

How could she have let him?

How could she have made love—no, *had sex*— with both Stonnor and Stonnor's son?

Dekkan's stomach churned at the vaguely incestuous overtones of his sordid situation. Perhaps such taboos were absent here on Mariposa, but back on Amity, even third cousins were considered consanguinally unhealthy.

And if he was going through such torments, what kind of woman could so easily open her body to both father and son?

What manner of woman was she?

Dekkan didn't know, but he sat a long time, deciding exactly how he could convince them both that such perverted intimacy must never occur again.

"If you're going to make a habit of hogging the cleanser, maybe I'd better consider adding a second unit." Ariel turned back to the cooker unit and removed the breakfast that had been keeping warm in the heater. Somehow, she just knew this was going to be a terrific morning. How could it not be after an evening of such incredibly, unbelievably, fabulously wonderful lovemaking?

Now that he was up and dressed, she was thrilled to see him. He was so handsome! In a forbidding kind of way, of course, but he was still the most attractive man she'd seen in ages.

Ariel's Dance

She'd awakened with the feeling that last night had plunged her far over the edge into the full maelstrom of being in love. She was even beginning to wonder if they might have some kind of future together—after all, she was smart and adaptable. Perhaps she'd find a way to enjoy being a farmer's wife. And based on his reactions to her, surely he must be feeling—Wait a minute!

Forbidding?

After a night like last night—and a good-morning kiss like the one they'd shared earlier—how could any man possibly be forbidding? Much less practically bristle with silent disapproval, as he was doing now?

"I apologize," Dekkan said with starched calm. Even his walk was stiff-legged and uncomfortable-looking. "I wasn't aware of causing a problem with the cleanser. I will try to be briefer in future."

Astonished that he'd taken her light comment so seriously, Ariel inspected him more closely as she began placing the food on the table. His face was as unyielding and prim as that of a justice condemning a *shallon* hustler to penal servitude. Whatever could be going on with him? "That's all right. I was only joking," she said slowly.

He nodded with a punctiliousness she'd never seen directed at her. "May I help you prepare anything?"

"No. It's all done." She put the last of the dishes on the small table and gestured him into a chair. Perhaps he merely needed his jolt of tea to start the day? Carefully she nudged a large mug filled with Amitan Master Brew toward his hand.

He obediently sipped it. Not that it made any difference in his demeanor.

"Um, are you feeling all right this morning?" she asked cautiously.

"Yes, thank you."

She noticed that he did not meet her eyes. "Is your food all right? I didn't know what you liked for breakfast, so I—"

"It's fine."

No help there. Her own spine was beginning to ache from watching him hold himself so stiffly erect. "Are you sure you're all right, love?"

She hadn't intended to let the endearment slip out. She wasn't even sure how true or false it was. And she regretted it even more when every muscle in Dekkan's body appeared to clench at the word.

"Ariel, there's something . . . I mean, I need to talk . . . I mean *we* need to talk."

His floundering at last clarified the situation for her. He wasn't upset or angry—he was merely embarrassed! Belatedly, she remembered that Dekkan had no experience with mornings-after. No doubt he was all but smothering in his own discomfort!

"Oh, Dekkan, don't worry about it! You're doing fine."

"That's nice, but—"

She was sure she understood what he was fretting over. "I want you to know that you might not have been very, uh, experienced, but believe me, you were *wonderful* last night. Surely you could tell that you made me very happy?"

His eyes seemed slightly glazed, and the merest hint of red crept up his cheeks. "Very happy?"

She took his hand and looked deep into his eyes. "Extremely happy."

"I did?" His voice had faded almost to a whisper.

She nodded.

"Well," he said, then cleared his throat, "that's, uh, gratifying. But we need to—"

"Of course! You want to finish those plans we were supposed to make last night. I thought we could talk about them after breakfast. Is that all right?"

Dekkan shook his head, nodded, then shook his head again. "Yes—no—I mean . . ." His hand gripped hers with steely intent. "That's not what I wanted to discuss."

"It's not?" *Oh, galaxy.* He wanted to have a *relationship* discussion! Ariel knew better than to get mired in one of those before she'd even had time to sort out her own feelings. Unfortunately, she couldn't see any way to head Dekkan off on the subject.

"No. It's not about getting the ring back."

Desperate, Ariel interrupted, speaking quickly to distract him. "I only wanted to mention that I know someone who can help us make the copy. One of my fans, Fedry is his name, is a, um, part-time jewelmaster. I'm sure he'd be willing to construct a copy for you."

"Part-time jewelmaster?"

The distraction had worked. She smiled in relief. "Well, it's sort of a hobby with Fedry. More of a, um, career sideline. He doesn't work with any of the official guilds, you see."

"Would his work be of high quality? I would not feel right substituting a ring of lesser quality."

"Oh, yes." She knew she was talking too fast, but she couldn't help it. "He's *very* well known here in Mariposa City."

Dekkan's eyes narrowed. "He's a copyist, isn't he?"

Drat the man! Why did he have to be so astute?

Maybe a show of innocence would throw him off the track. "Of course!" she said in her most agreeable tone. "That's what we need him to do for us, remember?"

"That's not what I meant. He makes sham jewels and sells them to gullible tourists, doesn't he?"

Caught! "Well, sometimes," she admitted grudgingly. "But he can do beautiful work—and we're not going to find a reputable jewelmaster who can do what we want as quickly as we need it done."

He sighed. "I suppose you're right. But I am not used to dealing with such people."

"That's all right. I'll explain things to him. Fedry's a big fan . . . of . . . mine. . . ." Her voice trailed off as she realized she'd reminded Dekkan of one detail too many.

His eyes narrowed again in new suspicion. "I suppose this Fedry is another man you've learned to manipulate."

Ignoring the hot tide that raced up her neck and cheeks, she said, "I don't know what you mean."

"Yes, you do. He's another of your men, isn't he?"

"Dekkan, he's a *fan* of mine. I have lots of fans. It doesn't mean anything."

"No, I don't suppose it does," he said with deliberate meaning. "Not when you cavil at so little."

Ariel's head ached with confusion. It was too early in the morning to keep up with Dekkan's masculine twists of logic. Why couldn't men be as clear-headed and logical as women? "I don't have any idea what you're talking about."

"Don't you?" He leaned forward to trace one hard finger down her cheek. "Such a beautiful woman—and one who doesn't mind sharing that beauty with many others."

Ariel's Dance

"My job is perfectly respectable here on Mariposa!"

"Perhaps so," he conceded. "But it's not your profession I'm referring to."

She gasped. He thought her a–a– "I told you I don't do personal pleasure contracts–*ever*."

"Maybe not, but your tastes are a bit kinkier than I'm comfortable with." He leaned very close, holding her gaze captive with his own laserlike stare. "Did you enjoy introducing the son to sin as much as you did the father?"

Every drop of blood seemed to drain from her face and pooled in her feet. For a desperate moment, she thought she might faint. "What do you mean?" she whispered with lips almost too tight to move.

"I mean, I did not enjoy being seduced by my own father's mistress!"

Ariel squeezed her eyes shut for a long moment. How could he think—? Didn't he realize—? What opinion must he have of her! Of his father too! The thoughts whirled through her, eddies of shock that coalesced into a hard, cold knot of rage in the pit of her stomach. When she opened her eyes, it was with the determination to make him pay for that slur.

Deliberately, she patted his cheek a little too hard to be a caress. "You shouldn't lie like that, Dekkan. Your ears will grow—remember the fairy tale?"

"Lie! I don't lie!"

A glimpse of her reflection in the shiny surface of a nearby cabinet sent a quivery chill down her spine. No smile should be so terrible. "Sure you do. You said you didn't enjoy taking me to bed. That's a lie."

To her surprise a dark tide of color washed over his face. "I—"

"Don't even think about denying it!" She would not let him destroy her memories of last night's joy.

He swallowed hard. "You are very good at making a man feel—"

"Love?" she asked silkily.

"Certainly not! What I meant to say is that you obviously have a way of seducing—"

"I don't recall being the seductress last night!" In a more rational mood, she knew Dekkan would immediately go into his professional negotiator mode and, no doubt, start apologizing for any lapse in manners. But by all the dimensions of hyperspace, she wasn't going to let him call her a *lapse* again! "Seems to me you're the one who hasn't been able to keep his hands off me ever since you arrived on Mariposa. If there's been any seduction going on around here, it's been from you, not me."

But Dekkan was too astute to stay off balance for long. "And what do you call those kisses you greeted me with this morning?"

She lifted her chin. "I call them a charming way to say good morning," she said with lofty precision. "And what do *you* call stripping me out of my robe within seconds? An ancient Amitan greeting ritual?"

"I wouldn't have stripped it off you if you had been wearing a respectable nightshirt underneath it."

His logic might be askew, but Ariel knew very well she'd pulled on that oh-so-easy-to-drop robe with the precise intention of having Dekkan slip it off her. Nevertheless, she'd never admit that to him! "And I might have had the opportunity to put on a 'respectable nightshirt' last night if you hadn't taken my shift off then, too! Seems to me you've got a real preoccupation with removing my clothes."

"Only because you so rarely wear any!"

"Is that right? Well, we can't have the ever-so-talented Dekkan um Stonnor proved wrong, now can we?" Gracefully she stood and stepped right in front of where he was seated, standing between his widespread knees. With deliberate movements, she slipped loose the knot of her robe's sash and let the tie fall to her sides. With a simple shrug of her shoulders, the silky robe fell to a small puddle of cloth at her feet, leaving her completely nude in the morning sunlight.

Time froze. Their argument withered under the sudden rush of passion that curled between them. He slowly wrapped her waist with his hands and pulled her closer to him. Her small defiance was meant to crush him, but the aching hunger she saw in his face dissolved her anger as the morning sun dissolved the crystalline frost of early spring.

Dekkan bent and lowered his head to rest it against her stomach. He whispered something she didn't quite catch.

"What is it?" she asked softly.

His hands holding her hips tightly against him, he looked up at her. "How do you make me want you so much?"

"I don't know. How do you?"

His lips began a soft tracery of her right breast. "How do I what?" he asked absently. His attention had obviously moved on to other topics.

Her fingers lacing through his sun-kissed hair, she said, "Make me want you so much."

He stilled and looked up at her again. "Is that true? Do you want me?"

She smiled. Silently she guided his hand between

her legs to the moist arousal already bedewing her. "Can you doubt it?"

Intently his gaze searched her face for something she couldn't define. She waited until she saw the light of acceptance on his face. Then she said, "Make love to me, Dekkan. Please."

Without a word, he lifted her hips to the tabletop with the effortless ease of well-trained muscles, and spread her legs. Bending his head, he kissed his way up her thigh to her feminine core. With his tongue he caressed her intimately until her whole body clenched in utter chaos. Only then did he stand, free himself of his pants, and ease himself inside her.

But despite the ecstasy that raged between them in their age-old dance of desire, Ariel couldn't quite forget his betrayal. He thought she'd loved his father too. How could he?

And how could she ever be happy with a man who trusted her so little?

Chapter Fourteen

Dekkan wasn't sure exactly when during that long day he started to respect Ariel. Oh, certainly, there was a strong element of lust mixed in with his respect. He'd already proved himself completely unable to resist her many charms. All he had to do was inhale a hint of her sweetly spicy scent or catch a glimpse of her incredibly beautiful body, and his staff engorged so quickly that he feared he'd injure himself.

No question about it. He was definitely a pervert.

That was the only explanation for the way he was so inexplicably attracted to a woman who was obviously utterly wrong for him. Or the way he was so willing to shove aside the thought of Ariel and Stonnor—no! He refused to think such thoughts about her!

Only belatedly did it occur to him that he was more worried about his reaction to Ariel's perfidy than that of his own father, who surely must have been an equal partner in any such affair. If such an affair had indeed happened, he reminded himself.

Oh, it was far too confusing. And, no doubt, none of his business. The only possible way he could deal with it was to put it out of his mind. He trusted Ariel—at least he thought he did—and he certainly trusted his father. And she wouldn't have made love to him if she'd also had sex with Stonnor—would she?

He definitely wasn't going to think about it anymore.

Besides, it was only midday and he'd already succumbed to her charms three times. Once at the breakfast table after their incomplete argument. Once just outside the front door as they were leaving. Luckily, the streets were quiet and no one seemed to notice him pulling her behind one of the oversize shrubs to bury himself in her with frantic urgency. And once, to his continuing embarrassment, in the ladies' retiring room of the public transit center. He'd pushed her inside the small compartment and against the door so quickly she hadn't been able to utter more than a squeak of protest. Once away from the prying eyes outside, he'd thrust into her so urgently the door had rattled.

At least he'd thought his passion caused the rattle, until he realized that a large woman just outside was shaking the handle in her attempts to enter.

But he'd needed to express that burst of passion so much, he hadn't even cared when the woman patted Ariel on the arm and congratulated her as they left the privacy of the small booth. The woman had eyed him up and down, then said in a whisper that no doubt echoed louder than the announcing system, "Practically felt every stroke, I did, dearie. If you feel like you want to share . . ."

Ariel, her hair in wild disarray and her dress slightly askew, merely smiled with kiss-swollen lips and shook her head.

The woman sighed. "I thought not. But next time, do try not to deprive the rest of us of the use of the retiring room, dearie."

He should have been embarrassed. Instead, seeing the glaze of happiness in Ariel's face, he merely felt proud.

But it wasn't until they arrived at Fedry's that his respect for her blossomed.

They'd caught a public tram to a slightly seedy part of town and walked a couple of blocks to Fedry's residence, an undistinguished cell in a hive complex. Dekkan had never visited one of the once-popular mass housing units before. For a brief period the Federation had experimented with nontraditional housing plans to alleviate crowded conditions on the more urbanized planets. Hives, with their individual cell units clustered around central resources such as cooking and bathing areas, seemed a natural solution. Unfortunately, most people hadn't enjoyed the communal living of insectoids, so the developments soon became the less prosperous areas of town, where low price outweighed personal preferences.

As they approached the announcement plate, Dekkan said, "Ariel, remember, I'll do the talking here. All right?"

"But Fedry's *my* fan! He'll expect me to say something."

"Fine. Tell him hello. Chat with him about anything—except the ring." He tried to frown her into agreement. "I negotiate contracts for a living. I do know what I'm doing."

"But—"

"Remember the trouble we got into the last time you interfered?" He recalled all too well his shock when she'd announced their phony engagement to her father. No way did he want her springing another surprise on him now!

"It worked, didn't it?"

"Yes, and we're now married because of it! Talk about cutting one's ears off to avoid a noise!" He realized belatedly that his apparent unhappiness with their temporarily married state wasn't the most flattering thing a bride wanted to hear. "Not that our marriage has been all bad, of course."

Naturally, that only made it worse. Ariel tapped her chin with one finger. "No," she drawled, "I suppose it's not so bad when you get to have sex on demand. With no long-term consequences to your Amitan *honor*."

"Ouch! You know I didn't mean it like that."

"Do I?" She turned away to place her palm against the announcer plate.

But Dekkan stopped her hand before she could touch it. "I *didn't* mean it like that." He shook his head ruefully. "For a man who makes his living being tactful and diplomatic, I sure manage to blunder around you. I wonder why that is?"

"A very good question. You might want to consider what the answer might be sometime."

"Ouch again." He tried his Fifth-Degree Charming Smile to Defuse Opposition Unhappiness. "I'm sorry. But you will let me do what I'm good at, won't you?"

"Would I interfere?"

With that unsatisfactory half-assurance, she

Ariel's Dance

pulled her hand away and pressed it against the plate.

Dekkan hated Fedry on sight.

The man who greeted them was a perfectly ordinary person. He was of ordinary height, neither unusually tall nor short. He was of ordinary attractiveness, neither ugly nor noticeably handsome. He was of ordinary coloring, with the Federation norm of ordinary brown hair and ordinary brown eyes with an ordinary light brown skin tone. He was so ordinary that Dekkan was sure not one person out of a hundred would notice him in a crowd—or be able to identify him to the security patrols, should such an occasion arise.

In fact, his very ordinariness made it difficult to identify anything about him that could possibly generate the dislike that surged through Dekkan's veins.

Except, perhaps, the way he looked at Ariel.

"Ariel! I am honored that you have come to visit me! Please, come in." Not bothering to greet Dekkan, Fedry ushered Ariel into his tiny cell, a combination of bedroom, parlor, and private dining areas. Hastily the man swept a collection of vid cartridges off the sofabed and ensconced Ariel on it with due ceremony.

Meanwhile, Dekkan loitered by the door, still waiting to be greeted.

"Ahem. Gentlesire Fedry . . ." he said, finally.

Reluctantly, Fedry turned away from his intense perusal of the cut of Ariel's neckline. "Ah, yes. And you are?"

"I am—"

But Ariel cut him off. "This is Dekkan um Stonnor. He has come with me to request your skilled assistance with a problem."

Fedry stroked his chin as if deep in thought. "I see. And this, er, Diklar is a friend of yours?"

"I am—"

"Yes!" Ariel said hastily, cutting Dekkan's answer off again. "He is a good friend and he pays well."

Fedry eyed Dekkan up and down with a speculative gleam. "Hmmm." Then apparently coming to a decision, he waved Dekkan to a seat on an uncomfortable-looking stone-and-wood chair. "Sit down, gentlesire, and tell me how I can be of help to you and Ariel, the most beauteous woman on Mariposa."

A delicate rose coloring shaded Ariel's cheeks, and she lowered her lashes in coy acknowledgment of the compliment. Dekkan swallowed the ire rising in his throat and concentrated on accomplishing his task.

"Gentlesire Fedry, I need a ring copied very quickly. It must be done in as perfect detail as you can manage in the available time." Dekkan went on to give an approximate description of the ring in terms of size, carat, stones, and so on.

But Fedry's attention had wandered again. He leaned toward Ariel from his seat beside her on the sofabed and clasped her hand. "Ah, Ariel, you remembered your old Fedry, didn't you? You have always looked after me in your own sweet way, haven't you?"

Dekkan decided he did not like the sound of that. But he didn't quite know how to find out what the older man meant. So he tapped him on the knee in a First-Degree Gesture to Reclaim Attention. "Gentlesire Fedry, I fear I have not much time to arrange my task's completion. If I could but have your attention for a few moments?"

Irritated, Fedry swung his head around to face

Ariel's Dance

Dekkan. "All right, all right. But my Ariel and I have some memories to catch up on. What exactly was it you wanted?"

From the corner of his eye, Dekkan noticed Ariel surreptitiously slip her hand from Fedry's grasp. Suppressing the sigh of relief that bubbled up inside him, Dekkan patiently repeated his request.

"A firestone, eh? Is it genuine?" Fedry's all-too-ordinary face took on a shrewd, assessing cast.

"Yes," Dekkan admitted. "But I believe a synthetic stone will suffice for the copy—as long as it is of premium quality."

The shrewdness intensified. "Only one ring I know of in Mariposa City matches that description. Floribunda's got one that sounds just like it."

Dekkan's eyes met Ariel's in a desperate question. Slowly, Ariel nodded, and Dekkan's breath escaped in a resigned puff. They were going to have to tell Fedry the truth.

"Fedry, the ring we want you to copy is indeed Floribunda's," Ariel said. "But it originally belonged to Dekkan's family. It was lost in a game of *shallon*. Now we're trying to replace it."

"*Shallon*, eh?" Fedry eyed Dekkan up and down one more time, this time with more than a hint of condescension. "Shouldn't play *shallon* if you don't know what you're doing."

"I was not the person who lost the ring." Ariel might glare, but Dekkan felt he had to defend himself against the implied criticism.

"Hmmmph. Heard tell Mistress Floribunda keeps that ring close by her most all the time. Can't copy what I don't see."

This was indeed shaky ground. Carefully, Dekkan started to formulate a reply, only to be interrupted by Ariel.

She took Fedry's hand in hers and leaned a bit closer. "The thing is, Fedry, we're going to borrow the original from Floribunda and bring it to you. Then you can make the copy with the original right in front of you. Would that work?"

The faintest trace of alarm, mixed with greed, flared in Fedry's avaricious eyes. "Aye," he said, rubbing his chin. "I could make a fine copy that way. But seems to me I won't have that original for long—will I?"

"No." Dekkan understood the question as the challenge it was meant to be. "A matter of a few hours only. You must complete the copy process within three standard hours so we can return the ring to Mistress Floribunda."

"And which one will you be returning to her, I'm wondering. The original—or the copy?"

Though Fedry's glance from one to the other requested confirmation of his suspicions, neither Ariel nor Dekkan complied. "The ring will be returned to her," Dekkan finally said.

Finally Fedry nodded. "So you want me to construct a near-perfect copy in three hours."

"Fedry, you're the only jewelmaster I know with the skill to do so in the time available."

"And well you know that I'm not a member of the jewelmaster guilds." A rough note entered his voice that Dekkan interpreted as regret, or perhaps resentment.

"Skill is far more important than guild membership," he said. "Ariel assures me that you are the most skilled jewelmaster in Mariposa City—perhaps on the planet—no matter what your current affiliations. Or lack of them."

Fedry turned with ill-disguised eagerness to Ariel. "You said that about old Fedry?"

Ariel's Dance

"You're not a bit old," Ariel said. "And yes, I did."

The man's spine straightened noticeably. So it wasn't just Dekkan she had that effect on! Absurdly, Dekkan was both reassured and dismayed. How many other men wanted Ariel as Fedry did?

As he did.

With none of his usual subtlety, Dekkan guided the conversation to the sticky matter of price. Of course he would pay for all materials—at retail rates, since the need was great and time was short. Of course he would cover the necessary bonding and tool use expenses. Of course he would pay guild rates for Fedry's services. Of course he would offer a bonus if the work were done in less time.

The terms Fedry proposed and Dekkan had tentatively accepted amounted to twice the value of the ring when Ariel stepped in. Couldn't Fedry see his way to offering a bit of a discount, considering that the work was being done for Dekkan? After all, a friend was dearer than credits, so the old saying went. When the man nodded in bemusement—Ariel's explanatory gestures managed to grant both men teasing glimpses of the upper curves of her breasts—she pointed out that Fedry already had all the tools and facilities needed to do the work, so asking Dekkan to pay for those items was really a bit—well, it was a bit like gouging a friend. And Ariel had never known Fedry to gouge a friend.

With persuasion from Ariel, Fedry was even convinced to reduce the bonus he requested in the name of his close friendship—and what did *that* mean? Dekkan wondered—with Ariel and her family. Why, he was practically blood kin to her, Ariel asserted. And family had to stick together in times like these.

Before Dekkan quite realized what Ariel had

done, he and Fedry were shaking hands over a price that amounted to the true value of the ring plus a twenty percent bonus. It was the neatest piece of negotiating he'd ever witnessed.

With the final arrangements of delivery and pickup complete, Fedry escorted Ariel and Dekkan out the door. Dekkan felt nearly as shell-shocked as Fedry looked. Ariel led the way out, but when Dekkan tried to follow, Fedry held him by the arm.

"That's a hell of a bargain you got from me, Diklan."

"The name's Dekkan. And I know."

"Wouldn't have given such good terms to anyone but Ariel. Know that, too, don't you?"

Dekkan nodded silently.

"Is it true she's leaving the theater?"

"That's what she says," Dekkan said slowly. He was only now beginning to realize that the thought of Ariel at an academy wasn't a bit ludicrous. Obviously the woman had brains aplenty—more than enough to match her beauty. "She hasn't said what she plans to study, though. Do you know?"

Fedry shrugged, but his eyes narrowed. "If you're such a good friend of hers, how come you don't know something like that?"

"I'm not a friend, exactly," Dekkan said. But before the suspicion in the man's eyes could transform to rage at being conned, he added, "I'm her husband."

The shock on Fedry's face was worth it, he decided as he hurried to catch up with Ariel. For the first time he'd publicly acknowledged his marriage.

And it felt damned good.

Ariel hustled Dekkan away from Fedry as quickly as she could. She could tell that he'd been disturbed

Ariel's Dance

by Fedry's claims of intimacy, but wasn't ready to explain that Fedry had been an admirer of her mother's after the liason with Jeccad had dissolved. He'd practically helped raise Ariel, acting as Jeccad's stand-in during the all-too-frequent periods when Jeccad and her mother weren't on speaking terms. Of course, she could have explained all that to Dekkan, but some perverse instinct inside her enjoyed watching him overreact to Fedry's perfectly normal attentions. Someday, if they stayed together long enough, maybe she'd explain to Dekkan how things really were between her and her mother's best friend.

But probably not.

"I suppose we need to decide how we're going to get the ring from Floribunda," Dekkan said. "We only have a few hours until we promised to deliver it to Fedry."

Ariel nodded. "I've been thinking about that. We might as well go on over to her House of Joy now."

Dekkan stopped dead. "Now?" he asked faintly. "You mean as in—right now?"

"Sure," she said, prodding him forward into the tram station. "Floribunda spends most afternoons sleeping, because she's up most of the night. By the time we get over there it'll be the perfect time to check in, get established in our rooms, and sneak into her apartments."

"You're right, of course. But I think we need to make one further stop on the way."

She frowned as a tram car pulled to a stop in front of them. "For what? We don't have a lot of time to spare."

Dekkan stepped onto the tram and pulled her on board. "This stop is necessary. We need to buy ourselves a marriage ring."

A marriage ring! Ariel's heart thumped so hard she pressed a hand to her chest to make sure it didn't beat through her rib cage. Marriage rings were never used in pro tem marriages. Never. So why did he . . . ? Could he possibly . . . ? Was it at all possible that he . . . ?

Questions fizzed in her mind like the bubbles in a glass of Denebian foambeer. Only after two tries was she able to squeak out a question from her suddenly dry throat. "Why do we need marriage rings?"

"*A* marriage ring," he corrected gently. "We'll have to find something that's a reasonably close substitute for the keep ring while Fedry's making the copy so Floribunda won't notice that the real ring is missing."

Her heart slammed down to her toes. "Oh."

Though she felt Dekkan's speculative gaze on her throughout the tram ride, she kept her head down so he couldn't see the disappointment on her face.

Chapter Fifteen

"Are you sure we have to do this?" Dekkan said.

Ariel tightened her grip on Dekkan's hand and walked determinedly toward the entrance to Floribunda's House of Joy. The ruby-and-topaz ring Dekkan had bought a few minutes ago weighed her hand down. Although far from identical to the Misthaven Keep ring, it still had a shape and weight close enough to the heirloom, they hoped, that Floribunda wouldn't notice the difference in a piece of jewelry generally kept tucked under her garments.

Dekkan decided Ariel had to wear the ruby-and-topaz ring openly so there'd be no question if anyone for any reason noticed that she'd somehow acquired a ring while within Floribunda's house. It was a good idea, she had to admit, but even wearing a fake marriage ring cut far too close to her feelings. She'd be glad when she could remove it.

At least that was what she told herself.

"Yes," she said in answer to the complaint he'd already voiced at least seven times. "Unless you have another idea of how we're going to get to her apartments without setting off the house's security system?"

"I don't. Damn it."

"Then stop grousing and start figuring out what holo-scene we're going to choose."

Dekkan stopped. "Choose? Damn it all, Ariel, when were you going to give me some warning?"

"We talked about it yesterday, remember?"

"I guess. But I'm not sure I really believed you."

"Believe it." She shoved open the door.

They were met by the same silently sepulchral attendant as before, and Ariel explained that they wanted to sample some of the house's offerings. He appeared not to remember them, but that wasn't incredibly strange considering the number of people he probably saw each day. One couple would mean nothing.

At the greeter's gesture, Dekkan handed over his credit disk for verification. Once it was handed back, they were ushered into a comfortably furnished private selection room, where they were met by an attendant from the smoke world of Ziene. Surrounded by a stasis field that kept the swirling vapors of his native environment in constant motion, the attendant was virtually invisible except for occasional brief glimpses through the half-meter-thick fog. Ariel couldn't even tell which of the six primary Zieneii genders this being might be.

"Gentlesssire, gentlelady, pleassse to choossse your preferenssse from our catalog." The sibilant whisper barely escaped the stasis field. "Would you prefer to do ssso in privacccy?"

Ariel's Dance

Ariel glanced at Dekkan's edgy expression and nodded. "Yes, please."

The attendant nodded and flipped some switches to start up a holo-recording. With another gesture he handed a control unit to Dekkan. "Thisss controlsss the catalog. Pressss here to advanccce to the next choicccce. Pressss here to reverssse. The priccces of each are indicated on the bottom of each holo-vid. When you find what you like, pressss thisss button and it will be arranged for you."

After seeing that Ariel and Dekkan had no further questions, the smoky being bowed one more time with unctuous deference and left them.

Dekkan said, "I don't think I've ever met a Zieneii before. Do they come to Mariposa a lot?"

She shook her head. "Floribunda told me once that she prefers to use them to help new customers arrive because their smoky aura prevents them from making eye contact with possibly nervous clients. Keeps them from bolting, you see."

"Oh." He sat on the thickly padded sofette in the center of the room. "I suppose we should choose something."

The holo-vid was still paused on the starting display that explained terms and conditions of the house. Ariel sank onto the sofette and gestured at the tasteful abstract design. "Why don't you choose something?"

Dekkan jerked and his eyes widened. "Me? I wouldn't know what to choose."

"Does it matter? It's just a ruse anyway."

Though he stared at her for a long moment, he didn't disagree. "You're right again."

Carefully, Dekkan pressed the advance button a few times to skim through the various offerings. Ariel watched him more than the images. What kind of scenario would he select? On the one hand, he didn't seem the type for anything really kinky or unusual. But, she had to admit, he certainly had given every indication that he enjoyed sex despite his lack of experience. What would he choose?

The catalog paused. Automatically, she looked at the image loop displayed in life-size accuracy—*So real you have to touch to disbelieve*, the label shrieked—and for the first time in a very long time, she blushed.

One man—very naked, with the largest fully aroused penis she'd ever seen—stood, legs apart, arms crossed in lordly disdain. The catalog had naturally spliced in Dekkan's head and shoulders on the man's image. Around him swarmed a plethora of equally naked women, each caressing a part of his body. One for each leg. One for each shoulder. As the image slowly rotated, Ariel could see another couple of women running hands over buttocks and shoulders. And then of course, one woman with Ariel's own face devoted to kissing the man's—

"I've never seen you blush before."

Ariel snapped her mouth closed and glared at Dekkan. She was as flustered as the first time she'd danced in body paint. "I was merely surprised that you were interested in such a *communal* scenario." She might be off balance, but it seemed wise to try to put him on the defensive.

"Interested?" He laughed, shaking his head. "I think not. It would offend my Amitan sensibilities."

She couldn't think of a good reply to that, so she gestured at the control. "Let's keep looking."

More images whizzed by, but she scarcely glanced at them. She was too busy trying to explain away the stab of relief she felt when Dekkan had denied wanting many women to service him. It didn't matter that all but one of them—her—would be simulacrums. She still didn't want him finding pleasure with many women.

The catalog paused again, this time with a similar scene as before. Except this time it was Ariel's image that stood naked while men kissed and caressed her all over. One man, whose face quickly became pressed urgently between the image's legs, clearly resembled Dekkan.

"You would prefer this scenario?" Dekkan asked.

"Certainly not!" she snapped.

"Sure? She looks like she's having a great time." In fact, the image had tossed her head back and was moaning softly in ecstatic release.

"Positive. Choose something else." Ariel resented the scenario for reasons she couldn't quite explain to herself. Perhaps it was merely that she resented those other men—even simulacrums—intervening between her and the pleasure she got from Dekkan's caresses.

She simply wasn't cut out for group sex.

When Dekkan didn't hit the button fast enough, she pressed the advance button and held it down, skimming quickly through the various orgy scenarios until she came to the part of the catalog that dealt with fantasy illusions.

"Why don't you check out some of these scenarios?" she suggested. "Maybe one of them will interest you."

The fantasy scenes were grouped by type. The space-pirate scenarios, with and without an innocent young captive, with female pirate or male pirate, fighting with every weapon from swords to laser pistols. On land. On the sea. In space. Even a few set in the cloud cities over the gas giant Skyland.

Then there were the plantation scenarios, with male master and female slave, or vice versa. With and without dominatrix effects. With and without punishment for trivial "crimes." Nude, or dressed in everything from rags to virtual-light ball gowns.

And of course there was the lost-on-a-deserted planet fantasy where the environment was either dangerous or benevolent. Where it snowed or rained or was a desert or a tropical paradise. With and without natives who might be friendly or unfriendly. And, of course, stranded nude or stranded with elegant wardrobes—nothing much in between, except one scenario in which every article of clothing was perfectly transparent.

After a while, Ariel stopped watching, leaving the choice entirely up to Dekkan. Though she did notice that he consistently paused on those scenarios with the female partner nude. Typical male.

"You know," he said at last, "I think I've noticed something. Take a look at this image."

Ariel glanced at the scene. This was one of the vampire scenarios in which the female was being overwhelmed by a male vampire dressed in formal evening wear. The setting was dark, spooky, and the handsome male with Dekkan's spliced-in face sported discreet fangs. The heroine wore a transparent peach gown that concealed nothing at all. Even as she watched the action loop, the vampire swept that useless covering away and pulled her against himself, one hand sweeping the long hair away from her neck and back while the other nestled intimately between her buttocks.

"So?" she asked Dekkan. "It's just another fantasy."

He fumbled with the control buttons, finally freezing the motion of the image with the eerie pair locked in that sensually intimate embrace. With a twist of a different control, the size of the image zoomed to larger-than-life.

"Look there. Between her shoulder blades."

Ariel looked again, but didn't notice anything in particular except . . .

"You see those faint scars?" Dekkan asked.

She should have known he'd find them. Maybe she could bluff her way out. "Scars?"

Dekkan stood and pointed to the fine, almost invisible lines threading the woman's back. He had to be careful to keep his distance and not actually touch her flesh, or the image dissolved. Still, it was far too easy to see exactly what he meant.

"See where his hand has rubbed away the body makeup? These marks look familiar," he said, holding her gaze with his. "They look like the scars on your back."

She tried to be casual about it. "It looks like my face too—and yours is on the vampire. It doesn't mean anything. The holo-image selector pastes these catalog together using the customer as a model. It personalizes the selection experience, Floribunda says."

For a long moment, he didn't reply. "Are you telling me that this isn't your body in these holo-images?"

Lying was always an option. Jeccad had instilled that truth in her since she was tiny. But . . . this was Dekkan, and she just couldn't do it. "It's me. I mean I. I mean—"

"You mean you posed for these scenarios. You're the heroine of them all." Darkness shrouded Dekkan's face with his disappointment and hurt. "I should have known."

After a moment, she said, "It's not what you think."

"Isn't it? Don't I have proof right in front of me of the many men you've had sex with? Hell, the holo-camera has recorded it in faithful detail—every second of it!" He grabbed the control and zoomed through the images until he found one in which the naked heroine was making love with passionate abandon on a wave-shrouded beach. "Was this fun?"

Ariel squeezed her eyes shut. She had to admit that based on the evidence he had, he was justified in his anger. The only unfortunate thing was that the evidence wasn't very truthful. "Dekkan, let me explain—"

"Explain what? That you're a liar? That you have no honor?" He rubbed his hands over his eyes, and when he took his fingers away, she thought she saw the gleam of moisture on them. "Aren't you going to tell me how *untutored* I was compared to your other lovers? How do I compare with *him*?" He gestured at the frantically coupling pair in the image. "Or are you going to insist I'm the very best you've ever had?"

She grabbed the control to turn off that false image, whizzing forward until the catalog paused on a simple cabin setting with no characters present at all. "Dekkan, please. You don't understand. *I didn't do those things.*"

"Didn't you? Then why are they so faithfully recorded? Complete with sound effects?" Bitterness had turned his voice harsh and grating.

She stretched her hand out to touch his taut arm, then pulled it away quickly when the muscles under her fingers flinched away. "Don't you know how easily images can be created within the selector? I didn't actually have to *do* any of those things—not even go through the motions. All I'm guilty of is letting Floribunda's holo-grapher record me dancing. And there certainly was no one else present at the time."

"You dance while men have sex with you? I can see why you have so many fans. Men must line up for miles to watch that."

"No! There was no one there except me and the holo-grapher—who was a woman in her sixties, before you ask! Floribunda paid me extra when I was reworking her security systems—enough to finance a whole year at an academy. She wanted the images stored and fed into the selector—I did that work myself to the selections she requested. That's all that happened. I swear."

Sadly, Dekkan shook his head. "You know, even now I want to believe you. Why is that, do you suppose?"

"Because you lo—like me?" This time he didn't flinch away from her hand.

"Galaxy help me. I have no self-control where you're concerned, do I?"

"I don't know. Do you?"

Dekkan stared down at her as if trying to penetrate the mysteries of her mind. Ariel held his gaze as straightforwardly as she could. She sensed that one faltering of her sincerity would destroy the tenuous relationship they'd built.

He looked away first. Staring at the image, he said, "Do you swear to me that none of these images are true? That every one of them is a computerized reconstruction?"

"Yes! Dekkan, you know I was not untouched when we first made love. But there have been very few men in my life. When have I had time? I've been dancing and working freelance computer jobs for the past ten years trying to save up enough money to finance my education. Between rehearsals and practices and jobs, I've had no time or energy to fool around with a man."

She held her breath, waiting for some indication that he believed her. It took four long, thudding heartbeats before he nodded.

"I believe you," he said. "I think I have to believe you or go mad."

"I've never lied to you, Dekkan. I never will."

He nodded, as if accepting a solemn vow. "All right." He dipped his head to kiss her in a way that seemed to Ariel both sweet and eternal. His lips enticed hers with a promise and a vow that she couldn't quite understand but that she wanted never to end.

So, of course, he lifted his lips far too soon.

After a pause to get her voice under control, Ariel pointed out, "We still have to make our selection. We've been in here long enough that they're going to get suspicious if we don't pick something soon."

He glanced at the current image, showing a firelit room with a wide, comfortable-looking bed to one side, a small dining table set with silver and candles next to the fire. "What about this one? It looks simple enough."

For the second time that day, Ariel blushed. "Dekkan, this isn't a good choice. It's—"

"What? Looks quite nice to me."

"But it's the honeymoon scenario," she blurted. "It's for those who wed for love—part of the happy-ever-after group."

Startled, he stared at the romantic image one more time, then looked over his shoulder at her with an odd smile on his face. Turning to face her

Ariel's Dance

fully, he tipped her chin up and stared into her eyes. "Sounds perfect to me."

"You mean the perfect cover story for our visit?" For some odd reason, her voice had sunk to a whisper.

Something clouded his eyes and he dropped his hand. "Exactly."

But as he turned away to make the formal selection, Ariel couldn't help thinking that it wasn't what he had meant at all.

Chapter Sixteen

Dekkan had never been so confused. Faced with clear evidence of Ariel's promiscuity, he had chosen to believe her when she claimed it was all a lie. Faced with the reality of a temporary liaison with a woman all too wrong for him, he chose to ignore the transitory aspect and concentrate on binding her to him with as many ties as he could manage.

He had to be losing his mind.

If it weren't for the fact that he was an engaged Amitan male with a fiancée devotedly waiting for him to marry her, he'd almost think—he'd almost believe he actually—

Had fallen in love?

Yes. The fact was, he loved Ariel. Irrationally, unbelievably, he loved her with a passion that showed no signs of abating. He loved her body, of course. But he also loved her spirit, her sassiness, even her sense of the absurd. Not to mention that she could drive as hard a bargain as he could. She wouldn't defer to him, except perhaps in bed, but if she ever loved him back, he was willing to bet a galactic hurricane wouldn't be strong enough to rip her from his side.

While he waited with her to be conducted to their private suite in Floribunda's House of Joy, Dekkan applied all his negotiator's logic to assess his current position. He was married to Ariel, whom he loved more than he'd ever thought possible. He was engaged to Sebella, whom he now regretted ever agreeing to marry. Somehow, he had to convince Sebella to back out of their engagement. Then he had to convince Ariel to make their temporary marriage permanent—which could be a serious problem, considering her ambitions to attend an academy and the realities of the restrictions of life on Amity. Not to mention that he was about to commit a theft that on Amity would get him summarily ejected from any position of responsibility.

It was—almost—enough to convince him to throw up his hands and walk away from the most difficult negotiating position of his life. And he might have chosen that path, except that if he did so, he would lose all hope of gaining the one thing of supreme importance to him: Ariel.

"Anything wrong?" Ariel whispered as she tucked her hand under his arm, sending a wave of musk-sweet scent to tease his senses. They were following the Zieneii attendant through a maze of corridors.

"No. Just thinking." Actually, he was floundering in a welter of confusion rather than thinking, but he saw no reason to tell her that. It didn't help that he'd caught a glimpse of another couple being conducted to a suite, and the woman's tall frame and golden hair had immediately reminded him of the wrong he was doing to Sebella. Was there an honorable way out of this mess? If so, he had yet to discover it.

"Well, don't think too hard," Ariel advised, dropping her voice to a whisper. "We'll have to get started on our little project quickly."

The Zieneii eventually stopped beside a doorway and dilated it for them. Waving them forward, the attendant keyed the access pad to each of their palms. Then he gestured for them to enter and closed the door, leaving them alone in the holographic suite.

It was exactly as the catalog had shown it to be. From all appearances, the room was in a small wood cabin, perhaps on one of the logging planets. A stone fireplace blazed with a cheery fire that radiated a warm glow into the otherwise unlit room. Before the fire stood a table just big enough for an intimate dinner for two. Honeyed wine chilled in an elegant silver bucket on a stand, while savory dishes scented the room with mouthwatering aromas, competing with the spice-and-flowers outdoorsy scents wafting through an apparently open window. And in the shadows away from the fireplace, a huge bed waited, suspended from the ceiling by golden chains and piled high with quilted furs and pillows.

Dekkan swiveled slowly to take in the entire seductive scene. "A man could decide never to leave a room like this."

Ariel cast him a wary glance. "You don't think it's a bit, um, primitive?"

"Primitive?" He caught her gaze with his own. "A man alone with his woman with no trace of vidphones or holo-news? Only the sound of the wind

Ariel's Dance

sighing outside—and his lover sighing inside? Sounds like perfection to me."

A spark of something unnameable lit her incredible turquoise eyes, then dimmed as she broke his gaze. She walked over to where the wine waited, tracing the icy condensation trails on the bottle with one finger. "Perhaps you're right," she said as if it didn't matter either way. "But we'll have to put this on hold for the moment. It's already early afternoon. We have to get that ring before Floribunda wakes for the evening trade."

Dekkan wasn't going to let her fob him off so easily. "Ariel. Wait."

His hand on her shoulder, which was bared by her dress, froze her in position, but she didn't turn to face him. "What?"

"You know we have to talk."

"About what?"

Galaxy, but she could be as stubbornly blind as a cavemole! "About us, of course. I feel bad because I've taken advantage of you. Of your affectionate nature."

He could almost see every muscle in her body stiffen. "My 'affectionate nature' is just fine, thank you very much. And we really have to get going."

Damn it, she was right. There was no time for this now. He raked his hands through his hair in utter frustration, then nodded. "All right. Let's go. But Ariel . . ."

"What?" She didn't look at him, and her pose and her voice exuded wariness.

"We *will* talk later. Count on it."

Though she didn't reply, she gave a short nod before heading toward the door.

"Um, Ariel? Aren't you going to change?" He gestured at her outfit, one she'd changed into before coming to Floribunda's house. It was a poufy dress in shades of turquoise and green that billowed into a nearly spherical segmented bulb that stretched between two coppery bands, one under her arms and another just below her hips. A few randomly placed narrow segments of the bulbous dress were translucent enough to yield tantalizing glimpses of her coppery flesh, while one section a few centimeters wide was completely transparent. Meanwhile, the whole dress slowly rotated around the neckline and hem bands with an irregular stop-and-start rhythm. Matching copper-colored sandals with soft soles and raised heels lent every step a seductive sway.

Like nearly all the garments he'd seen her wear, it made him nervous. He caught himself constantly checking to ensure that all the essential portions of her anatomy were properly—or at least mostly—covered. He'd never seen anything quite like that outfit and couldn't quite decide if it was indecently sexy or merely indecent.

"Of course not," she said in answer to his question. "Why do you think I changed into it in the first place?"

"To make me crazy?" he suggested seriously.

She grinned. "Besides that."

"To make everyone else crazy?"

"Not even close." She quickly pushed her hands between two of the segments of the round dress and came out holding a small, complex device about the size of her smallest finger. She held it up for him to get a good look.

"That's a sonic lockpick! Where did you—never mind. I don't want to know."

"That's why I had to wear this. Floribunda has her people check carefully through any luggage or

Ariel's Dance

bags that clients bring in. But when I set up her security system I realized she draws the line at personal searches. This dress has hidden pockets inside just big enough to hold what we'll need. Besides, I had to wear something loose so I could move freely."

Loose wasn't exactly the word Dekkan would have chosen to describe that dress, especially when its rotation had just positioned the see-through segment directly over her left breast. His heart thudded into immediate hyperdrive, and he had to force himself to look away.

He didn't say a word as he followed Ariel through the maze of hallways to the door to Floribunda's private suite. He couldn't. He was too busy concentrating on watching that dress slowly twirl around her—a dress he now suspected had no seams between the overlapping segments at all. If he was right, it would take little effort to slip his hand between the edges of the sections and touch her naked skin underneath.

The door opened with a quiet snick, and they crept inside. Dekkan let the door close and lock, holding Ariel motionless with his hand on her arm. Rather than letting her go once they were encased in the soft darkness of the unlit room, he deliberately grasped her at the waist, slipping his hands inside that enticingly deceptive dress. Before she could do more than utter a soft gasp, he covered her mouth with his, while his hands took firm possession of her breasts. The kiss was slow, luxurious, and as deliciously carnal as he could make it. Only when he felt her go limp in his arms did he raise his head slightly.

"What was that for?" Her voice was as breathy as a summer wind.

"I just wanted to prove something." His hands slipped down inside the dress to cup her bare buttocks underneath the very scanty panties she wore.

"Wh-what?"

His fingers delicately traced the cleft between her buttocks, each movement delving deeper than the one before. "That this dress really does make me crazy."

"Oh—*oooh!*" She tightened abruptly as he found just the right place to tease. "And does it?" Her question was little more than a soft gasp.

"Yes," he whispered, pressing harder on that delectable nerve. "Promise me something?"

"Any-anything. What?" Her wriggles directed his hand to an even more sensitive spot.

He put his lips next to her ear so the words would be as soft as a butterfly's caress. "When you come with me to Amity, I want you to bring your incredibly erotic wardrobe with you—but you have to promise you'll wear it only for me."

"For you." She sighed. "Just for you."

His mouth swallowed her soft moan of completion. He only wished he could be sure she realized what she'd just promised him.

He'd invited her to go to Amity with him!

Ariel's heart pounded with more than sexual satiation as she began to work her careful way through the pitch-blackness of Floribunda's sitting room. Had she really heard that invitation? Or was it all a figment of her crazed imagination?

Working slowly through the salon in utter darkness was hard enough without having half of her mind chewing over a question that might have arisen only from a lover's imagination gone wild.

Ariel's Dance

"Ouch!" Though Dekkan's exclamation was whisper-quiet, it sounded heartfelt.

"What's wrong?" She groped backward until her hand found him. "Did you knock something over?"

His hand took hers and moved it to one side. Only then did she realize she'd been about to grasp him in a hold more suited for a bedroom than a burglary.

"Just a bump. I'm all right." He moved forward just enough to whisper the words directly in her ear, sending a tickle of warm, moist breath against her cheek. The sensation flooded her with security and calmed her nerves. For no good reason at all, she suddenly felt calm and in control.

Still holding his hand, she inched forward again. Brief flicks of her tiny lightbeam gave only hints of obstacles waiting. Unlike the receiving salon where she and Dekkan had met Floribunda earlier, this room seemed stuffed with oversize chairs, ottomans, shelves, cabinets, and tables. Every horizontal surface was cluttered with ornamental objects ranging from a waist-high statue of a Pernian fire lizard in full flight to a crystalline scupture of a Redmondia shivertree the size of her hand. Unfortunately she located that one by nudging the table it stood on. The slight vibration sent the delicate crystal leaves quaking against one another, resulting in a soft, dirgelike song. Though she froze instantly, the damage was done. It took eternity-long moments until the tree stopped keening.

Despite her damp palms and ragged heartbeat, she finally located the door to the inner chamber of the suite. "I think this is it," she said, barely loud enough for Dekkan to hear.

But Dekkan stopped her from opening the door

with the lockpick. "What if she's not there alone? Does she have a current lover?"

"I hadn't thought of that," she admitted slowly. "I haven't heard of anyone, but . . ."

"But what?"

She shrugged. "Floribunda can keep her own affairs quiet when she wants to. She doesn't always bother, of course, but occasionally, when her current friend requests discretion, she makes sure no one knows about the relationship."

"Damn. We should have done a little research before we came." Dekkan's fingers drummed against the skin of her arm. Ariel tried not to notice the thrumming pattern. "Someone here must know if she's sleeping with someone. Who would have that information?"

"Of course! Staff always knows about things like that—it's impossible to keep it wholly a secret." She flicked the lightbeam around the room until its feeble illumination settled on a dusty compu-terminal in one corner.

"Do you know how to work that?" Dekkan asked.

She couldn't blame him for his skepticism; the terminal was likely as old as she was—or older—and was so dusty it appeared no one had touched it in a very long time.

"Yes," she said, carefully wending her way through the scattered objets d'art until she stood before the terminal. "This is like the one I used to reprogram her security systems." More confidently than she felt, she pressed the stud to turn on the terminal.

The machine beeped. A fan whirred softly.

And from the next room, someone moaned.

A purple glow lit up the room as the terminal warmed up.

Ariel's Dance

"Turn it off! They'll see the light!" Dekkan's fingers fumbled for the power stud.

She grabbed his hand and held it. "Don't worry. Floribunda's room is light-proofed. She won't see the glow." Ariel wasn't all that sure that was so, but it seemed reasonable. Her acquaintance with the older woman had left her with the distinct impression that Floribunda spared nothing to achieve her desired level of comfort.

Rapidly, Ariel stroked the controls for the terminal until the display focused on the in-suite meal requests for the last several days. "See? She's asking for only a single meal each time. I'd think that if she were entertaining someone, she'd at least offer breakfast in the morning."

Dekkan peered over her shoulder. "Maybe so, but—"

Another moan, this one distinctly deeper, issued from behind the closed door.

"—but that doesn't mean she hasn't found a new lover very recently."

A sound that resembled nothing so much as a grunt echoed from next door.

"I see what you mean." Quickly, Ariel backed out of the program and gave the terminal its shutdown command, being careful to erase all trace of her intrusion. "What do you suggest we do now?"

The room was lit only by the dying phosphors of the screen. She could see only the vaguest outline of Dekkan's face, and within seconds even that faded as the terminal finally shut down completely.

An odd *ribble-grnhh-ribble* issued from behind Fioribunda's door.

"At least we're sure we're in the right place," Dekkan said softly.

She felt more than saw his wry grin. "What do you suggest?"

She felt him take a deep breath and let it out slowly. "I think we have to take the chance anyway. Let's see if we can get in and out quickly. Maybe she's taken the ring off while she and her friend . . ."

Ariel nodded uselessly in the darkness, then took his hand and used her tiny lightbeam to guide them back over to the doorway. From this position, the rhythmic grunt-whistles in the other room sounded all too clear.

"Let's get down on the floor. That way, if they're awake in there when we open the door, there's a chance they won't notice us."

She felt him lower himself to hands and knees, then overrode the palm lock and silently dropped to her knees beside him.

The door snicked open, and the sound was suddenly almost stentorian. A pale starlight glow shone from the ceiling, offering a dim light sufficient to see the outlines of the room. A hanging bed similar to the one in their holosuite occupied at least three-quarters of the available space. Except for a broad set of bed stairs on the near side, she could see no other furniture in the room. And the bed, suspended a good meter above the floor, offered an obvious hiding place underneath its massive, two-meter-square area. Once in the safety of that lair, there would be no way anyone in the bed could possibly detect them.

Guided by a nudge from Dekkan's hand, she crawled after him toward the swaying bed with the grunting whistles of the bed's occupant, or occupants, covering any noise they might make.

Once safe under the slightly swaying bed, Ariel rolled onto her stomach, propping her chin in her

Ariel's Dance

hands and squashing her dress into a crumpled mess. "What now?" she whispered.

"I thought you had this all planned," Dekkan retorted.

Amazing how he managed to inject so much irony in a sound little louder than a chiva-cat's soft purr. "I got us in here," she whispered back. "It's up to you to get the ring."

He nodded. Now that her eyes had become accustomed to the darkness, she realized the imitation starlight gave a surprising amount of illumination. "Give me the marriage ring," he said, holding out his hand.

She tugged on the ring, ignoring the corresponding tug on her heartstrings. It was only a ring, after all. What did it matter that it was the first—the only—thing he'd ever given her? Deliberately, scraping her knuckle in the process, she pulled it off and dropped it in his palm.

He started to roll out from under the bed, but she stopped him. "Dekkan—"

He just looked at her.

"Be careful," she whispered. "There might be two of them up there."

He nodded and started to roll away again. But before he could get out of reach, she leaned over and kissed him on the mouth. "Good luck."

His hand cupped the back of her head, and he returned her kiss with an ardor she couldn't resist. "Just marking my place," he told her. Then he rolled out from under the bed and stood.

Years later, Ariel often described the ensuing minutes as some of the most nerve-racking of her life. Every creak and sway of the bed seemed portentous. Every tiny moan, real or imagined, strummed along nerves too taut for comfort. She could see Dekkan's legs as his weight shifted from side to side. What was he doing? Absurdly, the impulse to leap to her feet, grab the ring from Floribunda's neck, and run grew inside her until it took all her willpower to suppress it.

The bed creaked loudly and swayed so much the edge crashed into the bedside steps. Simultaneously, a heavy "Hmmmph!" and an unintelligible mutter sounded from the bed. Sweat popped out onto Ariel's brow. Her fingernails carved crescents into her palms. What in the galaxy was he doing up there?

Just as the tension had reached the point where she was sure she'd run shrieking from the room, Dekkan suddenly dropped to the floor and rolled under the bed.

In fact, he rolled right up against her, clutched her to him, and pressed his mouth against hers.

With her hands busily checking him for injury—at least, that was the excuse she gave herself for running them all over his body—she returned the kiss with a passion she'd only ever felt for this man.

She pulled her head away from him. "Did you get it?" she asked in a nearly silent whisper.

"Mmmm-hmmm." His mouth was more involved in tracing her eyebrows than forming words.

Enthusiastically, she kissed him again. Her lips had a disconcerting habit of clinging to his, she'd noticed. Did Amitan diets include some kind of magnetic feature? she wondered vaguely.

Above her, the bed shifted and creaked again.

Reluctantly, she pulled her mouth from his. "We've got to get out of here! She'll wake up and catch us if we're not careful."

Though every movement expressed his reluctance to break their embrace, Dekkan did let her go. Stealing one last kiss, he rolled away from her and crouched beside the bed. She followed him, and they quickly crawled to the door, where no lockpick was necessary. The palm plate on this side of the door was designed to open to anyone within the room.

Seconds later, the door closed behind them. Moments after that, they'd made their way out of the suite and into the hall.

"We did it!" Exuberantly, she threw her arms around his neck and gave him a hug. "I never thought we'd be able to get the ring."

"Let's get back to our suite quickly. We don't want to be caught hanging around the hall outside Floribunda's suite, just in case she notices that I've switched the ring."

"Good idea."

When they were back in their suite with the door securely locked against intruders, Dekkan guided her to the bed and helped her onto its high platform. He sat beside her and took her hand. With a sudden solemnity she didn't expect, he carefully nudged the Misthaven Keep ring onto the middle finger of her right hand. It felt heavy, and she stared down at the ornately carved setting with the glowing heartfire gem.

With the ring firmly in place, he said quietly, "If this were the ritual keepsake Ceremony, I would tell you that this ring symbolizes the security and heart of the Misthaven Keep. As you wear the ring, you guard the family and fortunes of Misthaven."

A lump in her throat forced her to swallow twice before she could speak. "And what should I reply?"

His fingers tightened around hers. He cleared his throat before he said, "You would tell me that the fire of the gem reflects the fire of your devotion to me, for my family, and for my keep. You would promise to uphold the honor of the keep and to help me build a family and a worthwhile life."

Her gaze locked with his. "I see. Is there nothing of love in these keep promises you exchange?"

"Oh, yes," he said, a smile dawning in his eyes. He gently maneuvered her fingers until the ring gleamed in the firelight.

In the subdued lighting, it seemed to Ariel that the fire in the gem was a living thing, leaping with turquoise and emerald sparks within a bright auburn blaze. She gasped, "It's so bright! I didn't think it was so vivid before."

Dekkan's gaze clung to the ring. "Yes." His voice dropped again to a husky pitch. "You asked about love. It's there, in the ring. Can't you see the flame of passion that ignites in the stone?"

She did think she saw something in the depths of the gem, a living flame that surged even as she watched. "Yes," she whispered, "I can see it."

"Will you give me the words of the ceremony?"

Her free hand crept up of its own volition and traced a crease in his cheek. "Of course, Dekkan. If this were such a ceremony, I would promise to uphold the honor of your Misthaven Keep and to help you build a family and a worthwhile life. I would willingly tell you that the fire of the gem reflects the fire of my love for you, and your family, and your keep. I would even promise to love you as passionately as the gem glows for as long as I lived." Her lips curved in a smile that felt more wistful than joyous. "If this were the ceremony I would tell you all that."

He raised her hand and caressed the ring and her fingers with his lips. "Thank you."

"For what?" Despite her flippant reply, her voice was barely above a whisper.

"For helping me retrieve the ring. For . . . everything."

His gaze snared hers and would not let it go. But all too soon, she realized they still had more work to do. "Dekkan, we have to get the ring to Fedry. We can't delay if he's going to have enough time to get the copy made."

"You're right, of course." His smile definitely had a wistful quality. "But once we deliver it, would you promise me something?"

"Another promise?"

He ignored that. "Would you come back here with me and let me make love to you as I want? Once the ring is copied and returned, our time together will be very short. You'll be going to the academy and I must return to Amity. I want—I want a memory of you to hold close in a corner of my heart."

Tears blurred her vision. How could she possibly refuse such a tenderly worded request? "Of course," she said. "I too will treasure the memory of you."

But as they traveled silently to Fedry's workshop, she couldn't help but wonder if Dekkan realized that the ring wasn't the only thing he'd stolen that day. He'd treacherously purloined every last corner of her heart.

Chapter Seventeen

By the time Dekkan returned from Fedry's workshop, his nerves were as taut as a lutestring. He and Ariel had separated after dropping off the ring, he to run an errand while Ariel went to her cottage to change clothes. Now, as he paused outside the suite's door, his mouth was dry as summer in the West Amitan mountains while his palms sweated. Did Ariel realize how much he loved her? Probably not. How could she? He'd never told her.

Nor would he.

In the clarity of thought that deep tension sometimes brought, he had realized while taking the ring from Floribunda's sleeping form that he could not stand in Ariel's way. She had her dreams of an education and a career. He would see to it that she got both. He would help her and guide her—but never, never would he tie her to being just a

Ariel's Dance

farmer's wife in the desolate loneliness of a vast Amitan keep.

He would have to break things off formally with Sebella, of course. For just as he could not stand in the way of Ariel's happiness, neither could he face marrying another—if any Amitan woman could be found who would accept a man such as he. Sebella hadn't exaggerated when she claimed it would shame her to wed a man who had shared the intimacies of marriage with another woman. Amitans rarely married other than virgins, and the occasional exceptions were always the subject of speculation and gossip.

Besides, by all the laws of Amity, he was already wed to Ariel. The vows they'd exchanged in their suite, though private and unwitnessed, were sufficient to tie him to her for life. She was not so bound, of course—and he had no intention of telling her the true consequences of what they'd done. But a deep glow in his heart warmed his realization that in this small, unacknowledged way, he would always be a part of her.

And perhaps someday he would be free to tell her the secret of the ring.

Clutching that faint hope to his heart, he palmed open the door to the suite and entered. As it softly closed behind him, he searched the suite for Ariel. The table was still set, the food still emitted delicious aromas. The fire still crackled merrily in the fireplace. And along the far wall, the suspended bed still tempted and lured with its promise of shared pleasures.

But where was she?

His question was soon answered as she stepped

from behind a small divider screen almost hidden in the shadowy corners.

"Hello, Dekkan."

He swallowed, then swallowed again. Ariel was so beautiful his voice deserted him. He'd seen her in everything from bare skin to outrageously revealing dresses to a skintight catsuit. But he'd never seen her as she stood before him now.

She wore an Amitan wedding dress.

The modest garment was made of delicate pink embroidered satin, with a simple round neckline and a hem that grazed the top of her toes. The fabric was draped in elaborate folds and closures in a most flattering way, emphasizing a charming figure while revealing only a hint of the details. Long sleeves tapered to a point on the back of each hand, and a slight, triangular train trailed behind. A delicate skim of flowers was braided through her long hair, forming an elaborate coif. And she held the traditional sheaf of grain and sweet herbs.

"What—how did you know?" he finally croaked.

She shrugged. "It was easy to find out. And my autotailor is very good. It's not really authentic, of course," she added when he didn't respond. "The herbs are wrong, and I couldn't get Amitan wheat here on Mariposa. But . . . I thought you wouldn't mind too much."

His gaze feasted on her for another long moment.

"Do you?" Her question was tremulous and uncertain, a trait he barely recognized in her.

"Do I what?"

"Mind that it's not completely authentic? I really tried to get everything right, but—"

Her anxiety to please him melted his shock. He stepped over to her and put a hushing finger against her lips. "But nothing. Ariel, you're the most beautiful thing I've ever seen. And I'm overwhelmed that you've chosen to honor my world's customs."

Her smile could have blinded a man less used to her beauty. "I wanted to please you," she whispered, looking him directly in the eyes. "I just wanted this to be—special."

"Everything with you is special." He smiled. "Do you know the tradition behind the Amitan wedding dress?" he asked casually. He lifted the sheaf of grain and herbs away and placed it on the table.

She shook her head.

"It's said that an Amitan male, faced with his first intimate experience on his wedding night, must be taught the virtues of patience. So the Amitan females have concocted a dress that takes hours to remove. Each closure and fold has elaborate significance that must be pondered and accepted as it is opened and removed."

"Hours?" A pleat of worry creased her brow. "But Dekkan, we don't have hours. Jeccad left a message at my cottage that he's expecting us to dine with him. He said it was important."

He shrugged that off. Your father can wait. We have some time before Fedry finishes the copy of the ring. And I don't care if we make that dinner or not. I plan to take advantage of every moment we have together." The first layer of satin abruptly fell to the floor. "You see? I'm a fast learner."

She giggled softly. "You don't think it's because you've had a lot of practice getting me out of my clothes the last few days?"

"Maybe." Another layer slid away. "I'm beginning to think I prefer you in those outrageous Mariposan costumes."

"There's nothing outrageous about my clothes!"

"Really? Then how come I've spent most of the

past few days wondering which intimate section of your body will be revealed to passersby next?"

She pretended to frown as another drape of cloth fell away. "Is that what you've spent your time worrying about recently?"

"Pretty much. I find the subject endlessly fascinating, you see."

"Oh. Sort of a hobby?"

"More of a vocation, I think." He smiled in satisfaction as the last of the gown slid aside, leaving her in nothing but her undergarment. "I see you decided that you needn't bother being fully authentic in your costume."

She looked down at herself, drawing his gaze, too. The dress might have been Amitan, but the undergarment was pure Mariposa. It was a chemise of sorts, made of the sheerest sarsilk. Its low neckline teased the tips of her breasts, letting them peek over the lacy edge with each breath. A lace-edged waistline pulled the material in just below her breasts in an Empire line. Longer than most of Ariel's dresses, the chemise ended at midthigh, though the provocative slit from hem to the raised waistline banished all notion of modesty. Not that modesty had anything to do with a garment as transparent as this one.

"Ah. Now I feel that I've found my Ariel again. Completely naked, or near enough as to make no difference."

"I thought it was supposed to take hours to remove that dress," she said. He noticed that her complaint was accompanied by an eager glitter in her eyes. "You managed it in only a couple of minutes."

"I have more incentive than most. When a man knows there's a treasure such as this waiting, he's not going to dawdle."

Ariel's Dance

Though his words obviously pleased her, he saw the sudden decision in her eyes and wondered what sweet torment she planned next.

"Well, a bit of dawdling is in order, I think," she said with determination. "I'm hungry."

"So am I," he said, slipping the strap of the chemise off one copper shoulder, and revealing her right breast in the process.

"I meant for food." She skipped around him to the table and seated herself there. But she didn't bother replacing the strap on her shoulder.

"You want to eat? Now? What about dinner with Jeccad?" With his mind clouded by her scent and her nearness, he couldn't imagine anything more useless than swallowing food.

"I never share a table with him if I can help it. We may have to make an appearance there, but he has dreadful taste in food." She leaned forward to lift the cover over one of the dishes. The movement allowed her other breast to spill over the top of that useless garment. "This, on the other hand, smells divine."

"I'll make a bargain with you," Dekkan said, ever the negotiator.

Speculation rampant in her expression, she asked, "What kind of bargain?"

"You can eat your dinner without interruption, if—"

"What?"

He allowed his triumph to glitter in his eyes. "If I get to choose what you wear when you eat it."

"You'll just have me naked. Not much imagination in that."

"If I promise you won't be naked—at least not all the time—will you agree?"

She eyed him speculatively, but he knew she'd

say yes. There was far more excitement than wariness in her gaze. "All right."

"Then take off that chemise."

"I *told* you you'd just have me naked again." But she rose to remove the useless garment.

Before she could sit down again, he sat in the other chair and pulled her onto his lap. "What can I serve you?" he asked as if his only concern were seeing that she had an enjoyable meal.

"Um, some salad?" Ariel requested, wondering what he might be up to. She heard the quaver in her voice and steadied it. She felt truly like a bride, and Dekkan was playing the part of devoted new husband to perfection. Quashing the regret that this was only make-believe, she allowed herself to revel in his attentions.

Obediently, he scooped some of the mixed blue and green leaves onto a small plate and drizzled some honeycheese dressing over it. Holding the plate before her as she sat sideways on his lap, he offered her a fork.

Still a shade uncertain what he intended, she speared a leaf and brought it to her mouth. But as her lips closed around the bite, he tipped the plate just enough to cause part of the salad to fall into her lap.

"Too bad! His fingers dived for the leafy bits, but missed. In the process he managed to spread her legs slightly. "Here, do you need more dressing?"

Without waiting for her reply, he drizzled a bit more on the remaining salad—then let still more drizzle over her stomach and groin.

"Do I assume that your clumsiness is not an accident?" she asked.

He ignored that, instead reaching for the next course, a plate of delicate smallfish, doused in a

Ariel's Dance

sweet sauce. By the time he'd served that to her, she had one delicious morsel firmly attached to her navel by the sticky sauce.

With each passing course, as much of the food ended up stuck to her as in her stomach. She knew exactly where this would end up—and she was proved right when, meal over, he lifted her in his arms and stood, carrying her to the bed. He placed her carefully on the covers, making sure that none of the food was dislodged.

"Now," he said, "it's time for my snack."

With a feminine core of lava-hot moisture begging for release, she was more than ready for his lovemaking. But Dekkan had other plans. First stripping off his own clothes to reveal the tanned, well-toned body she loved to touch, he started with the various morsels adhering to her lips and kissed them away. Then he moved downward, nibbling and licking and biting gently, taking the time to enjoy and savor each luscious bit. Though she tried to caress him, too, one hand held hers hostage over her head.

When she protested the unfairness of that, he lifted his head and said, "No, love. This time is for you. I want you to understand how beautiful I find you—all of you. This is your time to fly."

After that she stopped protesting and let him caress every millimeter of her skin. He spent a long time suckling her nipples, rousing them to rock-hard titillation and driving her to writhe in excitement. Gradually he moved farther down, licking his way across her stomach until he at last reached the feminine folds that were swollen and aching for him.

There he paused. His hands spread her legs wide, his face hovered only centimeters from her, and he looked his fill until at last he let his mouth settle on her. The hot warmth of his tongue spearing into her made her arch her back. She screamed aloud with the release his mouth and fingers brought her. And while she still shuddered with the aftermath of her climax, he moved upward, embedding himself deeply within her.

For long moments they lay that way. Ariel's chest pounded with excitement, but whether it was her heart thudding or his or both, she couldn't be sure. She grasped his hips to bring him more firmly to her, then was surprised when he suddenly rolled onto his back.

Straddling him, she began the up-and-down dance of intimacy. His hips bucked beneath her, and she watched his face closely for clues to his pleasure. She tried a little wriggle and heard him moan in response. She added an inner clenching and was rewarded with his gritted-out "Ariel!" She leaned forward to let her nipples scrape against his chest and treasured each gasp of shock from him. And, as she sensed his control slipping for his final release, she guided his hands, pressing his fingers until they found the sensitive nub of flesh that controlled her own climax—and she gave him the joy of sending her flying upward to the stars.

But as she collapsed, exhausted, within the shelter of his arms, she knew he'd imprinted himself on her heart forever. The realization frightened her. Despite his lighthearted "when I take you to Amity" invitation, in her heart she knew there was no way they could have a future together. She would always be the woman he didn't—couldn't—trust.

And each time they made love, she felt bound closer to him. Realistically, if she didn't put a stop to their intimacy, she knew she'd end up devastated when he headed back to Amity without her. Her arms tightened around him in a compulsive reaction; then she deliberately, willfully, loosened her grip and let her arms fall to her sides.

Somehow, she had to find a way to make him leave her while she still had a small piece of her heart to call her own.

"It certainly seems a shame for you to put that on," Dekkan commented from the bed. "You know I'll only take it off you again."

Exasperated, Ariel faced him, her hands on her hips. "Have you become a sex fiend, or what? Can't you manage to go five minutes without thinking about getting me naked?"

He eyed her nude figure and smiled evilly. "I can't as long as you look like that when you're naked."

She threw up her hands and spun away, giving him a view of a luscious behind that practically begged for attention. Climbing out of bed, he positioned himself behind her, grasped her hips, and guided her backward toward his ever-eager shaft. "You see?" he asked as he gently angled her for his entrance. "When you're naked, it saves time all around."

Though her hips automatically moved to accomodate his gentle surge, she glanced over her shoulder in mock dismay. "I'm pleased you're so interested in efficiency, but we *do* have work to do, you know. And I'm sure Jeccad is getting angry because we're so late. We can't spend all afternoon in bed."

"Pity," he muttered, as he felt her shudder into a climax. Only then did he grant himself the three or four more thrusts needed to finish his own release.

"Though as we've demonstrated, a bed isn't strictly necessary."

She immediately moved away. Grabbing his pants and shirt, she tossed them at him. "Put some clothes on, won't you? We really have to get out of here. And try not to spend all afternoon in the refresher."

Dekkan grimaced and headed for the small attached cleansing unit. He knew she was right. If they got started one more time, it could well be morning before they surfaced again. And they still had to collect the copy of the ring from Fedry and sneak it back around Floribunda's neck.

With nothing to distract him, he managed to wash and dress in record time—at least a record since he'd arrived on Mariposa. Ariel, wrapped in an enveloping drapery, immediately confiscated the refresher and disappeared inside.

When she reappeared, he was astonished again. Was she trying to make a good impression? Or did she have some other plan in mind? "If that's your notion of conservative, my sweet, I have to tell you that it's not working."

"Why not? Except for that dress you pulled off me before we, um, well, it's the most modest dress I own."

Truthfully, Dekkan thought, it wasn't this dress's lack of modesty that gave it such an impact. It was a simple sarong style, tied on one shoulder and wrapping around her tightly. One shoulder was bare, of course, and it separated too high on one thigh every time she took a step. All things considered, however, it *was* quite a conservative style for Ariel.

He stepped over to her and tipped up her chin, smiling ruefully. "Haven't you realized yet that it

Ariel's Dance

doesn't matter what you wear or don't wear? All I have to do is look at you and I picture you naked in my arms, wanting me. And then I want to 'um' with you." His hand toyed with the knot on her shoulder. "And a style like this merely tempts me to discover what would happen if I were to untie it."

Hastily she stepped away. "Enough! Are all Amitan males so *obsessed* with sex when they finally lose those patches?"

His lips curled into a smile. "Only the lucky ones. And it's not sex I fantasize about. It's lovemaking—with you." He watched her closely to see if she would acknowledge that their relationship was more than physical—but she turned away and changed the subject.

"We need to go now."

"Wait. You know we won't have time to come back here before we replace the ring. Don't you need to wear that round, bulby dress again so you can carry things?"

She shook her head. "We don't need the lockpick now. I reprogrammed the palm plates so they'll accept us. Replacing the ring should be easy."

"Let's go then," he said. "Fedry should have the copy ready shortly. Should we pick it up now, then stop in to see what Jeccad wants?"

Ariel tipped her head to the side, considering. "No. Let's see Jeccad first. Fedry may need a bit more time. And this way there won't be any possibility of anyone questioning why we have the ring with us."

Dekkan nodded his agreement. "Let's just stop in at the restaurant, deal with whatever Jeccad wants, and we'll be on our way." Simple. Easy. Quick. And once he'd restored the copy to Floribunda, he'd have the time and the privacy to have a heart-to-heart with Ariel and get their whole tangled relationship straightened out.

Ariel missed the weight of the Misthaven ring on her finger. She wasn't sure how that could be, given that she'd worn it only a short time before they'd left it with Fedry. She knew only that her right hand felt incomplete. Empty. Cold. Still, her head insisted she was better off not getting used to wearing it. It wasn't hers, after all. It belonged to Dekkan's true bride, the irritating Sebella. She had no right to feel even a modicum of grief at the thought of Sebella sporting the ring on her large, heavy-boned hand.

Even worse, she knew the moment they stepped inside the Nouvelle Age Moderno Restaurant that having come there was a mistake.

The restaurant was one of the most stylish eateries in all Mariposa City and prided itself on its exclusive, high-society clientele. Every effort had been made to exclude the riffraff, from setting the prices four times higher than any other restaurant, to employing a host that embodied aristocratic snobbishness. The cuisine was considered "modified archeoprimitive jungle modern" and consisted mostly of arachnoids and insectoids prepared in a variety of sauces flavored with liqueurs and spices. The waitstaff consisted of hunky young men dressed in extremely skimpy loincloths who, in contrast with the host, were so overly friendly that they kept customers informed of their every major life event.

Ariel hated the restaurant. She hated the too-intrusive waiters. She hated the vastly uncomfortable chairs—backless stones with roughly hewn logs as tables. She hated the combination of delicate silver and crystal precariously balanced on the rounded tops of the logs. She hated the hanging vines that draped over the diners' heads and shoulders—one never knew when one of the muscled waiters would swing across the room shrieking like a jungle maniac. She even hated the birds that flitted unchecked around the dining area—mostly because of one unfortunate incident on her first visit in which a bird had added its own unwanted contribution to the Laurentian tadpole soup. In fact, the only good thing she knew about the restaurant was that, despite its extraordinarily high prices, at least the servings were very small. One wouldn't want to eat very much of the multilegged cuisine offered.

It was still quite early for the dinner hour, so Jeccad had claimed the huge central table—log—in the middle of the main dining room. Stonnor sat opposite him, looking vastly uncomfortable on his rock-hard seat. Ariel noticed that Jeccad had prepared himself for the experience by bringing a large padded cushion to sit on and wearing a large-brimmed pith sombrero to fend off undesirable falling objects. At one end sat Sebella and Brolla, sharing a single large rock.

Perhaps because there were no other diners at this odd hour, four separate waiters hovered around the table. Most of them congregated around Sebella and Brolla. Ariel smothered a grin when she realized that Sebella was overwhelmed by the muscular male physiques so open to her inspection. Brolla, on the other hand, looked so sour that Ariel wondered if he'd already tasted some of the food the restaurant served.

Jeccad saw her and Dekkan hovering by the dining room door and waved them closer. "At last!

Took you long enough to get here, boy. Have a seat, you two. Just getting ready to order dinner."

"Good day, Gentlesire Jeccad." Dekkan's greeting was a model of diplomacy. He nodded in turn at each of the others. "Father. Sebella. Brolla."

"Dekkan, sit by me!" Sebella scrunched closer to Brolla, attempting to make room on her other side for Dekkan.

But Dekkan guided Ariel to the opposite end of the log, sitting with her on a large stone. "We cannot stay long, gentlesire. We have tasks that must be done shortly."

Stonnor visibly perked up. "Tasks? You mean. . . ?"

Dekkan nodded.

Ariel sent Stonnor a reassuring smile. She knew how important the retrieval of the ring was to her friend.

But Sebella misinterpreted the gesture. "How *brazen*! And right in front of her husband, too!"

Unwarily, Ariel said, "Brazen? To smile at a friend?"

"Friend, hmmmph! You can't fool me. They say there's no fool like an aged one. It's perfectly clear that Stonnor and you had a—have a—"

"A what?" Stonnor asked icily.

Based on the near-empty glass in front of her, Sebella had already swallowed at least one of the restaurant's famous Swinging Waters drinks, and she wasn't about to stop. "A relationship, that's what."

Stonnor looked hunted, but Ariel spoke up. "Certainly we have a relationship. He is my friend. And, at least for the moment, he is my father-in-law."

"That's not what I meant!"

Dekkan pierced her with an icy glare. "If you're implying that Ariel and my father have any sort of dishonorable relationship, then you may leave the table now. I will take stern measures against anyone who so impugns the honor of my house."

"What about *her*? She's not of your house! She's the one acting dishonorably!"

Dekkan's frigid voice could have shattered the vacuum of space. "Need I remind you that Ariel is my wife?"

Sebella turned paper white, but settled back in her seat, muttering something Ariel was glad she couldn't understand. In truth, she was stunned by Dekkan's ringing defense. She stared at her all-too-temporary husband with a wondering gaze.

He leaned over and whispered, "I know you and my father are just friends. I've always known it, I think. But when my own feelings for you began to overwhelm me, I needed something to drive you away. I have come to realize that you would never behave in such a way. I'm sorry."

Numb, she just nodded acceptance of the apology she'd never expected.

Stonnor leaned over and whispered to Dekkan, "What's in that Swinging Waters drink, anyway?" he asked, gesturing at the inebriated Sebella. "It sounded like the most innocuous thing on the drinks menu, but . . ."

Dekkan shrugged, obviously not knowing, so Ariel explained. "Let me just say that you really don't want to try it unless you're used to hard liquor. It's called that because after you drink one, you're usually swinging from the vines."

"What are you whispering about?" Sebella's loud demand drew yet another waiter to hover around the table. "Tell me what you said."

"I just pointed out that your drink is very strong and you probably shouldn't have any more."

"Ha! I'll show you! I can have what I like." Imperiously, she snapped her fingers at the nearest waiter and ordered a second. The waiter pressed a couple of buttons on the order pad dangling down the front of his loincloth, and Ariel winced because she knew what was coming. Sure enough, within moments a loud shriek sounded and yet another muscular young man appeared, swinging deftly through the hanging vines and landing nimbly on the log that served as their table. His bare toes clung to the rough surface as steadily as any gymnast's.

Sebella sat, obviously awed at the acrobatics by the almost naked man. He crouched down and presented her with her new drink. When she reached for the glass, she missed, so he guided her hand to wrap around the drink. With another leap and a shriek, he swung away again.

"Why don't we get service like that on Amity?" Sebella asked.

"Good taste?" Ariel whispered to Dekkan.

But Sebella overheard her. "Are you implying I have bad taste?"

Stonnor interrupted. "Sebella, I think you may be indulging too much. Ariel was just making conversation—weren't you?"

Ariel nodded and the conversation turned general. But she could tell that Sebella, her already questionable good sense impaired by the potent liquor, was still brooding over the issue.

Dekkan asked Jeccad why he'd thought this meal so important to insist on his and Ariel's presence.

"Stonnor tells me you plan to leave for Amity soon. Just wanted to make sure you've been treating my little Ariel right."

With an effort, Ariel suppressed the quiver of shock that rippled through her. Jeccad wasn't say-

Ariel's Dance

ing anything she didn't already know, of course, but hearing the words from someone else made Dekkan's departure so much more real.

Dekkan sipped from the mineral water, which was all he'd ordered. "And now that you've seen us? Have we passed your inspection?"

Ariel strove to keep a bland face as Jeccad eyed her closely. Her father might be a rogue and a scoundrel, but she knew he'd have no compunctions about punishing Dekkan—or Stonnor—if he suspected anything was wrong. Slowly, Jeccad nodded. "She looks—fine."

But Stonnor piped up, "She looks tense to me. Have you two had an argument?"

"Of course not!"

"No, sir."

Ariel looked at Dekkan and saw his slight nod. "We're just working on that little project you asked us to help you with. It's a bit difficult, that's all."

As an excuse, it mollified both Stonnor and Jeccad, both of whom at least partially understood about the ring. But Sebella and Brolla had no idea what the "project" was.

"What project? What are you talking about?"

Dekkan immediately strove to cut short the situation. He stood and bowed generally to them all. "Forgive us, but it's time we left. We have other duties we must attend to tonight."

"Wait! No! You can't go!" Sebella leaped up as Dekkan extended a hand down to help Ariel to her feet.

Automatically, Ariel stood, and, equally automatically, his arm folded around her, pulling her close against his body. Before she thought better of the gesture, she smiled up at him and said softly, "Thank you."

Big mistake. He bent his head and kissed her—a slow, tender kiss that would have made her believe in true love everlasting if she hadn't known that her love for Dekkan was doomed.

Sebella, enraged by the affection blazing between Dekkan and Ariel, leaped onto the log before Brolla could stop her, then leaped to catch a handy hanging vine, and gave her own imitation of the waiter's swoop—toward the couple. "Cut that out!" she yelled. "Dekkan is *mine*, not yours. Dekkan, what have you done?"

Startled, Ariel and Dekkan stepped away from the vine's trajectory. As a result, the vine swung back, leaving Sebella dangling limply an arm's length above the table.

Jeccad erupted into guffaws. "Funniest—ha, ha—thing I've seen—ha, ha—in ages! Swoop! Ha ha ha!"

Sebella glared impotently at him, obviously unwilling to drop the half-meter to the precariously rounded log.

Stonnor stood too, goggle-eyed and with his chest heaving Ariel thought for a moment that he might be having trouble breathing until she realized that he, too, was all but overcome with laughter. He was merely disguising it better than Jeccad.

The waiters were too busy slapping each other on the back and pointing to retrieve the woeful Sebella. Brolla, however, sprang into action, heaving himself onto the log and walking carefully along the length of it until he was directly under Sebella. "Let go. I have you."

Having the reassurance of being held must have sparked Sebella's spirit. "Make Dekkan let *her* go first!"

Brolla glared at his friend. "Let Ariel go."

Ariel's Dance

Dekkan glared back. "Ariel is my wife. I can hold her if I want to."

Ariel squirmed, trying to get away from Dekkan's unbreakable grip. "Dekkan, please. Let me go."

He shook his head, still locking glares with Brolla.

"Dekkan!" Sebella wailed. "I'm your fiancée! Let her go."

Brolla chose that moment to switch his glare to Sebella. "Release the rope. I have you."

As Brolla tried to talk Sebella into letting go, from the corner of her eye Ariel caught three of the waiters passing around an empty salt dish with coins in it. "I'll take the husky one on the table," one said.

"Naw. It'll be the one with the gorgeous armful," insisted another.

"No way. The drunk on the vine for sure."

That was when Ariel realized they were betting on who would throw the first punch. She dug her elbow into Dekkan's ribs. "Dekkan," she whispered urgently. "We have to get out of here. We can't afford to have the restaurant send out for the street monitors—we'll be locked up for the night!"

He stood watching the deteriorating situation a long moment, then sighed and nodded. "They'll be all right if we leave. We won't be around to set Sebella off again."

With Jeccad and Stonnor ineffectually offering useless advice to Brolla, Dekkan turned and quietly guided Ariel to the door. They were met at the restaurant's entry by the snooty host. "What's going on in there?" the man demanded.

Ariel met Dekkan's eyes and erupted into giggles. "Nothing much," she sputtered. "Just enjoying the floor show. Or should I say, the vine show?"

Dekkan hustled her out the door, still giggling, while behind them the host muttered bewilderedly, "Floor show? Vine show? But we don't provide entertainment."

Chapter Eighteen

Sneaking back into Floribunda's suite was as easy as Ariel had said it would be. Dekkan had taken Ariel to Fedry's workshop and picked up both the original ring and the copy. For safekeeping, and because he really liked to see it there, he solemnly placed the Misthaven ring on Ariel's finger as before. She curled her hand protectively. The copy he merely shoved in his pocket. It was a fine piece of jewelry, but nothing could compare to the spark he felt seeing the heartfire gem blaze on Ariel's hand.

Back at the House of Joy, they once again crept through the cluttered anteroom of Floribunda's suite. Muffled snores and snorts came through the closed door to the bedroom. Giving Ariel a kiss for good luck, he dropped to his knees and waited until she did so also. Then he reached up and keyed the palm plate to open the door.

With a soft snick the door opened, and they

crawled through. Again the dim starlit glow from the ceiling left plenty of light to guide them to their safe haven under the suspended bed. He took a deep breath, then rolled out from under the bed and stood.

Floribunda lay, still snoring, though more quietly than before. Carefully, guided by the soft glow from the ceiling, he reached toward her neck, lifting the massive curls away from her throat. The chain around her neck still glinted in the dim light. He reached for the clasp—

Floribunda's hand grabbed his in a viselike grip. He'd been caught in the act!

"You can come out from under the bed, Ariel," Floribunda said. "I know you're there."

Slowly, Ariel edged out from under the bed and stood. Floribunda sat up, still keeping a duranum-hard grip on Dekkan's hand. With her other hand, she waved at a control, causing the room lights to turn on. She was wrapped in a loose sleep-robe of pale yellow, the matching yellow curls of her wig spilling over her shoulders and into her lap. Dekkan had never known a woman who wore a wig to bed before.

"I suppose I don't need to ask why you're here. You were planning to steal that ring, weren't you?"

"No!" Ariel said. "It's nothing like that. We were going to return it to you."

"Return it?" Floribunda fished among the curls and draperies until she found the chain still around her neck. "You can't return it. It's still here." Triumphantly, she pulled out the chain until the substitute ruby-and-topaz ring Dekkan had placed on it in their first visit appeared.

Ariel glanced at Dekkan, then closed her mouth firmly. It was up to him to talk their way out of this.

Ariel's Dance

"Gentlelady Floribunda, this is not as it seems. I was indeed trying to replace the ring you wear." He held out the copy of the Misthaven ring on his palm.

"But if that's the ring I'm supposed to have . . ." Floribunda let go of Dekkan and undid the necklace's clasp, spilling the chain into her palm. "This isn't my ring!"

"Yes, we know, gentlelady. That's why we were going to replace it with this one." Again he proffered the copy.

Floribunda snatched the ring from his hand and grabbed a lamp to pull it closer. Squinting at the copy's workmanship, she said slowly, "It looks like my ring. . . ."

Ariel stared at Dekkan, wondering what he was going to do. Would he let Floribunda believe that the copy was the ring she owned? Or would he speak the truth?

Her question was answered when he took a deep breath. "It does resemble the Misthaven ring, gentlelady. But—it is another copy. I commissioned it especially for you of the finest materials and workmanship."

Floribunda's shrewd glance speared Ariel. "Fedry?"

Reluctantly, she nodded. "Yes."

Her fingers drumming on one plump knee, Floribunda eyed Dekkan shrewdly. "So where's the real ring? I see two imitations, but not the original."

Dekkan squeezed Ariel's hand—the one wearing the Misthaven ring—as if to tell her to keep silent. "That is what I would like to speak to you about. I would be honored if you would consent to accept both those rings for the true Misthaven ring."

Floribunda's eyes narrowed. "Are you willing to accept my original conditions, then?" She glanced down at his hand clasped with Ariel's. "But I'm too late, am I not? You've already yielded your virginity to Mistress Ariel."

"Ariel is my wife. It is to her I owe my fidelity. I could not share my body with another woman."

"Ha! Wife pro tem, is what I hear. Not much fidelity in that—not for long, anyway."

Before Dekkan could take issue with that, Ariel interjected, "Floribunda, couldn't you see your way clear to letting Dekkan keep the Misthaven ring? The other two rings are nearly twice the value of the Misthaven one. Think what a bargain that is!"

"No! That ring was mine, given to me by that weasel Jeccad. I'm not going to give that up anytime soon."

Ariel glanced at Dekkan, then said, "I'm sure Jeccad wouldn't mind if you gave his love token away. In fact, wouldn't it be a symbol of how little his feelings concern you if you didn't bother to keep even a valuable present from him?"

But to Ariel's surprise, the older woman's eyes suddenly glistened with tears—of anger or of sorrow? Ariel couldn't tell. "I'll not have him think he can arrange to take back his gifts from me! If he wants it, he'll have to ask me for it nicely."

"Not to put too fine a point on it, you might remember that you no longer have possession of the ring."

Ariel almost groaned. It was the worst thing Dekkan could have said.

Floribunda's smile turned sly, and she pressed a stud on the wall. "Perhaps I don't have the ring now, but I'll guarantee you know where it is. And I won't let you leave here until you tell me how to find it. Unless of course you'd prefer I call the street monitors to help straighten this out."

Ariel's Dance

"No!" Ariel said.

But Floribunda had pinpointed Dekkan's vulnerability with laser accuracy. "That would look good on the holo-news outlets, wouldn't it? Amity's key negotiator charged with grand theft on Mariposa. What would the people back home think?"

"Floribunda, don't do this!"

"Why not?"

Dekkan spoke. "I have a suggestion, gentlelady. Perhaps we should discuss this among all those involved. I have found that negotiations are useless unless all affected parties are included."

"That's what we're doing," Ariel said. "You, me, Floribunda."

The older woman just pursed her lips in a pout.

"Ah, but there is one more person who is of import here. Is there not, Floribunda?"

"I can't imagine who you are referring to."

Dekkan's voice gentled. "Gentlesire Jeccad is involved, is he not? After all, he gave you the ring. He has a vested interest in what you do with it."

Floribunda gave an elaborately casual shrug. "If you want to waste time getting him over here, it's all right with me, but your time would be better spent figuring out when you're going to tell me where to find my ring."

Dekkan bowed in acknowledgment of her tacit permission and moved toward the vid-phone on the wall. "Do you know the vid-phone ID of the restaurant?" he asked Ariel in a low tone. "With luck, he'll still be there."

Ariel rattled off the ID, and Dekkan placed the call.

Floribunda protested, "You mean he's dining at my favorite restaurant? That worm! He knows how much I love eating there. They have the most divine waiters."

Ariel coughed to cover the snicker that threatened to surface. It figured that Floribunda would like that hell hole of a restaurant.

While they waited for Jeccad to arrive, Floribunda eyed Dekkan speculatively. "So tell me, Ariel. How was he? Was he as good as they say Amitan virgins are?"

Ariel choked.

Dekkan raised an eyebrow. "I find this subject inappropriate for discussion."

"Oh, pooh. Men always hate it when women talk about how good they are in bed. Or not." Floribunda settled against the cushions and gave him a smirk. "How else are we to know when we've found a good one if we don't compare notes?"

"Perhaps, Floribunda, you could simply decide on the value of a lover based on your feelings for him?"

But the older woman snorted skeptically. "That's what I asked, isn't it? How you felt when you had sex. In other words, was he good in bed?"

It's hard to remember, when we so rarely used a bed. The irreverent crack almost popped out of her mouth. She met Dekkan's eyes and could see that he was thinking much the same thing. A warm thread of mirth connected them and teased her with might-have-beens.

Before Floribunda could press the point further, the door chime announced Jeccad's arrival.

"Enter!" Floribunda commanded, and the door snicked open.

What seemed like a flood of people tumbled into the room, bringing with them a cacophony of noise and jumbled complaints. When Ariel sorted out the

Ariel's Dance

mass, she counted only six newcomers, though it certainly seemed like more. There was Jeccad, of course, and Stonnor. And a still partially inebriated Sebella, supported heavily by Brolla on one side and a muscular, loincloth-clad waiter on the other. And, for some bizarre reason Ariel couldn't fathom, the host from the restaurant, complete in his tigrette-striped formal evening garb.

The noise level escalated as soon as Sebella caught sight of Dekkan and Ariel, until it was so loud only Floribunda's piercing whistle penetrated everyone's attention.

"Who *are* all these people? And what are they doing in my suite? I recognize Umberto from the restaurant," she said, giving him a nod, "and obviously that utterly delicious young man is one of the staff there. But why are they here?"

"Gentlelady Floribunda, I am loath to admit that one of our clients"—he pointed at the hapless Jeccad—"has attempted to depart from the restaurant without providing payment for the bill."

"I was going to pay it!" Jeccad grumbled. "Just had something important to do first."

Umberto sniffed, obviously skeptical.

Ariel tried to explain. "There's Jeccad."

"I know that!" Floribunda snapped. "I invited *him*!!

"And Stonnor, Dekkan's father. He is the one who, um, wagered the ring in a game with Jeccad."

Floribunda carefully eyed Stonnor up and down. "I don't suppose he's still a . . . ?"

When Ariel shook her head and reminded her that Stonnor was Dekkan's father, Floribunda said only, "A pity."

Before Ariel could continue the explanations, Jeccad wormed his way to the front of the crowd.

"Ah, Flossie, my love, it does my heart good to see you again."

"Ha! If you wanted to see me you could've hustled your butt over here once in a while." Floribunda's meaty arms crossed over her chest in a belligerent stance.

"But, Flossie! You said to get out! You told me to leave!"

"And you think I meant it?" She turned to Ariel. "Wouldn't you think a grown man would know better?"

"Yes, Floribunda." Ariel covered her mouth with her hand to hide her amusement.

But that, too, was the wrong gesture. Sebella took one look at the ring on Ariel's finger and shrieked, "You gave it to her! You worm! You snake! You low-down, rotten, slime-eating—" Her shaking finger pointed directly at the Misthaven ring firmly ensconced on Ariel's finger.

"So that's where it is! I might have known!"

"Son! When did you . . . ? Why did you . . . ?"

"You betrayed me, you stink-ridden churl!"

"It's not what you all think! Truly! I'm just wearing it for safekeeping. I'm giving it back."

Cutting through the hubbub of voices, Dekkan's resonant tones captured everyone's attention. "No, you're not giving it back." He turned to Sebella. "Sebella, I must announce that Ariel and I are formally wed in the full Amitan tradition."

"Dekkan! We're not!"

He ignored Ariel's shocked gasp. "My marriage to Ariel is permanent and lifelong. While I regret that this has caused you pain, I entreat you to accept the reality of what has been done."

Sebella's eyes narrowed to slits. "You'll owe me big-time for this, Dekkan. I'm a gentle Amitan maid, and you betrayed me for that slu—mmmph."

Brolla's hand muffled Sebella's further comments. "I congratulate you. Don't worry 'bout this one. I'll handle her."

Ariel stared at the usually silent Brolla. What did he mean? But there was something else. "Dekkan," she whispered, "you know we're not wed in the Amitan way, only with a pro tem Mariposan license. Once you go off-planet it becomes null."

He smiled down at her and tucked a stray curl behind her ear. "I can straighten this out. Trust me?"

"Well, yes, but—"

He touched his lips to hers in a kiss that squelched her protest. "I love you," he said quietly as he lifted his head and faced the others.

Stunned, Ariel just touched her lips, completely at a loss for what to say. Did he mean . . . ? What was going on?

Brolla had lifted his hand from Sebella's mouth. She gave Dekkan a glare that could have roasted a boar, then turned toward Stonnor, snubbing her former fiancé. "I believe we have some settlements to negotiate now. I claim half of Misthaven Keep as my rightful dowry."

Ariel gasped.

Floribunda gave Sebella an admiring look. "Good for you, girl. You got him where it hurts, now put on the squeeze."

Jeccad winced. Umberto pulled him aside and began a quiet haggle to get the bill settled.

"Now, Sebella, let's not be extreme. Half of the keep is a bit steep, don't you think?" Stonnor adopted a conciliatory mien. "Dekkan, what do you think is fair compensation for Sebella's loss?"

"I'll not negotiate with *him* in the room! He's not even chaste!"

With Sebella ignoring Dekkan and Stonnor trying to include his son, little progress was made. Ariel was still trying to figure out what exactly was going on when Floribunda gestured for Brolla to come to her side.

"You look familiar," she told him.

An uneasy look flickered across his face. "Just arrived from Amity. Haven't met before."

Floribunda eyed him up and down carefully. "Hmmm. You know, I never forget a face, Ariel—especially when they come attached to a body as charming as this one. I like to know who my customers are—and I'm sure I've seen this handsome gentlesire before."

But Floribunda must be mistaken, Ariel knew. She turned back to Dekkan as he said softly, "Sebella, I am a married man. Ariel will swear that I maintained my, uh, virginity until after the ceremony that made us man and wife."

"That's true," Ariel confirmed, and stretched out her hand to console the other woman. It was a lot easier to be sympathetic now that she knew that Sebella would not be Dekkan's final bride. "Sebella, I know you are hurt by this, but—"

Floribunda grabbed Ariel's hand. "Look at the ring!"

Everyone froze in place, staring at the ring blazing on Ariel's finger. Where before the heartfire gem had gleamed softly, now the stone burned with an intensity that was all but blinding. Turquoise and emerald flames surged with light and power, while the auburn background now resembled a red sun in intensity.

"That's not my ring!" Floribunda's shocked gasp

Ariel's Dance

astounded Ariel as much as the ring's sudden luminescence.

Stonnor patted Ariel on the shoulder then sent a shrewd glance at Dekkan. "So that's why you entangled yourself in this mess! Never knew you to cause such a to-do before now."

Dekkan met his father's gaze. "Yes."

Stonnor smiled down at Ariel. "Couldn't be happier for you, son."

Staring first at Stonnor, then at Dekkan, Ariel blurted, "Will one of you tell me what's going on here? Why is the ring so bright?"

"It's a heartfire gem," Dekkan said.

"So? You told me that before."

Stonnor said, "You don't see genuine heartfires much anymore. Synthetics are easier to make and they don't have the special problems heartfires do."

"What problems? Will you stop talking in riddles?"

Dekkan took her hand in his and spread out her fingers so the ring was visible. "A genuine heartfire doesn't have a stable structure. Most of the time it's a rather dull yellowish color—just as you originally remembered it being. But sometimes, when it is given and worn by appropriate people, the stone changes."

Ariel couldn't take her eyes off his face. "What do you mean by appropriate?"

Floribunda explained in a voice softer than Ariel had ever heard from her. "He means when it unites a couple deeply in love. Only then does the true beauty of the heartfire emerge. The deeper the love, the brighter the stone shines. At its brightest—like now—it is more brilliant than any other gem in the known universe."

Wonderingly, Ariel stared down at the fiery ring on her hand. "You mean—"

Floribunda looked rueful. "I mean that even if you gave me back the ring, it wouldn't have near the brilliance of the copy. So keep it. Who am I to interfere when true love casts its spell?"

"True love?" Ariel parroted, still in shock.

Dekkan said, "She means that I love you. And you must love me, too. Remember when I explained the Amitan ceremony in which I would give the ring to my bride?"

"Yes," she whispered.

"And you repeated the words back to me?"

"Yes."

He smiled. "From that moment you were my true Amitan bride. For the rest of my life, I will belong to you alone."

"But—there were no witnesses. No ceremony."

Stonnor interrupted. "Child, on Amity we presume the honor of all our citizens. If a couple of marriageable age says they repeated their vows—as you have just admitted—whether the vows were taken in public or privately, with or without witnesses, it is as binding as a ceremony held on the steps of the keep's chapel with every resident witnessing it."

Ariel stared down at the ring. It truly symbolized the love she felt for her husband. But . . .

"Ariel, I want you to know I won't stand in the way of your education. If you choose to ignore this marriage, I will accept that. I'll fulfill my promise to help you into the academy of your choice." Dekkan paused. "But you never told me what your choice was."

Jeccad snorted. "She couldn't be satisfied with an

Ariel's Dance

honorable job dancing. Oh, no. My Ariel has to go off and shame her family."

Ariel saw the faint trace of worry on Dekkan's brow. "It's not that bad, love," she said. "It's just that I had my heart set on attending the best academy on interstellar law in this sector. And that one is—"

"—on Amity." Dekkan stared at her. "You want to attend Amity Academy?"

"Uh-huh."

"To become an attorney? That's what Jeccad's so upset about?"

"Uh-huh. How would it look to his friends if his very own daughter were a *lawyer?*"

Dekkan pulled her into his arms and roared with laughter. "I see your point. I don't know how he'll live it down."

"Well, it won't be easy, young sir!" Jeccad said.

"What about me?" Sebella complained. "I'm the one who has been shamed by a fiancé who couldn't be bothered to maintain his chastity."

"Now I know where I've seen you before!" Floribunda pointed at Brolla. "You were a client here yesterday—and today, too, I think!"

Brolla's face flushed a dark red. "Must be mistaken."

"I told you I *never* forget a face. I can double-check the registration records, if you like. But you were with a lady—a blonde, if I remember rightly. Tall . . . and . . ."

All eyes focused on Sebella, now shrinking behind Brolla's bulky figure. "It's not true," she said weakly. "Tell them, Brolla."

But Brolla straightened. He faced Dekkan directly. "It is true. Sebella and I want to marry. But we can't afford it. Figured that if she wed you, you'd be gone a lot on your travels. She'd have the life she wants and me, too."

Dekkan's mouth dropped open in shock.

"Knew there was something fishy about that girl," Stonnor muttered. Louder he said, "So you and Sebella have violated chastity?"

"Yes."

At a nudge from Brolla, Sebella's proudly raised her head. "Yes. We threw away our patches for each other. I love him. I don't love Dekkan. Never did. But being mistress of Misthaven keep would have been . . . pleasant."

"Obviously all compensation claims against my son are now void," Stonnor said. "And I think we must plan a formal wedding ceremony as soon as possible to make right the wrong you two have done. Perhaps at a dinner somewhere?"

Umberto stepped forward. "May I offer my gracious restaurant as the ideal location to celebrate one's nuptials? Our cuisine is, as you know, exquisite."

Ariel buried her face in Dekkan's shoulder to muffle her chuckles. She would always treasure the private exchange of vows she and Dekkan had shared, but somehow that awful restaurant seemed perfect for Sebella and Brolla.

Dekkan tipped her head up while the others discussed the arrangements around them. "I won't stand in your way, you know. If you don't want to be tied to our marriage, I'll let you go. All I can offer is the life of an ordinary keepmaster."

She smiled at him. He held her heart in his hand and didn't even realize it. "If I'm with you, I'll have the universe in my hands. I'd like to attend the academy, of course, especially since it's right there on

Ariel's Dance

Amity. But I won't leave you. Maybe I can even learn to be a decent keepmistress."

Stonnor interrupted. "Um, about that keepmaster thing, Dekkan. I've been thinking about that."

She saw a cloud pass over Dekkan's eyes; then he determinedly smiled. "I know you wish me to settle down, Father, but . . ."

"Oh, it's not that. It's just that I know the position normally is handed from father to eldest son. But you know, son, you haven't shown much inclination lately to settle down to farming."

"I know. And I'll try to do better—"

Stonnor waved that aside. "The thing is, your little sister Jenna is really good at it. I've been wondering what it would take to persuade you to keep on doing what you're good at, negotiating contracts for us, and let Jenna take your place as keepmistress."

Dekkan's face paled: then a broad grin spread over it. "And of course, the one thing a good negotiator really needs at his side is a top-notch interstellar lawyer. Just to keep negotiations fair and on track."

"Exactly." Stonnor's beaming pride encompassed all of them.

Ariel stared at Stonnor. "Why do I have the strangest feeling that none of this is an accident?"

Stonnor cast a smug look at Jeccad, then put on a face of pure innocence. "Would I interfere with my eldest son's life?"

Dekkan cast a wry glance in his direction. "Without the slightest qualm." He pulled Ariel toward the door. "Tell the others that we've left, Father. We'll be in touch tomorrow."

"But—don't you want to attend Brolla and Sebella's marriage?"

Dekkan glanced down at Ariel, nestled snugly against his side. "Not a chance. I have more important things to do."

Once outside Floribunda's suite, Dekkan gave Ariel a kiss twice as fiery as the ring on her hand. "You have a choice. We can go back to our suite here and spend the rest of the night making love."

"Or?" Her fingers traced the lines of his cheek.

"We can go back to your place and spend the rest of the night making love."

"That's my choice?"

"Uh-huh. Which will it be?"

She pretended to consider. "Well, I guess I'll have to choose—yes."

He laughed and lifted her in his arms before heading toward the suite. It was much closer—and he hadn't forgotten that Jeccad had interrupted them once at Ariel's.

But as the door sealed behind them, shutting the rest of the world outside, Ariel cocked her head and said, "I just have one question."

"What's that, love?" He set her down, his hands having already undone her dress's knot, letting the garment fall gracefully to her feet. As he'd hoped, she was deliciously nude underneath it.

"Are you ever going to let me wear any clothes when we're alone?"

He pretended to consider that. Then he shook his head with mock solemnity. "I don't think it's too likely anytime soon. Maybe on our fiftieth wedding celebration. If you ask me as a special favor."

Ariel smiled and put her arms around his neck. "Oh, goody. That's what I thought you'd say."

ALL'S FAIR

ANNE AVERY

For five long years, Rhys Fairdane has roamed the universe, trying to forget Calista York, who seared his soul with white-hot longing, then cast him into space. Yet by a twist of fate, he and Calista are both named trade representatives of the planet Karta. It will take all his strength to resist her voluptuous curves, all his cunning to subdue her feminine wiles. But if in war, as in love, all truly is fair, Calista has concealed weapons that will bring Rhys to his knees before the battle has even begun.

_52257-8 $5.50 US/$6.50 CAN

Dorchester Publishing Co., Inc.
P.O. Box 6640
Wayne, PA 19087-8640

Please add $1.75 for shipping and handling for the first book and $.50 for each book thereafter. NY, NYC, and PA residents, please add appropriate sales tax. No cash, stamps, or C.O.D.s. All orders shipped within 6 weeks via postal service book rate. Canadian orders require $2.00 extra postage and must be paid in U.S. dollars through a U.S. banking facility.

Name_____
Address_____
City_____State_____Zip_____
I have enclosed $_____ in payment for the checked book(s).
Payment <u>must</u> accompany all orders. ❏ Please send a free catalog.
CHECK OUT OUR WEBSITE! www.dorchesterpub.com

Futuristic Romance

Star-Crossed

Saranne Dawson

Bestselling Author Of *Crystal Enchantment*

Rowena is a master artisan, a weaver of enchanted tapestries that whisper of past glories. Yet not even magic can help her foresee that she will be sent to assassinate an enemy leader. Her duty is clear—until the seductive beauty falls under the spell of the man she must kill.

His reputation says that he is a warmongering barbarian. But Zachary MacTavesh prefers conquering damsels' hearts over pillaging fallen cities. One look at Rowena tells him to gird his loins and prepare for the battle of his life. And if he has his way, his stunningly passionate rival will reign victorious as the mistress of his heart.

_51982-8 $4.99 US/$5.99 CAN

Dorchester Publishing Co., Inc.
P.O. Box 6640
Wayne, PA 19087-8640

Please add $1.75 for shipping and handling for the first book and $.50 for each book thereafter. NY, NYC, and PA residents, please add appropriate sales tax. No cash, stamps, or C.O.D.s. All orders shipped within 6 weeks via postal service book rate. Canadian orders require $2.00 extra postage and must be paid in U.S. dollars through a U.S. banking facility.

Name_____
Address_____
City_____State_____Zip_____
I have enclosed $_____ in payment for the checked book(s).
Payment <u>must</u> accompany all orders. ❏ Please send a free catalog.

To Touch The Stars
Tess Mallory

Eagle is enjoying the quiet serenity of Station One when suddenly it is attacked by a rebel spacecraft. Before he can defend himself, he is pinned by a beautiful droid who demands to know the whereabouts of a child. Skyra will let nothing—and no one—stand in the way of finding her little sister, for Mayla is the only hope of freedom for the rebels. But the more time she spends with Eagle, the more she feels something stronger than compassion for her prisoner, something that makes her burn with delicious turmoil when she envisions his sleek muscular form. And only in his arms does she find an ecstasy like none she's ever known, one that lifts her high enough to touch the stars.

___52253-5 $4.99 US/$5.99 CAN

Dorchester Publishing Co., Inc.
P.O. Box 6640
Wayne, PA 19087-8640

Please add $1.75 for shipping and handling for the first book and $.50 for each book thereafter. NY, NYC, and PA residents, please add appropriate sales tax. No cash, stamps, or C.O.Ds. All orders shipped within 6 weeks via postal service book rate. Canadian orders require $2.00 extra postage and must be paid in U.S. dollars through a U.S. banking facility.

Name_____
Address_____
City_____State_____Zip_____
I have enclosed $_____ in payment for the checked book(s).
Payment <u>must</u> accompany all orders. ❏ Please send a free catalog.

The Midnight Moon
Stobie Piel

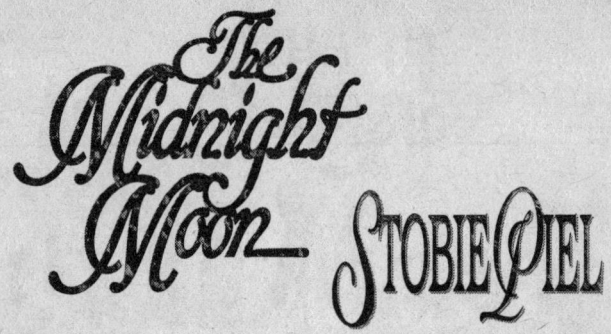

Dane Calydon knows there is more to the mysterious Aiyana than meets the eye, but when he removes her protective wrappings, he is unprepared for what he uncovers: a woman beautiful beyond his wildest imaginings. Though she claimed to be an amphibious creature, he was seduced by her sweet voice, and now, with her standing before him, he is powerless to resist her perfect form. Yet he knows she is more than a mere enchantress, for he has glimpsed her healing, caring side. But as secrets from her past overshadow their happiness, Dane realizes he must lift the veil of darkness surrounding her before she can surrender both body and soul to his tender kisses.

___52268-3 $5.50 US/$6.50 CAN

Dorchester Publishing Co., Inc.
P.O. Box 6640
Wayne, PA 19087-8640

Please add $1.75 for shipping and handling for the first book and $.50 for each book thereafter. NY, NYC, and PA residents, please add appropriate sales tax. No cash, stamps, or C.O.D.s. All orders shipped within 6 weeks via postal service book rate. Canadian orders require $2.00 extra postage and must be paid in U.S. dollars through a U.S. banking facility.

Name_____
Address_____
City_____State_____Zip_____
I have enclosed $_____ in payment for the checked book(s).
Payment <u>must</u> accompany all orders. ❏ Please send a free catalog.
         CHECK OUT OUR WEBSITE! www.dorchesterpub.com

The Magician's Lover
Flora Speer

Determined to locate his friend who disappeared during a spell gone awry, Warrick petitions a dying stargazer to help find him. But the astronomer will only assist Warrick if he promises to escort his daughter Sophia and a priceless crystal ball safely to Byzantium. Sharp-tongued and argumentative, Sophia meets her match in the powerful and intelligent Warrick. Try as she will to deny it, he holds her spellbound, longing to be the magician's lover.

___52263-2 $5.99 US/$6.99 CAN

Dorchester Publishing Co., Inc.
P.O. Box 6640
Wayne, PA 19087-8640

Please add $1.75 for shipping and handling for the first book and $.50 for each book thereafter. NY, NYC, and PA residents, please add appropriate sales tax. No cash, stamps, or C.O.D.s. All orders shipped within 6 weeks via postal service book rate. Canadian orders require $2.00 extra postage and must be paid in U.S. dollars through a U.S. banking facility.

Name_____
Address_____
City_____State_____Zip_____
I have enclosed $_____ in payment for the checked book(s).
Payment <u>must</u> accompany all orders. ❏ Please send a free catalog.
CHECK OUT OUR WEBSITE! www.dorchesterpub.com

DON'T MISS OTHER STARSWEPT FUTURISTIC ROMANCES FROM *LOVE SPELL!*

Nighthawk by Kristen Kyle. Determined to earn her father's approval, Kari Solis must capture the commander of the rebel forces wreaking havoc on their world. But she doesn't count on her plans being upset by a rogue smuggler—a handsome loner concealing a shadowy past and an even darker secret. Confronted by a dark menace, the two reluctantly join forces, igniting a firestorm of cosmic passion that takes them to a final battle—pitting the power of betrayal against the strength of their love.

_52184-9 $4.99 US/$5.99 CAN

Hidden Heart by Anne Avery. Determined to free her world, Marna has traveled to the planet Dilor with her own secret agenda. And her plans don't include being seduced by the first hard-bodied man she encounters. Although the enchanting beauty refuses to forget her mission, she can't deny the ache Tarl rouses in her. But the more Marna longs to surrender to unending bliss, the more she fears she is betraying everything she holds dear.

_52109-1 $5.99 US/$6.99 CAN

Dorchester Publishing Co., Inc.
P.O. Box 6640
Wayne, PA 19087-8640

Please add $1.75 for shipping and handling for the first book and $.50 for each book thereafter. NY, NYC, and PA residents, please add appropriate sales tax. No cash, stamps, or C.O.D.s. All orders shipped within 6 weeks via postal service book rate. Canadian orders require $2.00 extra postage and must be paid in U.S. dollars through a U.S. banking facility.

Name_____
Address_____
City_____ State_____ Zip_____
I have enclosed $_____ in payment for the checked book(s).
Payment <u>must</u> accompany all orders. ❏ Please send a free catalog.

DON'T MISS OTHER STAR-STUDDED *LOVE SPELL* ROMANCES!

Sword of MacLeod by Karen Fox. When his daughter leaves their planet to find their family's legendary sword, Beckett MacLeod is forced to enlist the help of the best tracker in the galaxy—and the most beautiful woman he has ever laid eyes on. But Beckett has no patience for the free-spirited adventurer—until one star-studded evening she gives him a glimpse of the final frontier. Raven doesn't like working with anyone, but being in desperate need of funds, she agrees to help Beckett, thinking the assignment will be a piece of cake. Instead she finds herself thrown into peril with a man whose archaic ways are out of a history book—and whose tender kisses are something from her wildest dreams.

_52160-1 $4.99 US/$5.99 CAN

The Dawn Star by Stobie Piel. Seneca's sinewy strength and chiseled features touch a chord deep inside Nisa Calydon—reminding her of a love long gone, of the cruel betrayal of a foolish girl's naive faith. But she's all grown up now, and to avert a potentially disastrous war, she has kidnapped the virile off-worlder to fullfill her responsibility. But the more time she spends with the primitive warrior, the less sure she becomes of how she wants this assignment to end. For behind Seneca's brawn she finds a man of a surprisingly wise and compassionate nature, and in his arms she finds a passion like none she's ever known.

_52148-2 $5.50 US/$6.50 CAN

Dorchester Publishing Co., Inc.
P.O. Box 6640
Wayne, PA 19087-8640

Please add $1.75 for shipping and handling for the first book and $.50 for each book thereafter. NY, NYC, and PA residents, please add appropriate sales tax. No cash, stamps, or C.O.D.s. All orders shipped within 6 weeks via postal service book rate. Canadian orders require $2.00 extra postage and must be paid in U.S. dollars through a U.S. banking facility.

Name_____
Address_____
City_____ State_____ Zip_____
I have enclosed $_____ in payment for the checked book(s).
Payment <u>must</u> accompany all orders. ❏ Please send a free catalog.

ATTENTION ROMANCE CUSTOMERS!

SPECIAL TOLL-FREE NUMBER
1-800-481-9191

*Call Monday through Friday
10 a.m. to 9 p.m.
Eastern Time
Get a free catalogue,
join the Romance Book Club,
and order books using your
Visa, MasterCard,
or Discover®*

Leisure
Books

LOVE SPELL

GO ONLINE WITH US AT DORCHESTERPUB.COM